LUCIFER'S CHAMPION

LUCIFER'S CHAMPION

Juliet Blyth

SEVERN HOUSE PUBLISHERS

This title first published in Great Britain 1988 and
simultaneously published in the U.S.A. 1988 by
SEVERN HOUSE PUBLISHERS LTD of
40–42 William IV Street, London WC2N 4DF.

British Library Cataloguing in Publication Data
Blyth, Juliet
Lucifer's champion.
I. Title
823′.914[F]
ISBN 0–7278–1638–1

Distributed in the U.S.A. by
Mercedes Distribution Center, Inc
62 Imlay Street, Brooklyn, New York, NY 11231

Printed and bound in Great Britain

For my Dad, with love

An Unexpected Encounter

Darkness closed in as the hired carriage bounded swiftly through the quiet Hampshire countryside. The tired horses stumbled and the coachman cursed under his breath.

'Travelling at night and all the way from Stockridge wi'out a stop,' he grumbled. 'She trying to kill the horses?'

'She sure be in an 'urry,' said the postilion. 'She'm determined to be in London afore morning.'

'Ah! Fine chance,' growled his friend. 'Why don't she put up at an inn like decent folk? There'd have been a good mug of ale at the George.' He shook his head regretfully as he thought of the inn they had passed a mile or so back.

Inside the carriage, Vanessa Tremaine watched the shadows lengthening with growing consternation. If only she could get to London without having to spend another night on the road! She had no maid, very little baggage and, worse still, scarcely any money; little more than she would need to pay the remainder of the post charges.

Leaning back, she reviewed the incidents of the past two weeks and sighed. Strange that so much could happen in so short a time – and yet it really was only a fortnight since Papa had emptied a bottle of port with his luncheon and taken a fatal fall on the hunting field some two hours later. And then, within forty-eight hours, grief had become bewilderment with the news that her father's estate was entailed on the heirs male. Penmarne, it seemed, passed intact to Sir Thomas' nephew and Vanessa was left with nothing but some nebulous legacy from her mother which no one had found occasion to explain.

Deprived at one stroke of both family and home, she was obviously in no position to lightly regard an offer of marriage; but it had come from her cousin Joseph and in such a way that there had been no preventing the lively quarrel which had resulted in Vanessa's departure from the house within twenty-four hours of Mr Wade's arrival in it. Her only consolation lay in the fact that, owing to Sir Thomas' addiction to the Turf, a great deal of the estate was mortgaged and Cousin Joseph was likely to find his inheritance more of a millstone than a windfall.

And so, having no relatives to whom she could go, Vanessa was making her way, unheralded, to the London home of the godmother she had never met. It was a situation fraught with potentially horrible pitfalls – compared to which her lack of money was a mere bagatelle.

It was almost dark and, peering through the window, Vanessa saw a bend in the road ahead and knew a vague wish that they were travelling slower. At that precise moment, there came around that bend another vehicle at breakneck speed. Vanessa had a split-second vision of horses bearing down upon her and then both drivers swung over, merely grazing the wheels of the carriage. The one in which Vanessa sat swayed drunkenly and landed in the ditch, while the other drew up at the opposite side of the road.

Immediately, the drivers leapt down from their boxes and began a fierce altercation, each blaming the other for the near-accident and accusing him of being a menace to every other road user.

'Look at my coach a-lying there in the ditch! How'm I going to get it out?'

'If you knew how to drive, it wouldn't *be* in the ditch!'

'You should talk! You took that bend like a madman – '

'At least I'm not mad enough to drive an old bone-shaker like *that!* And you better hope my horses ain't hurt!'

'My good creatures – am I to wait all night to resume my

journey?' A soft, almost purring voice cut off the promising argument in mid-flow. The gentleman had alighted from his carriage and stood confronting his coachman.

'Oh no, your Grace. Beg pardon, sir – but this fellow claims the fault to be mine and – '

'I do not believe I evinced any desire to converse with you, Strode. I care not where lay the fault. I do, however, wish to reach the George before morning.'

'Yes, your Grace.' The man hurried back to the coach.

'And you, fellow.' The soft-spoken gentleman turned his attention to Vanessa's coachman. 'I presume that you also have a passenger?' A faint tinge of sarcasm ran through the smooth tones.

'Yes, m'lord – a lady. But the coach is stuck and I don't see how I can get it out.'

'That,' came the cold reply, 'is your misfortune.'

By this time Vanessa had succeeded in opening the door of the coach – which was lying almost on its side. Scrambling up the sloping floor, she emerged from the doorway to find herself looking at the shadowy owner of the drawling voice.

'Permit me, madam,' he said, holding out his arm to her. Wordlessly, Vanessa laid her hand on it and jumped lightly down. 'It would appear,' continued the gentleman with a weariness he made no attempt to hide, 'that your conveyance is temporarily defunct. I suggest, therefore, that you grant me the inestimable honour of transporting you to the nearest inn.'

Vanessa swallowed, resolutely tempering indignation with commonsense. Then she said smoothly, 'You are all consideration, sir. Mother, of course, told me never to go with strange gentlemen – but I'm sure she would allow you to be an exception.'

There was a tiny pause and then, with a disquieting note that told Vanessa he had grasped her meaning exactly, the gentleman said, 'Are you? But everyone makes mistakes, you know.' And, with a brief, genuinely amused laugh, turned away to give instructions concerning her luggage.

Unlike the hired chaise, an aged and musty-smelling rattler, the gentleman's equipage was elegant and luxurious in the extreme. Vanessa sank gratefully against soft upholstery and drew a breath of pure appreciation before deciding that it behoved her to attempt some conversation.

'Will it take long to repair the carriage, sir?' she asked.

'I really have no idea,' he sighed. 'No doubt it will be done as soon as possible. Are you in such haste?'

'It's not so much a question of time, sir, as that my journey has proved more costly than I anticipated. I am . . . a little short of funds.'

'Indeed? Pray accept my condolences.' His tone, a nice blend of mockery and indifference, made the words unanswerable. Vanessa did not speak again and by the time the coach halted in the stable-yard of the George, she was acutely relieved that she would soon be able to remove herself.

Very leisurely, the gentleman stepped down, offered his arm to Vanessa and then acknowledged the landlord's greeting with a faint inclination of his head. He indicated Vanessa with a wave of one hand and said, 'This lady is the sole occupant of a . . . coach . . . yes, a coach which had the misfortune to land in the ditch. Doubtless the driver and postilion will arrive here shortly seeking aid. In the meantime, you may devote your energies to providing bedchambers for the lady and for myself.'

'Certainly, your Grace! At once, sir.' The landlord rubbed his plump hands together. 'And will your Grace be requiring dinner?'

'Naturally,' came the cool reply. 'You will reserve a private parlour and serve dinner . . . for two . . . in precisely half an hour from now.' He turned languidly to Vanessa. 'I trust that will suit your convenience, madam?' And without waiting for her answer, he walked away.

Bewildered and not a little ruffled, she watched him go. She could think of no reason why he should wish her to dine with him and as for his calm assurance that she would accept his invitation, well – it was plain that the gentleman was lamentably accustomed to having his own way. Vanessa had never before encountered his like and was not sure she was prepared to tolerate such high-handed manners. Thoroughly bemused, she followed the chambermaid upstairs to her room.

Half an hour later, having completed her very hasty toilet, she took a long, critical look at herself in the mirror and sighed. 'I look,' she told her reflection resignedly, 'like a dowdy schoolgirl. And if *that* doesn't make his overbearing Grace regret his impetuosity, I don't know what would.' And upon that note, she shrugged her shoulders, took a deep breath and went downstairs.

Her rescuer, meanwhile, gazed pensively into the fire and wondered just what had made him invite a perfectly strange and undoubtedly provincial girl to dine with him. He was not in general prone to acts of impulse; nor could it, he reflected sardonically, be attributed to motives of chivalry. Quite the reverse, in fact. His was usually the role which caused distress to the damsel – a thought which did not disturb him in the least.

Walking over to a small table at the side of the room, he poured himself a glass of wine. It was surprisingly palatable and, meditatively staring at the ruby-coloured liquid, he moved slowly back to the fireside. And then the door opened.

Vanessa entered the room and hesitated, her eyes widening and her confidence ebbing as she gazed at the striking figure before her. Clad exclusively in black and silver, diamonds on his fingers and in his cravat, he stood aloof and motionless, yet dominating the space between them with a strength that was almost tangible. His raven hair, though elaborately dressed, was worn unpowdered as though to deliberately enhance the natural pallor of his skin. The cheekbones were high, the mouth well-shaped but hard; and narrow, black brows were set above eyes which, though heavy-lidded and veiled by thick lashes, were strangely piercing, their topaz hue seeming too vivid for a man. A haughty, mask-like face but not unhandsome and, moreover, his Grace had an air. Vanessa was reluctantly impressed.

'I am sorry to hurry you,' mocked the gentleman indulgently, 'but the draught is causing the fire to smoke.'

Vanessa flushed and shut the door with a distinct snap.

'Thank you. Please sit down – and a glass of wine, perhaps?'

Without waiting for her reply he turned to the decanter, smiling faintly. Her face was an easy one to read and her reactions amused him. His own appraisal had, of course, been completed much quicker – and with less flattering results. Not tall but neatly proportioned and graceful, she had good bones and hair that gleamed bronze in the candlelight; but her nose was more *retroussée* than classical, her mouth too wide for beauty and she was dressed like a servant. Deplorably commonplace with nothing to attract a second glance, had been his initial verdict. Only then he looked into wide, dark grey eyes, heavily fringed with black; and changed his mind. 'My compliments, madam. You are remarkably prompt.'

Vanessa accepted the glass he offered and raised one ironic brow. 'I thought it was expected of me,' she explained sweetly.

For a moment, he held her gaze with trying impassivity and then, 'I believe I do not know your name.'

'It is Vanessa Tremaine, sir.'

'Indeed. I have some slight acquaintance with one Sir Thomas Tremaine. A connection, perhaps?'

Her flicker of surprise gave way to bleakness. 'My father. He . . . he sustained a fatal injury on the hunting field two weeks ago.'

The gentleman bowed coolly. 'My deepest sympathies, Mistress Tremaine. No doubt you are travelling to relatives – in London perhaps?'

'Yes. But to my godmother – Lady Maria Henley.' It seemed to Vanessa that the golden eyes gleamed with sudden interest but before she could be sure the heavy lids had veiled them and he was replying smoothly, 'I see. And will you then be making your curtsy to society?'

'I am not sure,' she replied candidly. 'You see, I have never met my Lady – nor does she know that I am coming.'

His brows lifted a little. 'Dear me! Your decision seems to have been made a trifle hastily.'

'There were . . . reasons.' Vanessa's voice was low and strained. Then, growing tired of his inquisition, 'I have told you my name, sir. Will you not tell me yours?'

'But certainly, mademoiselle. I am Francis Eugene Courtenay, fifth Duke of Lyndhurst – and wholly at your service.' He bowed elaborately and regarded her through half-closed lids. 'I am also known as Lucifer Courtenay. Perhaps you have heard of me?'

'No. How should I?'

A mocking smile dawned. 'Merely that my reputation generally precedes me.'

'Oh,' said Vanessa blankly. 'But then, I don't listen to gossip – and that's all reputation is made of, after all.'

'It seems only fair to tell you,' he remarked gently, 'that mine is not.'

'No?' She eyed him consideringly. 'Then, sir, no doubt you are content to have it so.'

The topaz eyes narrowed fractionally and then he gave the ghost of a smile. 'Your trick, Mistress Tremaine.'

Vanessa flushed and was on the brink of apologising when there came a tap on the door, followed by the smiling landlord announcing that dinner was served. Lyndhurst signified his approval and, while the first course was brought in, conducted Vanessa to her seat.

Suddenly realising that she was ravenously hungry, Vanessa looked eagerly on while the servant helped her to a portion of duck.

'You will bring a bottle of claret,' said Lyndhurst, 'and . . . some ratafia for the lady.'

'Yes, your Grace. At once, sir.' The man hurried away.

Across the table, Vanessa studied his Grace with an air of benign interest. 'Do people always treat you like this? As though they were Moslems and you Mecca?'

'But of course. It surprises you?'

She thought. And then, 'No. Perhaps not. I suppose that if I were a Duchess, they would do the same for me.'

'You aim high, mistress.'

His tone was sarcastic but Vanessa was singularly unimpressed. 'No. I don't. Or not in the way that you mean. No doubt rank and wealth are very pleasant commodities – but there are, surely, more important things in life?'

'Pray enumerate them,' mocked Lyndhurst gently.

'Happiness, I suppose,' said Vanessa thoughtfully. 'For example, I don't see the point in wedding a person one dislikes just for the sake of money. Only think how miserable it would be!'

His Grace looked upon her with astonished cynicism. 'Would you not find such an inconvenience trifling when set against the obvious advantages of such a union? You need, after all, see very little of your husband.'

'Quite,' replied Vanessa witheringly. 'But I want love and companionship . . . not a financial partnership.' She hesitated and then, with a hint of diffidence, asked, 'Are you married, sir?'

'I rejoice to say that I am not.'

'Oh. Then perhaps you haven't found what I am describing. When you do, I daresay you will feel differently.'

His mouth curled. 'I doubt it. And you must pardon me if I also take leave to question the . . . er . . . tenacity of *your* feelings. I imagine that when you enter the polite world they will undergo a change.'

She met his piercing gaze unflinchingly. 'I hope not.'

While the servant removed the remains of the duck and set a cream, two pigeons and a ham on the table, Vanessa felt herself to be under close surveillance but remained deliberately unresponsive to the implied challenge and tried a new tack. 'Shall I like Lady Henley, sir?'

'I am not a seer, mademoiselle,' came the cold reply.

'But you have met her, haven't you? Please tell me a little about her.'

'You had best wait to form your own opinions. I doubt you will find mine enlightening.'

Plunged suddenly into her own thoughts, Vanessa missed the forbidding note in his voice and said anxiously, 'It's foolish of me, I know, but I can't help being a little nervous. For all I know she may not even remember me. And, worse still, she may think that I should have accepted Cousin Joseph.'

The icy gaze sharpened. 'Cousin who?'

'Joseph.' She flushed a little. 'I shouldn't have mentioned that. Please forget it.'

8

'Certainly. And yet I apprehend that he is the hub of the matter.'

Vanessa looked at him. 'You are very acute, sir.'

'I have that reputation,' he agreed, bowing slightly.

'I thought it wouldn't be long before we returned to that,' she remarked with a sigh. 'It seems an immensely important feature in your life. But tell me – now that you have it, do you simply rest on your laurels or spend your time living up to it?'

His eyes gleamed. 'Why, the latter. What else?'

'And do you not consider it a waste of effort?'

'Not at all. I achieve it quite naturally, Mistress Tremaine.'

'Oh. Well I suppose,' she observed kindly, 'that everyone needs *some* sense of accomplishment.'

'However bizarre?' he asked mildly.

'Yes.'

And, quite without warning, he laughed. 'You are making a most creditable attempt to lower my self-esteem, are you not?'

'Not at all, your Grace.' She favoured him with a bland smile. 'Unlike Icarus, I know when to curb my ambition.'

Caught in the act of sipping his wine, the Duke narrowly avoided choking and simultaneously discovered that he was deriving no small pleasure from her company. He made a slight bow. 'I applaud your wit, mademoiselle.'

Vanessa, realising how impolite she had been, blushed furiously and shook her head. 'I – I beg your pardon. I have no right to criticise you.'

'No,' agreed his Grace sweetly.

She stiffened, good intentions forgotten.

'But I concede you both temptation and provocation,' he finished, throwing up one hand in a gesture of surrender.

Vanessa laughed and gave up. Whatever else he might lack, the gentleman clearly possessed a keen sense of humour; and when he allowed it to show, it rendered him much less formidable.

'Are you acquainted with my cousin, Joseph Wade, sir?' she asked.

'I believe not. This is the gentleman, I take it, who was brave enough to offer you his heart and hand?'

9

'Not quite,' grinned Vanessa. 'He merely felt obliged to make some provision for me – having inherited my home, you understand – and marriage seemed the most economical way of doing so. I was to be a very frugal wife, you see. My appearance was to be creditable but on no account extravagant – although he did say – ' her voice trembled with laughter – 'that he would be glad for me to have something done to my hair!'

The Duke looked back at her gravely. 'In truth, a most elegant proposal. I am amazed you found yourself unmoved by it.'

'But I *was* moved,' she objected. 'Right out of Cornwall!'

He was forced to laugh. And then, after a brief silence, 'And so you go to your godmama.'

The smile left Vanessa's lips and the constraint with which she answered did not escape him. 'Yes. I wish now that I had written asking if she would have me. But I was so angry that I did not think of it until it was too late.' She sighed and continued more wistfully than she knew, 'I only hope that she will want me.'

Lyndhurst did not reply and his expression was enigmatic. Silence fell again until, suddenly, they were jerked into awareness by sounds of commotion outside the room. Vanessa heard mine host expostulating with a gentleman of hearty voice and then, frowning, his Grace said, 'I think I know this traveller. Let us hope Wilkins does not feel it necessary to advertise my presence.'

'Why not?' asked Vanessa puzzled.

'It surprises me that you need ask,' he responded coldly. 'It can do you no good whatever to have it known that you spent the evening alone with a man, but to have it known that you spent it alone with *me* would ruin you.'

'Dear me!' she said placidly. 'I had no idea you were so dangerous. I wonder why?'

'Because Friday being my day of rest, I have given you no demonstration of it,' he snapped.

From the other side of the door they heard the gentleman say, 'Lyndhurst, you say? Why did you not tell me so before? Out of my way, man! I know his Grace.' And with that, the door burst open and he swept inside.

The Duke rose, smiling unpleasantly. 'What an unexpected pleasure, my dear Winthrop.'

'Like your return, Lucifer – like your return! When did you get back from Paris?' The gentleman divested himself of his cloak and then, suddenly noticing Vanessa, rolled an expressive eye at his Grace. 'Stap me! I had no idea you had company – that fool of a landlord should have told me. I'll remove myself directly . . . but won't you present me?'

'Of course,' said the Duke smoothly. 'Mistress Tremaine, may I present to you Mr James Winthrop . . . Mistress Vanessa Tremaine.'

Winthrop made a jerky bow and Vanessa her best curtsy. She said, 'Please do not go on my account, sir. I was just about to retire.' And turning to his Grace, 'I must thank you, sir, for your help – and for your patience.'

'The pleasure was mine, child.' He walked to the door and held it open while she curtsied to Winthrop and passed through it. Then he stepped after her and partly closed it behind him. 'As I make an early start it is unlikely that we shall meet in the morning and so I will wish you a safe journey.'

Impulsively, Vanessa turned to look up at him. 'Perhaps we shall meet in London?'

'I shall be desolate if we do not.' He bowed. And this time it was impossible to tell if he mocked or not.

For a moment after she had gone, Lyndhurst gazed enigmatically after her and then, smiling maliciously, re-entered the parlour.

Mr Winthrop looked owlishly at him and said, 'Charming – quite charming! But not your type, I shouldn't have thought. Where did you find her?'

'How like you to fall into vulgar error, my dear James. I . . . found her . . . as you so eloquently put it, on the road some two miles from here where her coach lay in the ditch.'

'And rescued her from the perils of the lonely wayside to dine *à deux* with you?' Mr Winthrop slapped his thigh. 'Stap me, but that's a good jest! She'd have been safer in the ditch!'

11

His Grace waited in frigid silence for his companion's hilarity to subside. Then he said, 'Astounding as it may seem to you, I do not make a point of seducing, raping, abducting or otherwise molesting quite *every* woman with whom I make contact.'

'Aye – of course. You know I wasn't serious.' His laughter gone, Winthrop looked ill at ease.

'Natrually not,' said Lyndhurst ironically.

'Tremaine, I think you said? A connection of old Tom's perhaps?'

'His daughter,' replied his Grace wearily. 'She is on her way to her godmother's home. Lady Henley, in fact.'

Winthrop's jaw dropped. 'Good God!'

The Duke rose, yawning delicately behind his hand. 'Just so. And now, if you will excuse me, I shall tear myself away from the delights of your society in favour of my bed.' The sarcasm in his voice was thinly veiled. 'I bid you goodnight, Winthrop.'

'Eh? Oh, yes. Goodnight,' replied Winthrop, startled.

His Grace walked with measured tread to the door and then turned, smiling faintly. 'By the way . . . my room is at the end of the passage on the first floor – should you feel it necessary to safeguard Mistress Tremaine's virtue by keeping watch.'

And with that he was gone, leaving Mr Winthrop to babble fruitlessly at the closing door; and, when it was safely shut, to pull a face.

Checkmate in Two Squares

At some time after two on the following day, the Duke of Lyndhurst presented himself at the Great Jermyn Street home of his only sister and her husband, Viscount Overton. Lady Blanche sat in the drawing-room setting rather petulant stitches in a piece of embroidery but, as his Grace was announced, she flung it aside and ran across the room to throw her arms around his neck.

'Francis – oh, Francis! I am vastly delighted to see you!'

Disengaging himself, Lyndhurst said, 'So it appears. I rejoice to find you within, Blanche, but must beg you to control your raptures. I am not accustomed to such violence.'

'Very well, very well! But come and sit down. How was Paris? When did you get back? Oh – tell me everything!'

'Your impatience is very fatiguing,' he complained gently as he selected a chair and seated himself. 'I am surprised that Laurence bears with you. And where, if one is permitted to ask, is your estimable husband?'

Blanche frowned. 'Indeed, Francis, you shall not sneer at Laurie! He is very good to me.'

'So you have often told me. But that does not answer my question.'

She laughed jerkily and sat down amidst a flurry of taffeta. 'It's horrid of you to tease me. But I am glad to see you – truly I am. Laurie is at his club and I had resolved to spend the day quietly but I was bored within an hour.'

'And even I am an improvement on solitude,' said her brother, bowing. *'Merci du compliment.'*

She gave a little trill of laughter. 'You know I didn't mean that. Now – tell me about Paris. Was it amusing?'

'Very. And you will doubtless be ecstatic to hear that you are still remembered . . . in particular by Monsieur de Villagnon.'

Blanche gave a crow of triumph and went on to chatter happily of her Paris acquaintances. After a time, she said, 'Your return is very sudden, Francis. When did you arrive?'

'This morning. I had not thought to find you still here. Have you finally persuaded Laurence to forsake the rural pleasures?'

'Oh no. You know he never likes to be in town for long. He wants to go to Audley Vale. Charles and Judith have asked us for a visit.' The wilful little face grew stormy. 'But nothing could induce me to go!'

'Ah. And why not?'

'Because I've no desire to be bored to distraction by Madam Judith!' she snapped.

Lyndhurst raised enquiring brows and his eyes mocked.

'All she can talk of are her child's doings and prattlings,' continued Blanche. 'And if it's not that, then it's her herbs and her still-room! Goodness knows it was bad enough here in town – but a whole month at Audley is more than I can bear!' His Grace smiled provokingly and his sister stood up with an angry stamp. 'You are all the same! Half the men in town are positively foolish about her. But I am amazed at *you*, Francis. She is quite bourgeoise . . . unless country manners are to your taste?'

The smile vanished and his eyes grew cold. 'Jealousy is a tedious emotion, my dear. You should strive to conquer it.'

She eyed him sulkily but heeded the warning. 'You are dreadfully ill-natured today, Francis. Don't you love me a little?'

'Like you, Blanche, I love only myself,' he replied. And then, less harshly, 'You would be happier if you could content yourself with less, my dear.'

'Like you, you mean? she demanded pettishly.

'Not in the least like me. I am precisely the same – but unlike you I have no one to please but myself.'

14

'And it's just as well,' said Blanche waspishly, 'for you are – '

'Pray refrain from enumerating my vices. I assure you that I am entirely aware of them and I lack the time to listen to a complete recital.' He rose and faced her, smiling a little. 'And now I believe I must take my leave.'

'Don't go!' She flew to his side in a swish of blue taffeta. 'I am sorry I was cross. Stay a little longer. Are you going to Lady Knightley's rout?' She laid a coaxing hand on his arm.

'I am. No doubt I shall see you there – and, of course, the saintly Laurence.' He removed her hand from his sleeve to raise it to his lips and then halted a moment. 'By the way – did you know of the somewhat sudden demise of Sir Thomas Tremaine?'

She looked up at him in surprise. 'Why, yes. It's all over town. It seems he went hunting whilst in his cups and took a fall. Why do you ask?'

'No reason. A thought, no more. *Au revoir*, my dear.' And he was gone.

As was his custom, Lyndhurst arrived late at the Knightley rout and walked coolly into the light of a great chandelier to stand beneath it. The diamonds on his fingers and in his cravat sparkled as he moved and though, as usual, he wore black, no dress in the room was more magnificent. Snowy lace lay at his throat and fell in deep ruffles over his hands and his dark hair was strikingly confined by long silver ribbons.

Having made his apologies to his hostess, he made his leisurely way through the main salon to the card-room where he found Gideon Vaughan playing with Milford and Drew.

'Lucifer!' said Milford. 'Falmouth said we could expect to see you tonight but I rather thought you'd be renewing your . . . friendship . . . with the captivating Mistress Charrington.'

His Grace looked blank and then light dawned. 'Ah. The dark-haired heiress from Yorkshire, was it not?'

'He had forgotten! Francis – how could you?'

'No doubt the smiles of La Pompadour are as effective as the waters of Lethe,' said Mr Vaughan quietly.

The Duke winced. *'Et tu, Bruté?'*

'The rumours were false then? We rather thought you had been forced to flee from fat Louis' wrath.'

'Did you so? How imaginative!' said his Grace admiringly. 'Don't play, Gideon.'

Mr Vaughan threw down his cards. 'Will you believe that I only get hands like that when you are nearby?'

The merest hint of a smile lurked in the Duke's eyes.

'Shall I apologise?'

'I doubt you know how!'

'That is quite possible. I have not had much practice, you know. Come – let us walk. Gentlemen.' Lyndhurst bowed and, followed by Mr Vaughan, moved slowly back to the salon. Raising his glass, he gazed across the room. 'Dear me! I rather fear that I perceive Lady Marchant beckoning to us. I think we had better obey, don't you?'

Lady Alicia Marchant, a lively dame nearing her seventieth year, grinned wickedly at the Duke and bade Mr Vaughan fetch her a glass of canary. Then, as Gideon walked good-humouredly away, she remarked approvingly, 'He's a nice boy.'

'Hardly a boy,' commented his Grace lazily.

'Ha! He seems one to me – and so, come to that, do you, Francis Courtenay. You forget I knew you before you were breeched!'

'And no matter how hard I try to do so, you invariably remind me.' His eyes gleamed.

Lady Alicia laughed. 'It's as well that *someone* stands up to you, my lad. Makes you more human.'

'You overwhelm me,' he drawled. 'Such concern for my welfare is most touching – but wholly unnecessary, I think.'

'Do you?' snorted her ladyship. 'It's time you were wed and setting up your nursery – unless you want Randolph to succeed you? A good gal who loved you but wouldn't let you wipe your boots on her the way you do with anyone who gives you the chance. That's what you need. Be the making of you.'

'You flatter me.' His voice was chilling. 'I am what you see – and, in all probability, will remain so. As you should know.'

16

Sighing, Lady Alicia fell silent as her mind slid back through the years and she recalled his father, a cold, hard man whose only passion had been the card-table; and his mother, a beauty of unrivalled, shrew-like selfishness. And from this, another face came to mind: the face of a Madonna, framed with hair of silver-gilt. How old had he been then? Twenty?

The arrival of Mr Vaughan with her wine prevented any further meditation on this theme and, as Lady Alicia received her glass, she heard the Duke say pensively, 'Ah. The charming mama of my so-dear friend Carlton Henley.'

'What devilry have you in mind now?' she asked sharply. 'It's seven years, I'll swear, since that business with Blanche.'

'Nearer nine,' he corrected. 'But, you see, I have not forgotten.'

'You challenged him, didn't you?' asked Gideon.

'Naturally. But we did not meet. A sudden indisposition occasioned his prolonged sojourn in the country.'

'He was afraid!' said Lady Alicia forcefully. 'And the story got about, of course, and he was the jest of the town for weeks. It was a far more fitting punishment than the sword could ever be!'

'Unfortunately,' said his Grace gently, 'I cannot agree with you.'

'You surely can't bear a grudge for nine years,' objected Gideon.

'A grudge? No. Let us say merely that I would rather have dealt with the matter . . . er . . . personally.'

'I'm told you've never spoken to him since?' queried my Lady.

'No. He . . . removes himself from my path. His mother, on the other hand, regards me with venom.' The topaz eyes rested on her with remote interest. 'What do you know of her, madam?'

'Of Maria Henley? Why, only that which all the world is aware of, I am happy to say!'

'Which is?'

'That she is proud, values her house more than her son and would probably manage to discover a secret vice in the Archangel Gabriel. What interest has she for you?'

'None, I think,' said the Duke, rising from his seat. 'I see

Viscount Burford bearing down upon us and, since it is plain that he is one of your most devoted admirers, we will undoubtedly be *de trop*. Come, Gideon.'

As they moved away, Lyndhurst asked casually, 'What is being said of Tremaine's death?'

'Only what you've no doubt heard. A glass too many and a fall on the hunting field. Why?'

'Oh – idle curiosity. Nothing more.'

Neat in brown velvet, Viscount Overton moved towards them and bowed slightly. 'You appear as suddenly as ever, Francis.'

'As you say,' replied Lyndhurst smoothly. 'My craving to be once more in the bosom of my family, you know.'

'Indeed,' said his lordship coldly. 'Then you will be pleased to hear that Randolph has also returned to the fold and is even now playing piquet in the small salon.'

'Touché!' muttered Gideon, under his breath.

'I thank you for the warning, Laurence. I shall curb my impatience to embrace him.'

'So he will be forced to borrow money elsewhere?' asked his lordship gently.

'How well you understand me,' came the equally gentle reply.

'It isn't difficult.'

A faint smile lurked in his Grace's eyes. 'You think so? But I delay you, Laurence. Pray tell Blanche that I am desolate to have missed her but will call on her in the next few days.'

'As you wish. Your servant, Vaughan.' The Viscount bowed curtly and walked away.

Once outside in the square, Lyndhurst and Mr Vaughan turned down Berkeley Street in the direction of Piccadilly.

'The lack of warmth between you and Overton is even more marked than it used to be,' remarked Gideon.

Lyndhurst laughed. 'Just so. He dislikes me cordially, you know.'

'I had noticed. Perhaps if you were to allow him a glimpse of your better self – ?'

'An impossibility, my dear. Unlike you, Laurence is fully

18

aware that I do not have one. And indeed, I am continually amazed that *you* remain undaunted in the fight to reform me.'

'I remain undaunted,' said Gideon with dignity, 'because, despite anything you may say to the contrary, I cannot believe that you are completely content. You are never in one place for more than a month at a time and you've had more mistresses these past two years than most men acquire in a lifetime. They have cost you a fortune and bored you in a matter of weeks. I know – you have always lived this way, eating from the trough at both ends; but since your affair with Judith it has become steadily worse.'

'Do I understand you to pity me?' asked Lyndhurst, quietly contemptuous. 'You overreach yourself. And your sympathy would be more usefully directed towards the wife you were doubtless about to advise me to take. She would need it; I do not.'

'Just so,' said Mr Vaughan, frostily.

A gleam of humour reappeared in his Grace's eyes. 'You should visit Lady Marchant. Only think how comfortably the two of you could discuss my depravity. Fortunately, it bothers me not at all.'

Gideon was forced to smile. 'That is quite typical. You have no conscience to trouble you.'

'None,' agreed his Grace blandly. 'Virtue goes unrewarded and vice unpunished. And since virtue and tedium so often go hand in hand, I much prefer the crooked path.'

'How can you know? You have never tried the moral one.'

'Nor have I the ambition to do so,' drawled the Duke. *'Better to reign in Hell than serve in Heaven . . .* It seems to have escaped your attention that we are about to pass my house. Will you enter my unhallowed portals for a rubber of piquet?'

'Only if we play for penny points,' laughed Gideon. 'I'd need the devil's own luck to match your skill!'

'And *I* am more likely to have that, am I not?' A soundless laugh shook him. 'Enter, my dear. We'll play for love.'

* * *

19

At about the same time that his Grace of Lyndhurst set out for the Knightley rout, Vanessa Tremaine stepped out on to the pavement in Portman Square, her mind in the grip of a fierce exhilaration. Her own small Odyssey was over and she had managed it alone and in spite of her cousin. Having paid off the postboys, she found she had arrived with less than a shilling in her purse and the thought of coming quite so close to disaster was a powerful one.

Her moment of triumph was destined to be short-lived. As she turned and looked up eagerly at the house, a most unwelcome sight met her eyes. Instead of the warmth of lights at the windows, she saw the shutters were up and the knocker off the door. The house bore every appearance of being uninhabited. Gathering her frozen wits, Vanessa found the gate to the area steps and descended to the basement door.

She knocked and waited. There was no response. Her heart began to behave rather oddly and, clenching her fist, she hammered on the offending portal with all her strength. It seemed that the silence following this assault lasted an age before she heard the sound of footsteps. For a second the relief of it coupled with hunger and exhaustion threatened to overcome her and she leaned heavily against the wall. There was a grating rattle as the bolts were drawn back and then the door swung open to reveal a large, sleepy young man in his shirtsleeves.

Pulling herself together, Vanessa said, 'I wish to see Lady Henley. Is she here?'

He thought about it and then shook his head.

'Then please tell me where I can find her.'

This required even more thought. He scratched his chin. 'Can't,' he said, at length.

'Why not?'

'Never 'eard of 'er.' He grinned as though it was a matter for congratulation.

Vanessa forced herself to speak patiently. 'But you must have. Don't you work for her?'

He stared perplexedly and then shook his head again. 'I works for my Lady Aster. This is 'er 'ouse, see.'

20

Chilly fingers closed tight round Vanessa's heart as, for the first time in her life, she felt and recognised paralysing fear. 'I daresay it's very late?' she asked, her voice seeming to come from a long way off.

'Aye,' agreed the servant amiably. 'Gone eleven. Mebbe.'

'Dear God!'

She turned and stumbled up the stairs. As she gained the street, she heard the door slam below and then a wave of shuddering blackness all but engulfed her. Clinging to the railings, she bent down, allowing her head to fall forward and slowly, gradually, the faintness receded leaving her shivering weakly. Cautiously, she stood up, pressing a hand to her throbbing temples.

'What are you doing hanging around here at this time of night?' The deep voice startled her and with a gasp, she wheeled to face its owner.

'Who are you?' she asked breathlessly.

'I'm the Watch. Who are *you* is more to the point. It wants but half an hour to midnight. A nice time for any decent wench to be abroad!'

Some of her panic evaporated. He was large and looked reassuringly stolid and dependable. 'I – I'm in a terrible mess. Can you help me?'

'What's this?' He was surprised. Her pure accent told him that this was no common girl but a lady – and ladies did not wander the town unaccompanied at any time, especially so late at night. 'Now then, Miss. Calm down and tell me what's wrong.

Slowly, Vanessa explained her situation and the Watch listened carefully without interrupting her. When she had finished, he said thoughtfully, 'Well, you were right. A rare mess, and no mistake.'

She nodded ruefully. 'I should have written first. A letter would have found her, wouldn't it?'

'Aye. And though we can locate her tomorrow, that don't solve your problem tonight. The only place I can take you is the lock-up – and that won't do. Not for the likes of you, it won't.'

21

'Why not? I assure you I am not likely to mind a little discomfort.'

The Watch regarded her with pitying sarcasm. 'Oh, you're not, are you? And I suppose you won't mind sharing a floor with all the drunks, whores and pickpockets we're likely to round up afore morning?'

Vanessa flushed. 'Oh. I didn't understand.'

'And ain't *that* the truth! Now, I want you to think. There must be someone else you can go to. Some old servant, perhaps?'

Vanessa thought. 'I'm sorry but there isn't anyone. I was never in London until today and I don't know – oh!' She broke off suddenly.

'You've thought of someone?'

'Yes – no – oh, no! I *couldn't*!' she said emphatically.

'Don't seem to me as you've a mort of choice, so you'd best tell me,' he replied firmly. 'Who is it?'

'Well, I . . . oh, it's the Duke of Lyndhurst,' she said in a rush. 'But I can't go to him. It's impossible. And useless because I don't know where he lives either.'

'St James Square,' said the Watch.

'W-What?' she asked faintly.

'St James Square – that's where Lyndhurst House is. Part of my job to know where the real nobs live,' he added with simple pride.

She looked at him helplessly. 'I doubt if his Grace is at home.'

'Well there's one way to find out.'

'But you don't understand!' she said in alarm. 'I scarcely know him. We met yesterday for the first time and quite by chance. He would think me totally mad – '

'Whatever he thinks, it's no use standing here half the night arguing. Beggars can't be choosers as you must know.'

Without more ado, he picked up her valise and bade her follow him. It was some distance and most of the way he kept up a monologue, warning her of the dangers likely to befall young and delicately reared ladies who roamed the streets alone at night. Vanessa felt a wild impulse to laugh, thinking that his Grace would doubtless claim to be one of them.

Lyndhurst House was a large and imposing residence faced with stone, with a wide flight of shallow steps leading up to a magnificent porticoed entrance. Too weary now to argue, Vanessa allowed the Watch to lead her up to the door and pull the bell. Worn out by the rigours of the day, hungry and miserable, she steeled herself to meet the coming ordeal.

St James Square: Lyndhurst House.

It was not without some inner quaking that Amos Benson opened the door to admit his Grace that night for he had been in the service of the Courtenays for more years than he cared to remember and was perfectly aware that nothing was less calculated to please Lyndhurst than the news that a dowdy female was at present ensconced in the morning-room.

'Claret, Benson. In the Library,' said the Duke, moving across the hall.

'Certainly, your Grace.' He bowed. 'If I might have a word, your Grace?'

His master sighed. 'Must it be now?'

'Yes, your Grace — if it please you.'

'It does not please me. However, let us get it over with.'

Benson hesitated and glanced questioningly at Mr Vaughan.

'Well?' asked Lyndhurst, very bored.

Nerves caused Benson to rush his fences. 'Your Grace, a lady has called. She desired to await your return so I took the liberty of placing her in the morning-room.' He held his breath.

Lyndhurst's eyes narrowed. 'I fear I must be a little stupid. It is your place, I had thought, to exclude unwanted visitors.'

'Yes, your Grace. But the lady was accompanied by the Watch and —'

'*The Watch*?' Lyndhurst was shaken from his habitual languor. 'And you let this trollop in?'

24

'No, your Grace! That is to say, I did let her in but she is not a person of that type,' said Benson, much hurt by this slur on his powers of discernment.

At this point Gideon could no longer conceal the mirth which threatened to consume him. His crack of laughter, belatedly turned into a fit of coughing, had the effect of diverting Lyndhurst's attention away from his ruffled butler.

'I fail to see the humour in this,' he said coldly. And then, restoring his piercing gaze to the unfortunate Benson, 'I presume that this . . . lady . . . has a name?'

'Yes, your Grace. Mistress Tremaine.'

The black brows drew together in a sudden frown. 'Ah. I see. Very well. You will bring claret to the library and then show in Mistress Tremaine.'

'Yes, your Grace.' Thankfully, Benson withdrew.

Still frowning a little, Lyndhurst ushered Mr Vaughan into the library, closed the doors and walked thoughtfully across the room to the fireside. In seeming abstraction, his eyes rested on the face of his friend, apparently oblivious of the surprised curiosity they saw there. The frown lifted and the topaz eyes gleamed as he said calmly, 'I fear that we shall have to postpone our game.'

Mr Vaughan laughed. 'Damn you, Francis! Do you really know this woman?'

'It might be said so,' said his Grace negligently. Then he also laughed. 'Since you do not intend to make a tactful exit, I imagine that you curiosity will soon be satisfied.'

'Do you wish me to leave?' Gideon rose from his seat only to be pressed back by his Grace's hand on his shoulder.

'No. I think I should prefer you to stay – in the role of chaperon.'

'For you or the mysterious Mistress Tremaine?'

'I think, perhaps, for both of us.'

A discreet tap heralded the arrival of Benson bearing claret on a silver tray. He set this down on a side-table and said, 'Shall I show in the lady now, your Grace?'

'Yes. Ah, Benson . . . how long has Mistress Tremaine been here?'

25

'Just over an hour, your Grace.'

'I see. Thank you. That is all.'

Benson bowed and went out.

'An odd hour for visiting, surely?' said Gideon.

'Yes. I am inclined to agree with you.'

'It's very intriguing.'

'Very,' agreed his Grace urbanely.

The doors opened again and, as Benson announced her name, Vanessa came slowly into the room. Her startled gaze took in Mr Vaughan's unexpected presence and then travelled to his Grace who moved unhurriedly forward to make an elaborate leg.

'I bid you good evening, Mistress Tremaine – or perhaps morning would be more appropriate – and welcome, somewhat belatedly it would seem, to my house.'

Vanessa curtsied nervously. 'Thank you, your Grace. It must appear strange to you, but I . . . it was . . .'

'Not at all,' murmured his Grace suavely. 'An honour – although an unexpected one. You must tell me to what I owe it. But first permit me to present the Honourable Gideon Vaughan.'

Vanessa, who had sustained what she devoutly hoped would prove the most trying hours of her life, hardly registered the Honourable Gideon's bow and conventional greeting. She responded automatically, aware only of the icy indifference in the Duke's eyes and wondering if the lock-up might not have been preferable. But what can't be cured must be endured, she thought desperately, and he can't eat me, after all! And on this heartening note, she stepped impulsively forward; her head swam dizzily and she swayed perilously before collapsing mutely at the Duke's feet.

Astounded, Gideon sprang forward but Lyndhurst was before him. Frowning, he stooped, lifted the inert form easily in his arms and carried it to a sofa. 'Open the window,' he said tersely. 'And get me some brandy.'

While Gideon hastened to do as he was bidden, his Grace untied the ribbons of Vanessa's shapeless bonnet, cast it aside

26

and unclasped her cloak from around her throat. He felt her pulse and proceeded to chafe her hands. By the time Mr Vaughan arrived with the brandy she was beginning to regain consciousness.

'Well, my dear, that was quite an entrance. No – don't try to move just yet. You'll feel very much better in a moment. The glass if you please, Gideon.'

Stupefied at the change, Mr Vaughan passed it to him. His Grace remained on one knee beside the couch and, sliding an arm behind her shoulders, he helped Vanessa to sit up. 'Drink this,' was all he said.

Vanessa looked at the contents of the glass with suspicion and then raised her eyes to his face. The world had now righted itself and things no longer spun unpleasantly round her although she still felt very sick. She looked searchingly into his eyes and then, apparently satisfied, took a sip from the glass. The fumes from the brandy made her cough but the warmth that ran through her veins instantly began to revive her. She leaned back against his arm and grinned weakly.

Lyndhurst looked down at her, a curious smile lurking in his eyes. 'Well, child?'

Vanessa found everything suddenly made simple. She said, 'My godmama has removed from Portman Square and I have nowhere to go. Will you help me, please?'

'Presently,' replied Lyndhurst calmly. 'First, I think you should sit up.' He stood and watched as Vanessa swung her feet to the floor and arranged her skirts about her. Then he pulled the bell. 'And I think you will be the better for some food.'

'Shall I?' she asked dubiously. 'It's true that I never faint and I *was* very hungry. But now I feel a little sick and I think that if I ate anything I might . . .' She stopped and looked enquiringly at Mr Vaughan who had uttered a choke of laughter. 'Have I said something I shouldn't?'

'Nothing that need concern you, child,' replied Lyndhurst gravely. 'Ah – Benson. Mistress Tremaine would like some supper. You may prepare a tray and serve it in here.'

'Very good, your Grace.' Benson bowed impassively and retired.

By this time, Gideon's curiosity was beginning to get the better of him. 'I do not wish to appear vulgarly intrusive,' he said, 'but will you please tell me how you come to be acquainted?'

'Yes, Gideon, I think I must – with your permission, Mistress Tremaine?' His Grace looked at Vanessa who nodded. 'Briefly, this is the daughter of the late Sir Thomas Tremaine. For a number of reasons into which we need not go, she decided to leave Cornwall for the home of her godmother, Lady Henley.'

'Good God!' exclaimed Gideon.

Lyndhurst smiled and continued smoothly, 'Just so. Last night our respective coaches were involved in a minor fracas resulting in the loss of a wheel to Mistress Tremaine's conveyance and making it necessary for me to ... er ... rescue her from the perils of the lonely wayside. We dined and were disturbed, most unfortunately, by the untimely arrival of James Winthrop.' He paused, the blue eyes glinting maliciously. 'Yes ... by Winthrop. I see you understand me, Gideon.'

'I'm not sure that I do,' returned his friend grimly. 'But please go on.'

'There is little to add. Mistress Tremaine very wisely retired to her room – and of the rest, you know as much as I.'

'Do I?' muttered Gideon, not quite beneath his breath.

The Duke met his searching gaze silently and with a touch of hauteur, while Vanessa looked from one to the other in some bewilderment, unable to comprehend the tension which had sprung up between them. She was just about to speak when Benson returned bearing a laden supper-tray which he set down beside her.

'Will there by anything else, your Grace?' asked Benson.

'No,' answered Lyndhurst slowly. 'Not for the moment. Eat, child,' he told Vanessa, 'and then you can complete the story for us. Gideon – I suggest that you sit and strive to contain your suspicions. Claret?'

Mr Vaughan nodded curtly and sat down while the Duke poured two glasses of wine and handed one to him. Lyndhurst himself remained standing, one arm resting on the mantelpiece and his eyes dwelling meditatively on Gideon's face. Then he said softly, 'Your apparent lack of faith in my word is almost insulting. I wonder why I bear with you?'

'Because you have to admit that you give me cause to doubt. But I *don't* doubt your word – when you give it.'

The black brows rose. 'Should I be grateful?'

Gideon gave a choke of reluctant laughter. 'Oh sit down, curse you! You're impossible.'

'Oh quite, my dear,' replied Lyndhurst with the ghost of a smile. But he sat down and proceeded to inquire languidly about the events in London during his absence. Gideon had little to relate and finally, in desperation, produced the only fragment of information he felt likely to be of interest. 'Charles and Judith Maynard paid a brief visit to town last month but it's said that Madam was anxious to return to Audley Vale.'

Lyndhurst's eyes narrowed almost imperceptibly but he said evenly, 'You see, Gideon, at best women are dull creatures. Even the lovely Judith.'

'It's over then? You don't care any more?'

'What do you think?'

It was at this point that Vanessa judged it time to remind them of her presence. She rose, walked over to the Duke and curtsied deeply before him. 'Your Grace, I can't express my gratitude but – '

'Then I suggest that you refrain from trying,' he said, pulling forward a chair. 'Instead, you might sit down and tell us the rest of your story.'

'I think there is little to add,' said Vanessa, doing as he bade her. 'You were right when you said I have been rash. I have no money and nowhere to go.'

'So it would appear,' he replied calmly. He sat down, his face in the shadow of the great carved mantel. 'But I should be glad if you will begin at the ... er ... beginning.'

So Vanessa told of her adventures, haltingly at first and then more fluently. Lyndhurst, meanwhile, exhibited neither sympathy nor impatience as he listened to the tired, husky voice of his uninvited guest. His face was a cool and expressionless mask, but he missed nothing and noted

29

dispassionately her total lack of self-pity despite the strain plainly evident on her face.

Describing her precipitate departure from the house in Portman Square and her apprehension by the Watch, Vanessa faltered and stopped, coughing a little. Lyndhurst rose unhurriedly and poured a glass of wine which he handed to her saying, 'One thing more I desire to understand. What made you decide to come here?'

Vanessa looked up, startled by the keenness of his gaze. 'I did not . . . well, not in the way I think you mean it.'

'And what way is that?'

'You seem to . . . well, to think that I took the decision lightly –that I wanted to come.'

'And did you?'

'Have done, Francis,' said Gideon. 'It's unnecessary.'

'Let be.' snapped Lyndhurst. 'Well?'

Vanessa swallowed. 'It was the Watch. He asked if there wasn't someone I might go to. I told him I didn't know anyone in London but he continued to press it.'

'Yes?' prompted the Duke relentlessly.

'I suddenly thought of you – I don't know why,' said the girl in weary agitation. 'I said I only knew one other person who lived in London but that it was out of the question. I was tired and confused. He asked me your name and I gave it. He knew your direction and he insisted on bringing me here because the lock-up wasn't suitable.'

'Quite right!' said Gideon, shocked.

The Duke relaxed a little and said provocatively, 'You think a night spent beneath my roof to be preferable?'

'That too has its disadvantages,' returned Gideon swiftly, 'but at least I am here to limit them. In the lock-up she would have been exposed to . . . all manner of undesirable persons.'

'I think I follow your meaning,' said Lyndhurst amused.

'And so do I,' announced Vanessa unexpectedly. 'You are referring to the type of female of whose existence a lady is supposed to be entirely unaware. I believe that you allude to them as *filles de joie*,' she added helpfully. And then, with a touch of regret, 'Although I have never met one myself.'

30

'I should think not,' said Gideon. 'Really, Mistress Tremaine – you shouldn't speak of such things, you know.'

'Papa told me never to be coy. He didn't like it.'

'And one cannot but appreciate his point,' interposed Lyndhurst. 'But you must spare Mr Vaughan's delicate sensibilities.'

Gideon uttered a choking sound somewhere between a splutter and an unwilling laugh. 'You're as bad as she is,' he told the Duke. 'Lady Henley will suffer an apoplexy if she hears Mistress Tremaine discussing such matters.'

'There is always that possibility,' agreed his Grace sweetly. Turning to Vanessa, he continued, 'It is, I think, too late to remedy your situation tonight so I will have Benson conduct you to a bedchamber. Tomorrow you shall go to Lady Henley and all will be well.

Gideon's open countenance expressed a lot of doubt and something more. 'Francis – it won't be if she stays here with you.'

Lyndhurst eyed him lazily. 'Then what do you suggest? That she spend the night in your lodging? I hardly think that would be an improvement.'

'No. But she can't stay here with you. You don't even have a housekeeper.'

'I fail to see what difference that would make,' said his Grace coolly. 'Come, Gideon, you try my patience. She is tired and you obviously have no alternative to suggest.' And he gazed mockingly at Mr Vaughan for an instant, then rang the bell.

Smiling, Vanessa crossed the room to stand before him. 'I wish to thank you. You have been extraordinarily kind and it's something I can never repay for I don't know what I should have done. Please accept my deepest gratitude.' And she sank into a low curtsy and kissed his hand.

A curious expression flickered in the topaz eyes and the hard mouth twisted a little. Then, raising her from her obeisance, he said in his most blighting manner, 'Pray reserve your gratitude for a more fitting recipient, my child. I believe I have already informed you that I am never kind – save for my own reasons.

Whatever I do, I do only because it pleases me. When it ceases to do so, you will needs look elsewhere for help. Last night you laughed at my reputation but you will do well to accept that it has been well-earned and charity has never formed any part of it.'

His tone had its customary effect and she turned away as if he had slapped her. Lyndhurst did not appear to be aware of her hurt and he turned to his butler with a series of smooth orders. Then, looking impersonally back Vanessa, he said, 'I trust that you will be comfortable, Mistress Tremaine.'

'Yes. Thank you. Good night, your Grace – sir.' Unaccountably close to tears, she curtsied mechanically and followed Benson from the room.

Silence fell as the door clicked shut. Then Gideon said, 'It makes me sick to see a child like that kissing your profligate hand; but why, in God's name, did you find it necessary to throw her gratitude in her face?'

Stung from his habitual languor, the Duke snapped, 'Damn you, I don't want her gratitude!' before, with a visible effort, he took hold of himself and resumed his usual sneer. 'You disappoint me. I expected you to applaud my honesty.'

'You even destroy that virtue, don't you? Not that I for one moment believe that's why you did it!'

'It is totally immaterial to me what you believe,' returned his Grace icily.

'Now that I can accept,' said Gideon furiously. 'But I know you, Francis – and I'm damned if I'll let you ruin that girl!'

'Will you not, my dear?' The drawling voice was silky smooth but the topaz eyes held twin demons. 'And just what makes you think that I shall await your permission?'

In Which Vanessa makes the Acquaintance of her Godmother

Despite her extreme exhaustion, Vanessa passed a restless night, her sleep troubled by vivid dreams in which his Grace of Lyndhurst figured as a tall and sinister knight completely encased in armour of black steel. Amber eyes shining behind the visor like those of a cat, the knight protected her from the dangers that threatened to engulf her; but when, safe at last, she turned to offer him her thanks, she found the visor raised and the armour empty of any human form.

She awoke with a start, beads of moisture forming on her brow and, with shaking hands, dragged herself out of bed to pull back the heavy curtains at the window. A rosy glow heralded the birth of the day and she sighed, looking down at the deserted square and suffering a sudden sharp longing for Cornwall. Impatiently, she brushed the back of her hand across her eyes and walked slowly back to bed, surprised to find that she was shivering. She lay quite still, eyes wide open, staring at the canopy of the bed and afraid to doze in case the dreams returned with sleep. Then, in the distance, church bells started to ring and brought her to the place of her hardest battle.

It's Sunday, she thought dully. Sunday the twenty-ninth. Less than three weeks. Three weeks ago today I went to church, spoke to the tenants, taught the Sunday-school, all as usual. And yet now it seems like another life. Only three weeks since that Sunday and five days later . . . Friday the thirteenth . . . We joked about it . . . and four hours later they brought him home

33

on a gate.' She turned her face into the pillow and pressed her hands over her ears to shut out the chiming bells. 'I won't think about it. I can't – not yet.'

When she awoke again the June sun was streaming through the open curtains and a smiling housemaid stood beside the bed, holding a tray. 'Good morning, Miss. Benson said not to wake you if you was asleep. I hope I didn't?'

'No,' said Vanessa sleepily. 'What time is it?'

'Gone eleven, Miss. Now don't you worry.' This as Vanessa gave a gasp of dismay and moved to scramble out of bed. 'You just stay put and eat your breakfast. There's no hurry. His Grace went out over an hour ago and so far as I know never asked nor expected to see you.'

Vanessa sighed and sank back against the pillows. Then, smiling, she asked, 'What is your name?'

'Jassy, miss.' The girl grinned. 'Short for Jasmine, see. Not that I've ever been called aught but Jassy as long as I can remember. Now, Miss – you drink your chocolate while it's hot. You still look ever so pale.'

'Do I? Then stay and keep me company. I should be glad of someone to talk to – if you can spare the time, that is.'

'Bless you, Miss – 'course I can. Had a bad night, did you?'

'I . . . I dreamed a lot. I'd rather not think of it. I'd like to hear about you, if you don't mind telling me.'

'Me, Miss? Not much to tell. I've been here nigh on three years and it suits me well enough for all they say about his Grace being a devil and so on. Oh – I beg pardon, Miss!' She coloured hotly. 'My tongue'll get me hung one of these days!'

Vanessa laughed. 'Don't worry – I'm the same myself. You're London-bred, aren't you?'

'That's right, Miss. Southwark.'

Jassy talked on about her home and family (of whom there seemed to be a great number), often making Vanessa laugh and gradually chasing away the miasmas of the night. She looked with uncritical concern on Vanessa's two dresses and asked which of them she intended to wear that day.

'The green,' replied Vanessa with a grimace.

34

'Right then, Miss. You just stay there. I'll get this pressed and be back in a jiffy to help you. Now just stay where you are, mind! You'll catch your death wandering around in that thin night-rail.' And she took herself off, the despised green gown caught over her arm.

When Jassy reappeared there was no sign of the green dress. Instead, she carried a large rectangular package and a gaily striped band-box, both of which she laid triumphantly on the bed.

'What are they?' asked Vanessa suspiciously.

'Open 'em and see!' laughed the maid.

Slowly, Vanessa lifted the lid, parted layers of tissue and gasped as her gaze fell on a gown of pale grey grosgrain, tastefully trimmed with a darker grey French braid. Of their own volition, her hands lifted it from the box and stroked it reverently. 'Oh – it's beautiful!'

'Yes, Miss. And just the thing for you, if I may say so,' said Jassy as if she had fashioned the gown with her own hands. 'And look at the bonnet, Miss!'

Obediently, Vanessa opened the band-box to disclose a hat of black straw adorned with grey satin roses and matching ribbons. Leaping out of bed, she ran over to the mirror and placed it carefully on her dishevelled curls.

'Oh, Miss – you'll look a picture,' said her enthusiastic handmaiden.

Vanessa came down to earth with a jolt. 'Where did they come from?'

'Oh, Miss Vanessa – it was so funny! I was just about to come back up with your old dress when Thomas came down and said as Benson wanted me in the hall. And when I got there, his Grace was standing there holding these two.' She gestured to the boxes and giggled. 'I'd lay my life he's never carried a band-box before and he says to me, "Take these to Mistress Tremaine and return *that* – " meaning your old gown what I'd just pressed – "back to the . . . er . . . laundry-room."'

'I see,' said Vanessa bleakly. 'But, naturally, I can't accept such a gift. Please fetch my own gown, Jassy.'

The maid looked blank. 'But why? He must have had a terrible time getting 'em – it being Sunday and all.'

'That,' returned Vanessa hardily, 'is not the point.'

Jassy decided that it behoved her to tread carefully. 'As you say, Miss. But, although he's had no end of particulars, I've never known him put himself out to choose anything for one of them. Alphonse does it for him. But not today 'cause he hasn't been out of the house.'

'Oh,' said Vanessa, visibly weakening.

Pressing her advantage, Jassy (who neither believed in nor cared for Lyndhurst's feelings) said earnestly, 'It'd be a shame to snub him – after all his trouble.'

Vanessa found some attraction in the idea that her strange benefactor might be hurt if she repudiated his gift and was guiltily glad of an excuse to placate her conscience. 'Oh – very well, Jassy. You've persuaded me.'

Clapping her hands, face wreathed in smiles, Jassy bustled over to where Vanessa's other gown lay and proceeded to measure its waist against the new grey one. 'Best to see what sort of fit it's likely to be afore I lace your stays for his Grace must've had to guess. Not that I reckon he'll be much out – there!' She pointed smugly to the dresses. 'Only half an inch difference!'

Vanessa gazed in fascination at this evidence of his Grace's accuracy, recognising the amount of practice that must have made it possible and beginning to realise on what sort of foundation his reputation had been built.

Forty minutes later she stood ready before the mirror. Her hair was piled on top of her head with three long chestnut ringlets falling down her back. The black straw hat accentuated the pure oval of her face and grey stuff of the gown showed her creamy skin off to advantage. Vanessa studied her reflection in disbelief and said, 'Why, I look almost pretty!'

Jassy laughed. 'You look beautiful, Miss. Now – off you go downstairs. I'll show you the way.'

A few minutes later, Vanessa was again shown into the exquisitely furnished library. The Duke rose from his desk and immediately her new-found confidence began to ebb. There seemed to be some element in his presence that invariably made her feel stupid and gauche.

He made a deep formal bow, 'Good day to you, child. You look decidedly refreshed.'

'It's the gown,' said Vanessa. And then stopped abruptly, wondering what he would say if she tried to thank him and quite unaware that her dilemma was clearly written on her face. She drew a deep breath and went on with the daring born of desperation. 'Thank you for thinking of it. And don't say anything. If you don't care to be thanked, then you shouldn't make it necessary!' She looked at him severely and then, baffled by his silence and the tiny smile lurking in his eyes, 'Please – why did you do it?'

The smile gave way to a guarded expression. 'A whim, my dear. Do not let it concern you. Unlike me, you are too young to wear black; but it occurred to me that you would perhaps not wish to wear colours so soon.'

'Do you always wear black?' she asked. And realised just a moment too late how adroitly he had turned the subject.

'Always. I have worn nothing else for nearly twenty years. And I fear that if I broke the habit now, London would be as stunned as if Elector George turned Jacobite.'

She laughed. 'I see. Then it's fortunate that it suits you.'

She looked at him appraisingly, noting his splendid height and strong but elegant shoulders set off by a superb coat of black velvet; the pale fine-boned face and the thick, black hair neatly confined at the nape. Encountering his gaze, her eyes fell and she flushed without knowing why.

'You overwhelm me, mademoiselle,' he said with a slight, ironic bow. The topaz eyes mocked but the smile in them was not unpleasant. 'And now, I think, we must discuss more serious matters.' He indicated his wish that Vanessa be seated but himself remained standing. 'It would, of course, be a simple matter to convey you to Grosvenor Square – where your Godmother now resides – in my own carriage, but for several reasons I deem it better not to do so.'

'Oh,' said Vanessa, disappointed. 'You . . . you won't go with me yourself, then?'

'No, child. I think not.'

'Oh,' she said again, looking carefully down at her hands.

Lyndhurst toyed idly with his quizzing-glass, a slight frown creasing his brow. 'Your reception will be . . . shall we say, less than cordial, if your Godmama is made privy to the circumstances of your having spent last night in this house. You will not need to ask the reason for this if you recall our old friend, my reputation.'

Vanessa looked up and grinned appreciatively.

'Though you may be reluctant to accept the fact,' he went on, 'there is probably not one person in London who would believe you innocent this morning if they knew you had stayed a night under my roof – with the possible exception of Mr Vaughan, and I imagine that even *he* has his doubts.'

Vanessa digested this. 'May I ask if you make a habit of seducing innocent females?' she enquired blandly.

'I am well known for it, Mistress Tremaine.' His eyes glinted strangely.

'That isn't what I asked but we will let it pass. And these unfortunate girls – they have no say in the matter?'

'None at all – though I am forced to admit that it is usually necessary to arrange an abduction. I am rarely so lucky as to have my . . . victims . . . walk blithely in at my front door.'

'As I did?'

'Just so.'

'I see. And do none of them fall . . . victim . . . to your charm? Or do you merely have a natural preference for the unwilling?'

His Grace was struck by the unfamiliar sensation that, not only was he failing to impress Vanessa with the gravity of her situation, but that she was systematically cutting the ground from beneath his feet. He found himself admiring her tactics.

'Upon occasion – yes.'

'In fact, you specialise in rape?' she asked pleasantly.

His eyes widened a little but he said nothing, merely bowing.

The growing conviction that had been taking possession of Vanessa's mind flared into blinding realisation. On the one hand, he was telling her the truth about himself and on the other she strongly suspected him of trying to alarm her. She rose and faced him with a teasing smile. 'Then perhaps Saturday isn't your day for ravishment – else why not add me to your reputation?'

Lyndhurst looked at her, his expression unreadable. Then he gave the ghost of a smile and, taking her hand, he kissed it. 'I make you my compliments, child. But I cannot conceive of why you are so determined to think the best of me.'

Vanessa's reply was simply to look up and smile. His fingers tightened on hers like a vice and then, abruptly, he released her, saying harshly, 'You do not answer my question. Why do you persist in disbelieving me?'

'But I don't,' she replied gently.

'No?' The word cracked like a pistol shot.

'No. You told me that you had earned your notoriety and you have told me how – at least, in part. That much I believe. But no amount of words can outweigh the kindness you have shown me – no matter what your reasons may be.'

'You are very certain,' he remarked grimly.

'Yes. Should I discover my mistake, however, I will engage to tell you so.'

Her dignified sincerity was impressive, yet Lyndhurst's face wore its most shuttered expression. 'How old are you?' he asked.

'Almost twenty-one.'

'And you have spent those years in Cornwall?'

'Yes.'

'I am nearly forty and have lived the greater part of my life in London. You will perceive, therefore, that I am amply qualified to offer you advice.'

'None better, your Grace,' she agreed meekly.

'*Bien*. Then I suggest that you on no account inform Lady Henley of our acquaintance.'

Vanessa's face grew troubled. 'I . . . would prefer not to lie.'

He sighed. 'I trust you will not need to do so.'

She thought for a moment. 'And that is why I am to go to Grosvenor Square in a carriage that is not decorated with your ducal crest?'

'Just so,' came the absent reply. 'I think . . . yes, I think you must be accompanied by your maid.'

'But I don't have a maid,' Vanessa objected. And then, jumping up with a brilliant smile, 'Oh – Jassy! You mean I may take Jassy?'

'Jassy?' queried Lyndhurst in faint bewilderment.

'Yes. It's short for Jasmine, you know,' she rushed on, misunderstanding. And then, 'Oh I see. You don't know her, do you? She is the housemaid who attended to me this morning.'

'She appears to have found favour in your eyes,' he remarked, ringing the bell for Benson.

'Oh yes. She is the most redoubtable girl. She – '

'Pray spare me a eulogy. I am sure she has many excellent qualities. Ah, Benson. You will locate the housemaid rejoicing under the name of . . . Jassy . . . and instruct her to be ready to accompany Mistress Tremaine out in five minutes. You will also obtain a hired carriage.'

'A hired carriage, your Grace?' repeated Benson, faintly.

'Precisely. My own, you see, are all conspicuously . . . er . . . decorated with the arms of Lyndhurst.'

'I see, your Grace.' The butler's face was wooden.

'I doubt it,' murmured the Duke. 'That is all.' The doors closed behind Benson and his Grace turned to Vanessa. 'Benson is undoubtedly shocked. Not a cause for mirth, I think?' He surveyed her merriment with raised brows. 'And now we must say farewell. We shall almost certainly meet at some time in the future but we will naturally do so as strangers.'

Vanessa found the prospect oddly daunting but she nodded submissively. 'Very well, your Grace. But please believe that I shall not forget you.'

He made an elaborate leg and offered her his arm. Out in the hall, Benson announced that the carriage was at the door and Jassy waiting within it. Vanessa turned impulsively to the Duke, suddenly nervous and loth to leave.

'Come, child,' he said calmly. 'Where is your courage?'

Perversely, the lack of sympathy in his tone helped. Releasing his arm, she smiled and curtsied. 'Goodbye, then,' she said softly; and descended the steps to the waiting carriage. At its door she looked back, but he had already vanished.

Vanessa advanced into the drawing-room of the house in Grosvenor Square with some uncertainty. She wished it was possible to have Jassy beside her but that, of course, was out of the question.

Lady Henley was seated upon a small sofa and Vanessa found nothing in her appearance to soothe her quaking nerves. She saw a large lady whose face was decidedly hard and whose mouth bordered on the predatory. Worse still, the basilisk stare showed no sign of relaxing as it dwelt on her. Trying to smile, Vanessa made a careful curtsy but found that she could think of nothing to say.

'You may be seated, Mistress Tremaine,' pronounced her ladyship in glacial tones.

'Thank you, ma'am.' Vanessa swallowed and sank weakly down upon the nearest chair.

Her Godmother continued to regard her in frozen silence for a full minute and then she said, 'Oblige me by stating your business.'

Dismayed, Vanessa stammered, 'I think, ma'am, that you cannot be unaware of the death of my father.' The turbaned head inclined almost imperceptibly but the bracketed mouth did not move. 'The estate was inherited, not by me, but by my cousin. He and I . . . quarrelled . . . and my presence at Penmarne was unwelcome. I left in rather a hurry. I realise that I should have written to you but . . .' And there she found it impossible to go on in the face of her ladyship's look of cold distaste.

'And why have you come to me?' asked her ladyship relentlessly.

Vanessa looked down at her tightly-clasped hands. 'I . . . you are my godmother, ma'am. I hoped – for the sake of my mother, if not for my own – that you might be prepared to give me a temporary home.'

Silence fell and in that instant she felt that no greater misery

41

or humiliation could be heaped on her. It was perfectly plain that she was about to be repudiated.

'And for precisely what reason, Mistress Tremaine,' came the inexorable voice, 'did you suppose me for a fool?'

Vanessa's head jerked up and she made a helples gesture with her hands. 'I don't understand you, ma'am.'

'Oh, I think you do,' answered the other with grim satisfaction. 'You have but now arrived from Cornwall?' This appeared a complete *non-sequitur* but none the less dangerous for that.

'I . . . no. I arrived last night . . . but I thought it too late to trouble you. I thought you might have guests,' said Vanessa uneasily.

'And you stayed at an hotel, I presume?'

'No. That is . . . I was most kindly offered accommodation by a – fellow-traveller,' she replied, unwilling to perjure herself.

'I see,' said Lady Maria silkily. 'And did you find Lyndhurst House comfortable, Mistress Tremaine?' Vanessa started guiltily and a deep flush crept into her cheeks. 'You understand me now, I see,' said her ladyship sarcastically.

Chaotic thoughts tumbled through Vanessa's brain. She was shocked to find the Duke's part in her affairs was not unknown as she had supposed and felt foolish at having been caught out trying to hide the fact. She rose from her seat. 'Pray allow me to explain. I realise that it must appear odd to you, but – '

'Then you are in error. I assure you that I understand perfectly.'

Vanessa frowned. 'Forgive me, ma'am, but you don't. Please let me explain – '

'It will do you no good,' broke in Lady Henley bitingly. 'I have no wish to listen to further fabrication. The situation is quite clear to me and I am merely amazed at your effrontery in daring to enter my house.'

Vanessa stared as though unable to believe her ears. 'I met his Grace on the road – our carriages collided. He invited me to dine with him at the inn and I did so. That is all, I promise you!'

'Your promises are of no consequence to me. Lyndhurst's

profligacy is well known and no decent girl would spend a minute in his company of her own volition – let alone a night in his house as I gather you have done.'

'But it was quite innocent and I had nowhere else to go when I found you had removed from Portman Square. He did not invite me but he was kind enough to allow me to stay in his house. Even this dress I am wearing – ' She broke off, burningly aware of having said too much.

Lady Henley rose majestically from the sofa like Titan from the depths. 'So! I was not mistaken. You are that man's mistress and he is seeking to insinuate you into my home.'

'*No!*' cried Vanessa. 'He only set eyes on me two days ago. He –'

'You are wasting your time, miss. I know Francis Courtenay for an evil and corrupt libertine who has long nourished a grudge against me and mine.'

'I know nothing of that, my lady, but you are wrong to be influenced by past grievances. He showed me nothing but kindness and is quite innocent of – '

'Innocent?' sneered her ladyship. 'You are raving! There never was a time when he was so. He is vicious and dissolute. He – '

'How dare you?' snapped Vanessa, her eyes blazing with sudden wrath. 'You have no right to condemn him so – or me!'

'When he sent you here filled with lies, he gave me every right,' retorted her ladyship. 'And now that I see you in your true colours, I have no doubt that you suit him very well. But, of course, one could expect no better from one with such a sire as yours.'

White with anger the like of which she had never before experienced, Vanessa said furiously, 'You wicked, spiteful woman! You are determined to believe this – this *filth*! You call his Grace corrupt and evil but I'm beginning to think that he's a – a gilded saint compared to you! And, for whatever satisfaction it may be to you, I'll tell you here and now that, though I'm not his whore, I think I'd prefer it to living with you!'

Her face an unbecoming shade of puce, Lady Henley

appeared to swell with rage. She raised a shaking hand and pointed to the door. 'Go! And don't set foot in my house again! The world shall hear of this – I shall see to it. Yes – and of your liaison with that depraved reprobate.'

The girl's eyes flashed sparks in her colourless face and she laughed derisively. 'Pray do so. There is no surer way of making yourself ridiculous. Or do you seriously suppose that his Grace is not more than a match for your petty spite?' And with that she swept to the doors and flung them wide. She brushed unceremoniously past the willowy exquisite who stood in her way, collected Jassy with a single, crisp word and stalked out of the house without a backward glance.

His mouth still slightly agape, the peach-clad gentleman minced carefully into the room to stare at Lady Maria. 'Dash it, ma'am – plaguey wench near knocked me off m'feet! Something upset her?'

Her ladyship eyed him with icy scorn and ignored the question. 'And just where have you been? Not that it matters, of course. I am perfectly accustomed to being left alone to deal with the consequences of your folly. Sit down.'

He scowled. 'Hang it all, mama – '

'*Sit down!*'

Carlton sat, tugging nervously at his cravat. 'If it's about last night at White's, I can explain. It wasn't my idea – it was Jerry Manders. Upon my honour – '

'Since even I am bound to own that you have none, I suggest that you refrain from using that particular expression in public,' she interrupted acidly. 'What I wish to discuss has nothing to do with your most recent escapade – of which I should prefer to remain in ignorance.'

'Oh,' said Carlton, stupidly.

'Just so. No doubt I should find your unnecessary confession diverting; but I am never amused by idiocy – especially in my son.' He cleared his throat and stared petulantly at the floor. 'And now you may oblige me by attempting to concentrate,' went on Lady Maria coldly. 'The girl you have just seen is one Vanessa Tremaine and my goddaughter. I have never laid eyes on her before today but her mother and I came out in the same season. Eliza died years ago and Sir Thomas killed himself recently in a hunting accident.'

Her son looked up, vaguely interested. 'Drunk, wasn't he?'

'Very probably. He usually was. But my concern – and yours – is with the girl.'

'Because she's your godchild?'

'No. Because, if James Winthrop is to be believed, she is the Duke of Lyndhurst's latest mistress.'

Carlton jumped. 'W-what?'

'She is Lyndhurst's mistress,' repeated his mother concisely. 'And since she has just attempted to foist herself on to me, I can only assume that he is using her to make mischief. You don't, I imagine, need to ask why?'

Carlton did not, for the events of nine years ago were enshrined in his memory like flies in amber. His courtship of Blanche Courtenay, her refusal, a foolish, angry embrace and the awful discovery that Lyndhurst had witnessed it; then the Duke's sarcastic and humiliating dismissal that still had the power to make him cringe even now.

And that had only been the beginning for, resentful and angry, Carlton had proceeded to set the town ablaze with a damaging rumour concerning Lady Blanche's virtue – the satisfaction of which had been abruptly terminated when Lyndhurst challenged him to a duel. The shock of that had brought Carlton quickly to his senses for the mere thought of physical violence made him sick; and Lyndhurst was reputed to possess an unnatural degree of skill with both sword and pistol. Without pausing for thought, Carlton had gathered the remnants of his discretion and decamped with all possible speed for Yorkshire on a plea of ill-health – leaving behind a sort of collective snigger from Tyburn to St Paul's.

He passed a shaking hand across his face and said, 'But it's all so long ago.'

Lady Maria shrugged irritably. 'Lyndhurst is a dangerous man. And he has a long memory. It is fortunate that I met Winthrop last night or I might have taken the girl in. As it is, we

45

should be safe enough for I've made sure that she knows better than to return here.' She paused and impaled Carlton in her gaze. 'It is a great pity you did not stand your ground and meet Lyndhurst nine years ago. He would scarcely have been stupid enough to make it a killing matter and it would have spared me a great deal of embarrassment and trouble.'

He flushed sulkily. 'I was unwell. And anyway – you may be wrong about this. The man's a devil, I know – but I don't see what you think he's trying to do.'

'No. You wouldn't,' snapped his mother. 'I'll put it in words of one syllable for you. It's my belief that Lyndhurst hoped I would accept the girl and introduce her to society so that he could then make me a laughing-stock by publicly acknowledging her as his mistress. He also probably hoped she would ensnare you. *Now* do you understand?'

'Yes.' Carlton stood up. 'And I'd like to grind my heel in his face!'

'No doubt. But you had your opportunity and declined to take advantage of it,' came the inflexible reply. 'All you can do now is pray he tries nothing else.'

Some of Carlton's bravado evaporated. 'Do you think he will?'

'Possibly not – unless you add fuel to the fire by gossiping about today's work.' Lady Maria rose and moved majestically to the door. 'I advise you to keep a still tongue in your head and stay out of his way. Not, I feel sure,' she added sardonically, 'that the latter will present any problems. Avoiding Lyndhurst has become quite a habit with you, hasn't it?'

The Surprising Behaviour of Lucifer Courtenay

Seated at the escritoire in the library, the Duke was writing and his long-fingered, white hand travelled with smooth precision across the page. Then, pausing for thought, he became aware of the distracting sound of a somewhat noisy arrival. Frowning a little, he remained, pen poised and then, disbelievingly, recognised Vanessa's voice crisply demanding his whereabouts. A second later the door burst open and she flew into the room, shutting the door with a snap.

Coolly, the Duke leaned back in his chair and looked appraisingly at her from beneath narrowed lids. The contrast between the girl who had left the house little over an hour ago and the one now facing him was quite startling and he waited with amused interest to discover the cause of this metamorphosis.

Vanessa swept across the room to lean with both hands on the corner of his desk. Her eyes blazed into his and she said unevenly, 'Tell me, sir, just what you did to inspire that – that *vixen* with such a virulent hatred of you?'

The heavy lids flickered and he drawled, 'Do you need ask?'

'I wouldn't else have done so,' she snapped. 'You knew, didn't you? And yet you never said a word. You – '

'Yes, child. I knew. But I believe I warned you that I have no heart.'

'*You* have no heart? Oh!' Words no longer seemed sufficient, she snatched up a small porcelain vase from the bureau and hurled it across the room, watching its progress with detatched interest till it struck the marble fireplace and disintegrated into tiny fragments on the hearth. Then, suddenly sobered, her wrath fled and she surveyed the results of her handiwork with horror before turning reluctantly to face her host. Wide grey eyes met astounded topaz ones and then, 'I'm sorry,' she faltered, inwardly ridiculing the futility of the words. 'W-was it very valuable?'

'Meissen. A piece imported specially by my father,' he replied, his voice not completely under control.

'Oh,' said Vanessa, deflated. Then hopefully, 'It was rather ugly, wasn't it?'

'Was it?' He rose unhurriedly and inspected the debris through his glass. 'It is of a certainty no more beautiful now.' Vanessa squirmed apprehensively. 'But yes . . . on the whole, I am inclined to agree with you.' She gave a sigh of relief. 'On the other hand, I could wish that you had chosen to rid the world of one of its monstrosities in a less . . . spectacular fashion.'

'Oh?'

'You see,' he complained gently, 'my entire household will be of the opinion that you threw it at *me*.'

She choked. 'I wouldn't dare.'

'No?' Laughter stirred in his eyes. 'I hope not. And now you had best be seated and tell me the cause of your . . . irritation.'

She smiled at the deliberate understatement. Suddenly tired, she sank dispiritedly down upon a couch. 'I don't think I've ever been so angry in my life. Anger is too small a word for it. I wanted to call down fire and destroy her with a wave of my hand. Can you understand that?'

He gave her a swift and unexpectedly charming smile. 'Oh yes.'

Vanessa stared at him, a little shaken. Then she said, 'I hoped you might. It frightens me to know that I have such violence in me and never before suspected it.' She fell silent for a moment and then went on, 'She knew everything. Did you realise?'

His brows drew together. 'I did not – and I ask your pardon

for it. I am not usually so maladroit. Doubtless she took you for my mistress and accused you of complicity in my . . . foul villainy.'

The grey eyes widened. 'How did you know?'

'It rather leaps to the eye.'

'Oh. Well, at first I tried to explain but she . . . she made certain remarks and I lost my temper. She said you were trying to insinuate me into her house and that . . .'

'Pray do not spare me,' begged his Grace. 'I am not easily hurt, you know.'

She regarded him dubiously. 'No? Well, she said that you were evil and corrupt . . . and vicious and dissolute.'

'Ah.' The black lashes veiled his eyes. 'And?'

'And that was when I grew angry,' replied Vanessa, looking down at her hands. 'Then she . . . made a remark about my father and I – I said a number of things that perhaps I shouldn't. I was fuming, you see.'

'I do see. And precisely what were you insired to say?'

Vanessa's face became tinged with pink. 'I said that you might be corrupt and – and so on, but that in comparison with her, you were a . . . gilded saint.'

His Grace raised his glass and examined her in astonishment. 'Did you indeed?' His voice shook slightly. 'How very original. Is there more?'

'Yes.' Vanessa shifted uncomfortably in her seat. 'I told her that I wasn't your mistress but that I'd prefer it to living with her. I suppose I went a bit too far really – even though . . .'

'Yes?'

'Even though I meant it,' she finished defiantly. The Duke regarded her in enigmatic silence. 'I'm sorry if you're shocked – but, indeed – '

'I am never shocked,' he said placidly.

'No,' she agreed with a sudden flash of humour. 'At least you aren't stuffed with hypocritical morality.'

The hard mouth curled. 'My one virtue, I believe.'

Vanessa refused to be diverted. 'Possibly. But if my revered godmama were as virtuous as she'd appear, she wouldn't have

49

prejudged us.' And then, guiltily, 'Oh. I've just remembered something else.'

His Grace sat down and took snuff. 'Well, child?'

She flushed and fidgeted a little. 'It's just that – that she threatened to tell everyone that you . . . that I . . .'

'I see. That, of course, was deplorably predictable.'

'I'm very sorry,' said Vanessa in hollow accents. 'I had no idea I'd caused you so much trouble. The scandal – '

'Need not concern you,' interrupted Lyndhurst indifferently. 'Firstly, because my name is already tarnished beyond repair and secondly, because although a few will believe it because they wish to, the majority will not be so credulous.'

Vanessa considered this. 'Are you sure?'

'As much as one may be of such things.'

'Well, thank goodness for that! I'd feel dreadful if you were slandered on my account.'

He regarded her steadily. 'Has it occurred to you that the person who will suffer most from any gossip is you, Mistress Tremaine?'

'Since I don't move in your circles, it won't matter,' she smiled. And then her face grew grave again with the dawning realisation of her predicament.

He read her thoughts without difficulty but said nothing and transferred his attention to the ruby on his finger. Her situation was extreme and he wondered idly if she saw the full extent of it. His decision already made, he calmly awaited the anticipated request for his help.

'I've been very stupid, haven't I?' she asked with a bitter smile. 'If I write to Mr Culver in Truro he will send me money for I believe I inherited something from my mother but that will take time so I must find work. Is it possible that you could recommend me for some position?'

A satirical gleam lit his eyes. 'I could, of course. But I doubt you would find it a help.'

Vanessa was obliged to laugh. 'No. I suppose not.' She rested her chin on her hand and relapsed into deep thought. Gently swinging his glass, Lyndhurst watched and waited for the inevitable. Abruptly Vanessa stood up, tense with excitement. 'But of course! How stupid of me!' She turned to him eagerly. 'There are many theatres in London, aren't there?'

His eyes widened disbelievingly. 'Theatres? You propose to become an actress?'

'Not exactly. I shall sing. I can, you know – it's the only thing I do at all well.'

'Are you serious?'

She nodded. 'I have to be. There is no other choice.'

'There is always an alternative, child.' He rose and looked at her disquietingly. 'You could ask my help.'

'No,' came the immediate and positive response. 'You've been more than kind and I've caused you enough trouble already.'

'You are quite sure?'

'Quite. It was good of you to suggest it, but no.'

'You are very independent.'

'Yes. Montaigne said – '

' – that the greatest thing in the world is to know how to be self-sufficient,' he interposed. 'Yes, I know. But I believe the trick is to know not how, but when. You understand what appearing on the stage will mean?'

'I think so,' she replied gravely. 'I don't expect it to be easy. But I will manage somehow. There is just one thing you could do. I hate having to ask, but would you . . . could you lend me a small sum of money? I'll repay you as soon as I'm able but I have to get to the theatre and find a lodging.'

Lyndhurst did not reply immediately. Then he said slowly, 'No, child. I will not.'

'You – you won't?'

'No. I am desolated to disoblige you but I am afraid that I really cannot allow you to embrace a theatrical career.'

'But I must!' she insisted. 'You don't understand!'

'But I do, my dear. Only too well. And the stage is no fit place for you.'

Vanessa blinked sudden tears away at this unexpected kindness. Angry with this unfamiliar weakness she said tartly, 'I

51

hadn't imagined you to be so strait-laced, sir. Lucifer Courtenay should surely applaud my choice.'

'You will do well,' he said coldly, 'not to use that tone with me.'

Ashamed, she flushed and hung her head. 'I . . . am sorry.'

'It is well.'

'Then what shall I do?' she asked, raising despairing eyes.

Silence stretched out like a long, invisible thread. Then he said, 'You will place yourself in my hands – figuratively speaking – and allow me to arrange matters as I deem best. And you will not argue with me because I am not accustomed to it and am likely to be put out of temper.' He paused and watched her sit down, hands folded and mouth resolutely closed. He gave the merest hint of a smile. 'Thank you. I intend to . . . adopt you as my ward, surrounded by a positive fog of respectability. In due course you will make your curtsy to the polite world and this will doubtless achieve the usual result.'

For a moment Vanessa was too stunned to do more than stare at him. Then she yielded to the overriding consideration. 'Why?' she asked baldly.

'For a number of reasons. Content yourself that it pleases me to displease your godmama. Also, it is a sure way to silence wagging tongues and I think I owe you that much. Unless you are worried that I plan to seduce you?'

'No! Of course not! It isn't *that*,' she said indignantly.

'Then we may regard it as settled.'

Eyeing him with misgiving, she said weakly, 'I don't know what to say.'

'I am glad to hear it. And now I shall leave you for there are arrangements to be made. Ah!' He looked towards the door. 'If I am not mistaken, we are about to be joined by Mr Vaughan. I must own to some astonishment that he was not with us much earlier.'

No sooner were the words out than the doors opened to admit Gideon whose eyes rested in quick surprise on Vanessa and then flew enquiringly to his Grace.

'As always, your timing is impeccable, my dear,' purred

Lyndhurst. 'I must visit Blanche and should be glad for you to bear Mistress Tremaine company while I am gone.'

'Certainly,' replied Gideon, taken aback. 'I shall be happy to do so.'

'I thought you might be.' The Duke proceeded serenely to the door. Pausing on the threshold, he turned and addressed Vanessa. 'Mr Vaughan is doubtless consumed with curiosity. You have my permission to tell him . . . everything.' And upon this valediction, he left the room smiling softly to himself.

It was but a short time later that he presented himself in Great Jermyn Street. Having refused the services of the butler, he walked in unannounced to discover Lady Blanche reclining on a sofa perusing a volume of sermons. She was clad in an afternoon gown of her favourite blue, lavishly trimmed with lace and her blonde hair was unpowdered. Her brother's sudden appearance caused her to utter a little shriek and drop the book which slid to the floor with a thud.

Retrieving the volume from beneath the couch, the Duke inspected its title through his glass.

'Sermons? My dear Blanche!' he said mockingly before she could open her mouth to greet him. 'I had no notion that "thou keepest holy the Sabbath day" quite so . . . religiously.'

'Don't be disagreeable, Francis,' said his sister, sitting up and offering her hand. 'I will not be provoked today.'

His Grace saluted the white, dimpled wrist and moved slowly to a chair. 'I am delighted to hear it for I want your help.'

Blanche eyed him with petulant resignation. 'Oh – money!'

'No, my dear. Not money. You know very well I never borrow from Laurence now. I require your assistance on quite another matter.'

'Oh!' cooed her ladyship, suddenly interested and fluttering over to sit beside him. 'Tell me!'

'I have every intention of so doing.' He paused for a moment and regarded the foaming lace at his wrists. 'You will recall, I think, that I made some passing enquiry when last I honoured you with my presence, about the death of Thomas Tremaine.'

She nodded. 'Yesterday.'

'Was it? Yes, you may be right. The late Sir Thomas was possessed of a daughter. Fate decreed that this daughter should cross my path . . . somewhere in the vicinity of Hook.'

'Hook?' echoed his sister blankly.

'Just so. An accident to her carriage forced me to convey her to the nearest inn and it was there that I discovered her to be en route for the house of her godmother . . . Lady Henley.'

'That woman!' snapped Blanche, sitting suddenly upright.

'Yes. A situation fraught with possibilities as you will perceive. We conversed, were interrupted by the arrival of James Winthrop – yes, I see you share my feelings – and Mistress Tremaine effaced herself.' He smiled sardonically at her ladyship's raised brows. 'I, not unnaturally, assumed that I had seen the last of her but Fate was once more waiting to intervene. Last night I returned from the Knightley rout to the tidings that Mistress Tremaine was awaiting me – having been escorted to my door by the Watch.'

'Good God! What sort of girl is she?'

'Not what you so obviously think, my dear,' came the bland reply. 'She had failed to find Lady Henley in Portman Square – you will recall that she resided there whilst waiting for the dowager to die – and had no money. She was extremely fortunate to encounter a benevolent watchman who took her to the only other person in London whose name she knew – myself.'

Blanche shuddered eloquently. 'And then?'

'Then she slept . . . unmolested . . . in my house and this morning set off for Grosvenor Square. Again I regarded the matter as closed but Nemesis had one more trick to play. It transpired that her ladyship was completely au fait with my role in the proceedings and had jumped to obvious but mistaken conclusions.'

'Winthrop,' said his sister succinctly.

'Quite. The child came back to me and formed the resourceful intention of seeking employment at Covent Garden in order to support herself.'

'Is she a lady?'

'Unquestionably.'

'Then the stage is out of the question. She would be in some man's keeping within a week.'

'I entirely agree with you. I have therefore induced her to accept my help,' said his Grace nonchalantly.

Blanche was astounded. 'You – did – what? It's madness, Francis! Why *should* you do so?'

'I have numerous reasons – not least the undeniable lure of Maria Henley's discomfiture. Also, when Fate takes a hand in one's affairs, it is never wise to disregard it.'

'Fate?' scoffed her ladyship. 'Nonsense! That you plan the Henleys' undoing I am ready to believe – but *Fate*? It's rubbish! And what, in heaven's name, do you propose to do with her?'

'That remains to be seen,' he replied enigmatically. 'To begin, I wish to bring her to you for a few days.'

'Do you indeed?' Blanche opened her eyes wide. 'Why?'

'I had thought it painfully obvious. My . . . ward . . . has already spent a night at Lyndhurst House. If she is to retain any semblance of respectability she cannot do so again. I wish to place her in your care until I can arrange a duenna. Then she shall go to Lyndhurst.'

Blanche regarded him in lively amazement and then gave a little trill of laughter. 'I can't believe it! The thought of you engaging a chaperon and interesting yourself in the proprieties is – '

'Inconceivable,' he finished with a smile. 'Quite. I will admit that the situation is not without irony. As for the duenna – is not our cousin, the lamentable Lilian, but recently widowed?'

'Of course,' cried Blanche, clapping her hands. 'The very thing! She will be ecstatic to be invited to take up residence at the Court.'

His Grace wrinkled his nose expressively. 'A sentiment which I fear I am unable to share.' He looked pensively at her for a moment and then said, 'Well, my dear – will you take the child? I should, perhaps, warn you that Lady Maria will be

55

busy informing the world that Vanessa – that, by the way, is her name – is my mistress.'

Her ladyship sniffed. 'No one will believe that!'

'Your estimable husband may be somewhat displeased,' he suggested with gentle malice.

She tossed her head. 'Laurie will not mind if I don't.'

'Then you will do it?'

'Yes. For you – and to spite that woman!'

Smiling, his Grace rose and kissed her hand. 'Thank you. When do you leave for Audley?'

The little face clouded and she replied sulkily, 'On Friday.'

'That will do very well. I will engage to install our cousin at Lyndhurst by then. Vanessa can travel with you and you may deposit her on your way to Audley. Do you care to return with me now to collect her?'

The sulkiness vanished as if by magic. 'Yes – oh, yes! Let us go immediately!'

'By all means,' drawled his Grace. 'On this occasion your impetuosity has some constructive value. A diverting thought.'

Returning to St James Square, the Duke and Lady Blanche entered the library to discover that their arrival had been narrowly preceded by that of a tall young man of somewhat rakish appearance. Lord Nicholas Courtenay resembled the Duke only in the aquiline cast of his features and Lady Blanche only in his blue-eyed fairness. His face was characterised by a look of casual good humour and his eyes held a merry twinkle that accorded well with a mouth made for laughter. His slim person was wonderfully clad in a coat of deep apricot satin with an embroidered vest and in his hand was a smart tricorne hat. On registering the presence of his sister, his mobile brows flew up and he said boisterously, 'Blister it! Quite a family gathering. Servant, Blanche.' He bowed with careless grace.

Her ladyship acknowledged this greeting with an unenthusiastic inclination of her golden head while her eyes moved past him to rest critically on Vanessa.

Lyndhurst examined his brother with languid interest. 'And

to what do I owe this unlooked-for pleasure, Nicholas? Not another loan, I trust?'

'Devil a bit!' replied Nicholas with unabashed cheerfulness. 'I've come to pay you back!'

'But how charming of you! This is plainly a day of surprises,' marvelled his Grace. 'I take it you have only now arrived?'

'Aye. You followed me in.'

'Then it clearly behoves me to make the introductions. Child – ' He beckoned to Vanessa who moved slowly to his side. 'I have the honour to present you to my sister, Lady Overton, who has kindly offered to have you stay with her for a few days.' He watched with seeming approval as the girl made her curtsy and said shyly, 'It's very generous of you, ma'am. I am grateful.'

'Tush, child – I'm happy to help you!' exclaimed Blanche with a bright smile.

Observing his protegée to be lost for words, the Duke continued smoothly, 'This graceless young fool is, as you may have guessed, our brother Lord Nicholas Courtenay. You will be advised to pay him little heed.'

Ignoring this cavalier introduction, Nicholas smiled engagingly, bowed over Vanessa's hand and said daringly, 'My brother has a peculiar sense of humour. I swear I'm a paragon of all the virtues – as things go in our family. Enchanted, Mistress – ?' He broke off, looking questioningly at his Grace.

'This is Mistress Vanessa Tremaine, Nicholas. My ward.'

His lordship choked and fixed the Duke with a fascinated eye. *'Your ward?'*

'Even so,' replied his Grace, calmly taking a pinch of snuff from his enamelled box. 'Your hearing would appear to be defective.' He paused as Nicholas hastily turned his snort of incredulous laughter into an unconvincing cough. 'Yes? You wish to make some comment?' The soft voice held a note of warning which his brother was quick to recognise.

'Not me,' he said with a comic glance at Gideon.

'How refreshing,' drawled Lyndhurst. 'I need hardly say that you will refrain from discussing Mistress Tremaine's presence in this house. Or, in fact, from discussing her at all.'

'Oh. Like that, is it?' asked Nicholas with cryptic wisdom.

The Duke inspected him through his glass. 'I am not at all certain,' he said with gentle sarcasm. 'Unblessed as I am with your . . . lightning perceptions.'

Bored with this interchange, Blanche took Vanessa's hand and led her away towards the fire. 'Do go away, Nicky. You are in the way.'

He laughed. 'Aren't I always? Oh – I'm off – no need to flash your eyes. I'm promised to Deveraux for six.'

'Then pray do not allow us to detain you,' begged Lyndhurst politely holding open the door.

'I won't. Servant, Mistress Tremaine – Vaughan. Ah! If I had not almost forgotten – two hundred, Francis. And my thanks.'

Lyndhurst accepted the bills with his peculiar glinting smile. 'Think nothing of it.'

Blue eyes alight with amusement, Nicholas bowed deeply in return and said with exaggerated courtesy, 'Your Grace's most obedient!' upon which he sauntered from the room.

'He is quite impossible,' remarked Lady Blanche.

Gideon laughed. 'Merely young, I think. He may one day surprise you.'

'He has already done so,' observed Lyndhurst. 'Here are two hundred guineas I never expected to see again. One can at least say of Nicholas that he has the delightful merit of being less expensive than Randolph.'

'Randolph is detestable,' said my Lady firmly.

'I am not enamoured of him myself.' And then, noticing Vanessa's look of incomprehension, his Grace explained, 'Randolph is the only one of us you have not met. He . . . fits in . . . between Blanche and myself. I doubt he will find favour in your eyes.' He directed a glance of malicious enquiry at Gideon. 'The child has told you?'

'Yes. I was shocked – and amazed.'

'Naturally,' murmured his Grace, ringing the bell. 'I have therefore arranged that she return to Great Jermyn Street with Blanche until such time as I can produce Lilian Erskine to chaperon her at the Court. Ah, Benson. Instruct . . . Jassy . . . to pack Mistress Tremaine's belongings and have them brought downstairs. Further inform her that I shall require her to be ready to accompany Mistress Tremaine to Lyndhurst on Friday. I trust that meets your approval, child?' he asked Vanessa.

'Yes, sir. Thank you,' she replied, subdued but faintly cheered.

'Blanche – I am not likely to return before Friday so I beg you will take steps to equip the child suitably.'

Eyes brightening, her ladyship nodded briskly. 'It will be a pleasure. For the immediate future she will need mourning. Black?'

'I think not. Half-mourning, perhaps. You may also place orders for such apparel as she will require later in London. For these you will discard mourning.'

'The cost?'

'Need not concern you.'

Blanche's brows rose to impossible heights. 'Paris must have proved lucky,' she mocked.

'Do not forget Nemesis, my dear,' came the masterly reply.

Vanessa rose and laid a coaxing hand on his sleeve. 'Your Grace I can't accept so much. It's – '

'Vanessa, I believe I have already requested you not to argue with me. You will do as I bid you because it is my will – if for no other reason. I trust I make myself clear?'

'Perfectly, your Grace,' she replied, crushed by his cool tone.

'I hope so. Do not fight me, my dear. I always win – and who knows? You may even enjoy being my ward.'

'Yes, sir.'

He looked with not unsympathetic amusement into grey eyes alight with unspoken questions and said calmly, 'Yes, child. I know.' Perversely, these cryptic words did much to soothe her.

She said slowly, 'Yes. I think perhaps you do.'

'I wish *I* did,' remarked Gideon to no one in particular.

Blanche, meanwhile, had watched this interchange with some suspicion but as usual her brother's face gave no clue to his thoughts and well she knew how useless it was to demand an explanation. She rose and shook out her skirts.

'I shall look to see you on Friday, Francis.'

'You may reasonably expect to do so. I hope to find Lilian in Oxfordshire. If she has removed to Scotland, I will engage to send you word and, in that event, it will become necessary that you either delay your departure or take Vanessa with you to Audley. I leave such details to you . . . and the worthy Laurence.'

Irritated, but unwilling to show it, Blanche turned to Vanessa and said, 'Come, Mistress Tremaine. I think it's time we took our leave.'

Vanessa was conscious of a sudden desire to beg the Duke not to send her away but she held her head proudly, made a formal curtsy and said evenly, 'You have been more than kind, your Grace. Thank you.'

He walked to the doors and opened them to allow the ladies to pass into the hall where Benson stood beside a battered valise. Then, taking Vanessa's hand, he said with something less than his usual sneer, 'You need have no fears. Go with Lady Blanche and . . . perhaps I shall visit you at Lyndhurst.' He kissed her hand and released it immediately to turn to his sister. 'You have my gratitude, Blanche. Pray convey my greetings to Laurence. *Au revoir*, my dear.'

As her ladyship led Vanessa out to the carriage, the Duke strolled unhurriedly to rejoin Gideon in the library.

'What new madness is this?' came the forthright question.

Lyndhurst leant one elbow on the mantelpiece and twirled his quizzing-glass on its silver ribbon. 'I wonder? "*Though this be madness, yet there's method in't.*" I had thought that you might tell me. You are always so perceptive, my dear.'

'I know you well enough to perceive that you've some plan in mind – else what can you want with that child?'

'You are very persistent. But I believe that my reasons are my own.'

'Are you "in love" with her?' asked Gideon with blunt significance.

'My dear!'

'Then let her go to my mother. If you want to help her – '

60

'I thought you said you knew me?' enquired his Grace sweetly.

'Then, damn it all, Francis, you must know why I'm concerned. She's an innocent and she trusts you and – '

'Spare me the lecture, Gideon. Suffice it to say I mean no harm by her. I find her trust a novel and amusing sensation – but it is not misplaced.'

'Then it's as she said? You'll use her to be avenged on the Henleys?'

'How dramatic!' sighed his Grace. 'Revenge is an inappropriate word. Rather say I . . . inconvenience them. Should I avenge myself, it will be, you may be sure, in a less subtle fashion.'

Mr Vaughan stared searchingly at his friend's face. 'I almost believe you've conceived a liking for the child,' he said in slow amazement.

The Duke's eyes flickered. Then he said politely, 'Take care you do not mistake me for a hero. I am persuaded you would regret it.'

'There's no doubt of it. I wish to God you'd give up this life you lead before it ruins you.'

'I find you a trifle inconsistent, my dear. I understand you to think that I was already . . . er . . . ruined. You will notice that I do not express my own opinion.'

'No. I don't feel that it's too late, even now. Two years ago, after your affair with Judith – '

'Hardly an affair, Gideon.'

' – I said that though she wouldn't take you, she had at least taught you to be a human being.'

'Always so deep,' murmured his Grace.

'At the time you had something approaching a heart. You said you loved her. But now it's gone and it seems I was wrong.'

'Dear me! How so?'

'If your love for Judith isn't to blame for your various – '

'Crimes. Enticingly wicked and too numerous to mention,' offered his Grace helpfully.

' – your various excesses,' continued Gideon manfully, 'it is clear that she changed nothing in you.'

61

'Ah. Then you admit me beyond redemption?'

'No,' he replied slowly. 'Just that Judith wasn't the right girl.'

The Duke was amused. 'You are so determined to see me wed for love of a good woman, are you not? But if you hope to persuade me you should take your own advice.' To his astonishment, Mr Vaughan flushed slightly. 'Can it be that you *have* fallen in love at last?' asked Lyndhurst with raised brows. 'Ah – I perceive that you have. How mortifying! I really had no idea.'

Gideon exhibited some embarrassment. 'It could hardly be called love. I don't really know the lady. I merely . . . met her once, in Bath. I don't even know her name.'

'But how romantic!' remarked his Grace admiringly. 'No – I assure you that I do not sneer. You have my warmest felicitations – for what they are worth.'

Gideon laughed. 'You are, to say the least of it, a trifle premature.'

'Possibly. But I feel impelled to drink to the day when you will applaud my foresight.'

He poured two glasses of wine and handed one of them to Mr Vaughan. Then, raising his own, a mocking but not unpleasant smile in his eyes, he said, 'To marriage, my dear. Yours – not mine!'

Introducing Mistress Elizabeth Tierney

In newly-built Hanover Square dwelt an alderman by the name of Tierney. A man of considerable astuteness and ambition was he and his shrewd and businesslike brain had built him a large fortune and the reputation of a man hard to cheat. Self-made and proud of it, he had but one foible: the desire to marry his daughter into some family of proud and ancient lineage.

With this in mind, Elizabeth had been placed in an expensively select seminary but when, her education completed, she returned to her opulent home, it seemed that no good had come of it save a ladylike manner and a certain elegance of deportment. Joshua was pardonably annoyed and had much to say on the subject of slow-witted and ungrateful daughters, but then Elizabeth was bidden to visit her erstwhile schoolfriend, Mistress Jennifer Crichton, in Bath. Miss Jenny's papa was not possessed of a title but Mr Tierney was able to establish that his pedigree was a long one and his connections quite excellent.

Elizabeth was duly despatched to Bath with many injunctions to make the most of her opportunities and, on her return, it appeared that, for once, she had done so. Not only had Jenny's mama offered to procure invitations and chaperon Elizabeth to parties in London, but there was also a certain Lord paying her distinguished and flattering attentions.

True, it did not seem that his gentle daughter quite appreciated her good fortune, but her delighted parent found it easy to dismiss such trivial irritations when he finally drew from her the identity of her admirer. That Colonel Lord Randolph

Courtenay was well known to be perpetually at a low financial ebb Joshua deemed an advantage, for had he been wealthy Mr Tierney knew that he was unlikely to wish to ally his name with that of a tradesman. His other great satisfaction was that, as things stood, his lordship was heir to a Dukedom and, since the present Duke's way of life was a byword and he was at the age when one might reasonably expect him to remain single, Mr Tierney could indulge the hope of seeing his Lizzie become a Duchess.

Neither he nor his wife attempted to determine what Elizabeth's feelings were and she thought it best to keep her own counsel. Gentle and retiring, she was possessed of an unworldliness wholly alien to her father. A pretty girl with pale blonde hair and large blue eyes, she lacked only that spark of confident vivacity that could have made her beautiful and she gazed on the world with a soft tranquillity that knew not what to make of Colonel Courtenay's unexpected attentions. Elizabeth was not a clever girl but intuition hinted at the undesirability of Lord Randolph. Try as she might, she could not quite explain her dislike of him nor the faint quiver of fear he awakened in her, for his behaviour had always been perfectly correct and she knew her friend Jenny found him charming. In her mind's eye, another face replaced his lordship's florid good looks. A face seen only once but somehow unforgotten, with its pleasant but unremarkable features and its rather dreamy grey eyes. Elizabeth sighed and inwardly rebuked herself for her folly.

It was on a cool day some three weeks after her return from Bath that Lord Randolph paid his promised visit. He was admitted to the house by the butler who then entered the drawing-room to enquire if the ladies were at home to visitors. Cast into sudden affliction, Elizabeth attempted to make her mother deny him but, mindful of her spouse's instructions, Madam Tierney refused to listen and gave her permission for the Colonel's admittance.

Looking critically at Elizabeth, she said, 'For the Lord's sake, Lizzie, bite your lips to put some colour in 'em – and do try to smile!' She rustled to the mirror and patted her elaborate coiffure, glad that she had chosen to wear her new striped armazine and her best cameo brooch.

Colonel Lord Randolph Courtenay entered the room with all his usual languor. A tall man, he wore an elaborately curled and powdered wig, a coat of gold-laced purple velvet and an expression of singular boredom. He exuded an air of arrogant assurance coupled with a certain dissipation which caused Madam Tierney to feel a momentary pang of misgiving.

Making a profound leg, Lord Randolph moved forward saying, 'It's very good of you to receive me, madam – a stranger and uninvited.'

'La, no, my lord – I am sure we're honoured! And as for saying you are a stranger – well, I know you're no stranger to my little Lizzie here,' said Madam in flustered effusion.

He bowed again. 'You are most kind. Indeed, I have come to renew my acquaintance with Mistress Tierney,' he smiled at Elizabeth who sat frozen and still in her chair, 'in whose memory I hope I hold some place?'

Urged by a sharp glance from her mother, Elizabeth replied in low tones, 'I have not forgot you, sir.'

Madam Tierney laughed. ''Deed she has not, my Lord! Why, I vow she's talked more of you than any other she met in Bath.'

His brow rose and the hard eyes glinted maliciously. 'I fear you flatter me, ma'am.'

'Oh no! To be sure, Lizzie has been agog for your coming – though she's too shy to show it – are you not, my love?'

Elizabeth flushed and glanced fleetingly at Lord Randolph to discover if he was at all put out by such obvious tactics.

If he was, he gave no sign of it, saying merely, 'Then perhaps you will permit me to take her for a short drive – if she will honour me?'

'But of course she will! Come, Lizzie – thank my lord prettily.'

'It's very kind of you, sir. But I am not dressed for such an expedition,' answered Elizabeth, deceptively calm.

'Silly child! You may change in a trice,' said her mama looking significantly at her. 'You'll wait a moment, my lord?'

'Certainly. There is no hurry.'

65

In the face of such opposition, Elizabeth was forced to capitulate. She rose, made a graceful curtsy and left the room. Alone with the Colonel, her mama smiled archly and patted the sofa beside her. 'Do pray sit down, my lord.'

He inclined his head and did so. 'I am delighted to make your acquaintance, ma'am. You have a most charming daughter.'

'I am sure I am pleased you think so,' beamed the lady. 'I have said times out of mind that it's better for a girl to be a mite quiet like my Lizzie than one of your harum-scarum misses. But as you likely know, she was educated at a most select school – and a pretty penny it cost us all told! I can't approve of modern manners, as I'm sure you'll agree, my lord?'

Lord Randolph suppressed a yawn. 'Just so.'

Madam's brain skipped a notch. 'I believe Viscountess Overton is your sister? I declare, she is a monstrously elegant lady. I saw her last week at the play and I make no doubt that her hoop was the widest there. And such a coiffure . . .'

Maintaining an expression of polite interest, Lord Randolph allowed his mind to wander. It was a great pity, he thought, that his obligations should be such that he was forced to consider matrimony as a solution. He had no desire to be married and although Elizabeth was well enough, she was not the type of girl he really admired. Neither had he any wish to acquire a 'bundle of Cits' as his relatives; but as no wealthy family of his own order was likely to welcome him as a son-in-law, his choice was somewhat limited.

He repressed a shudder at the probable reaction of his elder brother. Despite his own peccadilloes, Francis had very decided views on what was owed to the family name and Randolph could recall with the utmost clarity the Duke's attitude towards their cousin who had, in the opinion of the family, married beneath her. And the late Mr Erskine had not been a City merchant, thought the Colonel gloomily.

It was at that moment that Elizabeth re-entered the room clad in a carriage dress of deep blue and a chip-straw bonnet trimmed with forget-me-nots. Lord Randolph rose, bowed admiringly and turned back to Madam Tierney. 'Pray accept my assurance that I shall take the greatest care of her, ma'am. And I hope I may be permitted to call again?'

'La, sir – I hope you will,' laughed Madam. 'Off you go with his lordship, Lizzie – and have a good time.'

Elizabeth smiled perfunctorily and allowed Randolph to lead her out to his carriage. That she had virtually been forced to drive out with him was bad enough, but, in addition, all hope that her parents would refuse to allow my lord's title to blind them to her dislike of him had been thoroughly dashed by her mother's reception of him that afternoon. She sighed inwardly and prayed that he would not feel moved to demonstrate whatever affection he felt for her.

She need not have worried. Randolph was well aware of her reservations and far too experienced to aggravate them by a display of ardour. He therefore maintained a flow of easy conversation to which Elizabeth replied with largely monosyllabic answers. Bored but determined, my lord persevered as they bowled in a leisurely fashion around the park. The season being far advanced, they encountered few persons with whom the Colonel was acquainted and this he felt to be an advantage since he wished to carry off the prize before other impoverished peers could essay it. It was, therefore, with a sense of surprise mingled with irritation that he perceived the Honourable Gideon Vaughan riding towards them astride his chestnut mare.

Mr Vaughan noted the approach of Lord Randolph's equipage and, having no fondness for its owner, might well have turned his direction had this not been impossible without appearing rude. Consequently, he rode gently on and reined in beside the carriage with the intention of exchanging no more than a conventional greeting before continuing on his way. One glance at the girl seated beside the Colonel and this idea fled forgotten and unregretted from his mind.

He stared into Elizabeth's flower-like countenance and saw his own look of startled recognition reflected in her wide gaze. Too stunned to wonder how she came to be driving, unchaperoned, with Randolph Courtenay, he sat very still, a sudden spark blazing in his grey eyes. This highly charged exchange of glances lasted but an instant till, blushing furiously, Elizabeth looked quickly away.

'Well, Gideon?' The Colonel observed Mr Vaughan between narrowed lids. 'I must own to some surprise at your continued presence in town.'

'I'm waiting for Francis,' returned Gideon, pulled unpleasantly back to reality. 'He found it necessary to journey into Oxfordshire.'

'Did he so? How very peculiar of him,' mocked Randolph. 'But then, my dear brother is always so . . . mysterious, is he not?'

Declining to reply, Gideon looked again at Elizabeth and said gently, 'Will you not present me?'

Something akin to suspicion awoke in his lordship's eyes. 'Certainly. But I had the oddest idea, you know, that an introduction was unnecessary.' He paused but as Gideon vouchsafed no reply, turned to Elizabeth and continued smoothly, 'My dear, pray allow me to present to you the Honourable Gideon Vaughan – a close friend of my brother's. And this, Gideon, is Mistress Elizabeth Tierney.'

Mr Vaughan bowed smilingly. 'I am honoured, Mistress Tierney.'

Elizabeth raised shy eyes to his face. 'And I, sir.'

'I wonder how I came by the notion that you were already acquainted?' mused the Colonel pensively.

'I can't imagine,' answered Gideon pleasantly. 'Do you live in London, Mistress Tierney?'

'Yes, sir . . . Hanover Square,' replied Elizabeth. And blushed afresh at her own temerity.

Gideon's eye held a lurking twinkle. 'It's odd, then, that we haven't met – here or there?'

He won an answering gleam as she replied, 'It is, isn't it?'

'Mistress Tierney has but recently returned from Bath,' remarked Lord Randolph. 'And I seem to recall that you were there some weeks ago, Gideon. Or am I mistaken?'

'You are not.'

'Ah,' breathed the Colonel. 'I thought not.' He paused for a moment, smiling maliciously. 'Well . . . I think we must not detain you. Pray give Francis my . . . love . . . when next you see him.' And he set his horses in motion before Gideon could reply.

No sooner had Elizabeth entered the drawing-room than her mama began plying her with questions.

'But surely, Lizzie, you must've met *someone?*'

'There – there was a gentleman,' admitted Elizabeth at last, driven.

Her mother's eyes brightened. 'Well, child? Who was he?'

'A Mr Vaughan. I think that Lord Randolph described him as a friend of his Grace, the Duke.'

'Oh!' Madam was impressed and delighted. 'A friend of the Duke? Well! Mr Vaughan . . . I'll swear I never heard the name before. I wonder he is not mentioned in the Court journals. Vaughan . . . we must ask your father. And what did you think of him, Lizzie? Was he an agreeable sort of a man?'

'He seemed most pleasant,' said her daughter cautiously.

Madam snorted with irritable scorn. 'Pleasant? *Pleasant?* Is that all you can find to say? I declare I can't understand you, child! A fashionable lord asks you out driving and are you pleased? No. You try to refuse – silly girl. You meet a young gentleman – I suppose he was young?'

'Not very, mama. Perhaps a little over thirty.'

'There, then! You meet a young man, the friend of a duke so he must *be* somebody – and all you can say is that he was pleasant. I vow you are the most provoking girl!'

'We scarcely exchanged two words, mama. But if you really wish to know, I thought Mr Vaughan vastly more agreeable than my lord – for it can't have escaped your attention that I don't like him at all,' said Elizabeth with unaccustomed asperity.

'Well, Lizzie! If that isn't just like you!' retorted her mother, nettled. 'I've no doubt you only say it to be difficult.'

'No, mama. Indeed, I don't. You asked my opinion and I have given it. I knew it wouldn't please you.'

'Please me? I should think not! What's the friend of the Duke – and a commoner to boot – compared with the heir to the Dukedom?'

Elizabeth looked at her sadly and sighed. 'In effect, you and Papa wish to buy a title – and the higher the better?'

Ruffled and a little flustered, Madam Tierney made a pretence of arranging the lace at her elbows. 'My goodness, Lizzie – you should know your papa and I only think of your good. But you are young and you hardly know Lord Randolph and he's very fine, with elegant manners and all. Why, I shouldn't be surprised if you soon forget you ever thought you disliked him. It's just a silly girlish fancy, you mark my words!'

'I see.' Elizabeth realised that it was pointless to argue and wisely decided that no good could come of pursuing the subject till she was forced by circumstances to do so.

As she had expected, Joshua's initial reaction was identical to that of his wife. Much to Madam Tierney's disappointment, he could give her no extra information about the mysterious Mr Vaughan, but within two days he was able not only to satisfy her curiosity but also to form some opinions of his own.

'A good family, m'dear, but no title. This Mr Gideon is the younger son and don't inherit,' was his succinct verdict. 'He ain't what we want for our Lizzie and, to say truth, I'd as soon she didn't meet him again.'

His wife was surprised. 'Why not? She don't seem to fancy him particular, if that's what you mean.'

'No, Rachel, likely not. But that ain't it. He's a friend of this Duke, and I don't want Lizzie brought to his notice – not yet. I'll not hide from you that if there's a fly in the ointment, he's it.'

'Mr Vaughan?' she asked, baffled.

'No!' said Joshua, irritably. And then, with commendable patience, 'The Duke. It's a fact that the Courtenays are hard put to know where the next penny's coming from – gamesters, all of 'em – and the land's mostly mortgaged. But his Grace is well known for his haughty ways and I daresay he's daft enough to cut off his nose, as the saying is, and stop his lordship a-courting our Lizzie.'

'Well, my dear, I don't say you're wrong but I can't see as how he could! Lord Randolph's no minor, is he?'

Her husband regarded her in gloomy silence. 'You don't know the half, Rachel – and I hope you never do. Take my word that this Duke is an ugly customer – in more ways than one – and when he wants to do something, he does it.'

She had certain difficulties in visualising a noble duke who was also an 'ugly customer', but she refrained from admitting it and later communicated Joshua's wishes to their daughter. Having no expectation of encountering Mr Vaughan again before winter, Elizabeth was able to accept this edict with almost disinterested calm; and so it was with a mixture of pleasure, shock and guilt, that she found herself face to face with him in Bond Street only two days later.

'Mistress Tierney! It seems we are destined to meet by fortunate coincidence.' His voice was full of suppressed amusement and this caused her to wonder if coincidence were not, perhaps, the wrong word.

She smiled shyly. 'Indeed, sir – it does seem so.'

He laughed. 'May I walk a little way with you?'

Elizabeth saw where her duty lay and resolutely ignored it. She nodded and signed her youthful and inexperienced abigail to fall behind them.

'You are well acquainted with Lord Randolph?' asked Vaughan, coming directly to the point.

'Not – not well. We met in Bath a few times.'

He heard the constraint in her voice but could not bring himself to do the courteous thing and drop the subject. 'Unless I am mistaken, he felt my presence in the park to be rather inconvenient. He must admire you very much.'

Elizabeth flushed faintly and looked distressed. Instantly, Gideon regretted his words and said quickly, 'I beg your pardon! I had no right to say that. You will think me a boorish fellow. Pray forgive me.'

'There is nothing to forgive, sir,' came the low-voiced reply.

Gideon looked sharply at her. 'Do you like him?'

The blue eyes flew to meet his and then she replied hesitantly, 'Not . . . very much. I don't know why but I think I am a little afraid of him.'

He suffered a sudden insane impulse to grin. 'Very sensible. He's no fit companion for you. But how did you come to be driving with him? You can't have wished to.'

'I – I didn't. It was mama. She and my father . . .' She halted uncertainly, aware of saying too much.

Gideon frowned. 'Your parents would appear to know very little of Randolph Courtenay,' he remarked drily.

'No. Papa hasn't met him at all.' Elizabeth was torn between a desire to confide in Mr Vaughan and a reluctance to explain her family's ambition and social status. She was not in the least ashamed that she came of merchant stock but she was heartily embarrassed by her fond papa's determination to marry her to a title; and it seemed that the one necessarily followed the other.

'I don't want to appear vulgarly intrusive, Mistress Tierney, but I must own that I am somewhat confused.'

'I don't doubt it, sir,' she sighed. 'But I think my problems can be of little interest to you.'

'Indeed, they can,' he assured her warmly, 'and I would be honoured by your confidence. My dear – will you not tell me?'

The caring note in his voice shook her and she swallowed before replying breathlessly, 'It's easily explained, sir. My father is a merchant in the City. He has made a good deal of money and now he . . . he wishes to invest it in a husband for me.' She kept her eyes steadfastly ahead, unwilling to meet his gaze and see the disgust or patronage she dreaded to find there.

'I see. And Lord Randolph is a suitable candidate for this . . . investment . . . having a mountain of debts coupled with an ancient name and a title,' said Gideon grimly.

'Yes. He also has the distinction of being heir to a dukedom.'

Gideon's brows rose and then he laughed. Elizabeth nerved herself to peep into his face. 'What is so funny, sir?'

'Simply that although Francis – Lyndhurst, that is – has so far remained single, I wouldn't wager a groat on Randolph's

72

chances of stepping into his ducal shoes. They dislike each other cordially, you know, and at some time or other Francis is certain to take a bride – if only to annoy his brother.'

'Oh,' said Elizabeth blankly. 'His Grace must be a . . . rather unusual gentleman.'

'It's not the word. He's extraordinary,' was the ironic reply.

'But if he's your friend,' she said diffidently, 'I suppose that you know best what he is likely to do.'

'I doubt if anyone knows Francis *that* well. And Randolph is very like him – save that he lacks in equal measure his brother's wit, intelligence and experienced devilry. Though I think you'd find Randolph devil enough.' He paused and then said, 'Mistress Tierney, may I have your permission to call on you and your parents?'

Elizabeth felt a startled joy at this sudden request, followed by an unpleasant sinking sensation in the pit of her stomach as she recalled her mother's instructions. 'I – I'm sorry, Mr Vaughan. It's impossible. Papa has said that he doesn't wish me to meet you.'

'Good God! Why not?'

'For fear you reveal Lord Randolph's interest in me to his Grace,' she replied wretchedly.

Once more, he astonished her by laughing. 'So. Your father knows enough of Francis to beware, does he? Then he should also know that Francis will discover his brother's activities with or without my help. It's a habit with him.' He stopped walking and turned to face her, taking her hand and looking deep into her eyes. 'So our friendship is to be a secret, is it?'

Her heart gave a queer little leap and her fingers trembled in his but she did not pretend to mistake the implication in his words. 'Yes,' she whispered.

'And you'll not forget me – even though we may not meet again till winter?'

Elizabeth smiled with gentle brilliance. 'No, Mr Vaughan. I won't forget.'

Lyndhurst Court

An imposing residence of pale stone and warm amber brick, Lyndhurst had been erected by a long-dead Elizabethan Courtenay who had followed the fashion of his time in designing it himself. Cunningly, he had incorporated the fourteenth-century monastery church into the eastern wing of his dwelling and now, over a century and a half later, he might have congratulated himself on the result for it blended with quiet dignity into the mellow whole.

Successive generations had wisely refrained from adding to the original structure and so it stood, seemingly impervious to the passing years. Over the walls climbed ivy, glossy and dark, its tendrils clinging fiercely to the ancient brick, and bright-flowering honeysuckle and clematis softened the deliberate symmetry of the house. The ground floor boasted leaded windows built in squared bays with scrolls of stonework set beneath, while above them oriels were supported by stone corbels. Higher still, above small attic windows and ornately-carved gables, tall and intricately patterned chimneys stood stark against the sky.

Built on a rise in the ground, the house looked down across stone terraces bounded by low, balustraded walls from which flights of shallow steps gave access to the formal gardens below. Wide, gravel paths led between geometric rose-beds and, at their centre was a circular pond. Here stood Aphrodite, cast in bronze, and beneath whose feet fell a rippling cascade so gentle it scarcely disturbed the goldfish which lazed amongst the lilypads. Beyond the gardens, smooth green lawns ran down to the river, along whose banks grew weeping willows and tall wild iris, their flaunting, yellow petals tinged with burgundy brown.

Only to the keener eye was the beauty brittle, the timelessness an illusion, for Lyndhurst was becoming increasingly affected by the gradual decline in the Courtenay fortunes. No longer was there an army of gardeners to tend the grounds; now Bates struggled on single-handed, complaining bitterly and long of the impossibility of his task. He fought a constant battle with persistent weeds in the wide, gravelled drive and cursed the low privet hedges that grew too fast for one man's shears; he shook his fist at the willows and beeches when their leaves blew wildly across his new-scythed grass; but most of all he raged at the family of Courtenay, whose wanton extravagance he blamed for his futile crusade against encroaching nature.

Vanessa, arriving in the early evening of a glorious day in late June, saw all of the beauty and none of the need, and fell instantly under the spell of Lyndhurst's gracious tranquillity. Her sojourn in Great Jermyn Street had been spent in endless visits to modistes, milliners, haberdashers and the like – so many that she had quite lost count and remembered none of them. The number of purchases deemed necessary by Lady Blanche had left her stunned, exhausted and too weak to protest; and after the first day, she had given up trying to calculate the cost – for the items that they carried home with them or had delivered by various mantua-makers, seemed hopelessly insignificant beside the countless orders placed by her ladyship 'for next season'.

It had not taken Vanessa long to form a tolerably accurate picture of Lady Blanche. She quickly recognised her essential selfishness but also that, at the bottom of her rather shallow heart, Blanche was genuinely fond of her husband and of the eldest brother. It was also clear that Blanche did not want to visit Charles and Judith Maynard and from certain of her remarks, Vanessa gained the impression of some past trouble between them which also concerned the Duke. But events were moving too fast for her to devote much thought to this matter and she soon forgot all about it.

The serenity she experienced when first setting eyes on the house sustained her through the almost immediate departure of Lord and Lady Overton and the introduction to Lilian Erskine – whom she found placid, goodnatured and garrulous. Clearly, madam was so grateful to his Grace for installing her in his home that she had no wish to question or criticise his behaviour and, accepting Vanessa in the same spirit, she kissed her and begged to be addressed as Cousin Lilian.

Next morning, Vanessa woke early. For a few minutes she lay, relaxed and sleepy, and then, flinging back the covers, leapt energetically out of bed to look out of her window. Bright, early – morning sunlight enhanced the brilliant colours of the roses and turned the fountain to droplets of silver. The magnet lured and beckoned; and Vanessa exploded into activity.

By the time Jassy came to wake her, she was about to go downstairs, resplendent in lavender cambric with violet ribbons.

'Miss Vanessa!' exclaimed Jassy, indignantly. 'You should've rung. Whatever are you doing up at this hour?'

'It's such a beautiful day,' pleaded Vanessa. 'Don't scold – I'll try to remember in future. But today – oh, today I feel almost myself again and it's so long since I did that I'm quite shy of myself.' She looked at her reflection and said, 'Perhaps we should be introduced?'

Jassy smiled indulgently. 'Well, you look better than you did a week ago – and that's a fact.'

Vanessa dropped a mock-curtsy. 'We thank you. Is madam still abed?' Jassy nodded. 'Good. Then lead me to my breakfast for I can't wait to go outside.'

Vanessa partook alone of chocolate and bread and butter in the sunny breakfast parlour, then found her way to the front door and slipped unnoticed from the house. For a moment she stood on the stone terrace and then she skimmed lightly down the wide steps and into the rose garden. She was still there, sitting on the rim of the lily pond when Bates entered the garden to tend the rose bushes. Acknowledging her greeting with a taciturn nod and a grunt, he stumped over to a nearby bed of large golden blooms and began snipping off the dead blossoms.

'You must be very proud of your roses,' remarked Vanessa in a friendly tone. 'They are very beautiful.'

'Aye.' Bates disdained to look round and continued his pruning. 'I used to grow them myself – in Cornwall – but I was never very successful.' She paused, received no answer and, smiling faintly, tried again. 'I doubt I have the knack of it but I did wonder if the salt breeze might not have been harmful?'

He still did not turn to look at her but he ceased working. 'Could be. Near sea, were 'ee?'

'Very near.'

'Then 'twas poor soil belike. No nature in it.' And, as if regretting this display of interest, he fell to snipping fiercely.

Encouraged by this success, Vanessa considered her next remark carefully. 'Such a garden as this must mean a lot of work.'

'Aye. It do.'

'So I daresay his Grace employs many gardeners?'

Bates snorted and attacked the next bush. 'Aye. He did – once.'

'Oh. You mean you take care of all this *alone*? But surely one man couldn't do it!'

'Couldn't he though?' Bates turned at last and faced her sardonically. 'But it ain't easy. I can tell 'ee that!'

'No. I can't imagine how you manage,' said Vanessa in simple admiration. 'His Grace is fortunate to have the benefit of your obvious experience. But no doubt you've been here many years?'

'Aye. And my father before me and his father afore him. Bates have always served Courtenay.'

'Well, I am delighted to meet you, Mr Bates,' said Vanessa with friendly and winning courtesy. 'I am . . . his Grace's ward.'

'Aye. Mistress Tremaine.' He was patently unsurprised. 'I do hear all about 'ee from yon dim-witted wench in kitchen.'

'Oh.' Realising for the first time that her presence must be providing much food for speculative gossip among the servants,

77

she rose absently and shook out her skirts. 'You are doubtless finding me a terrible nuisance, Mr Bates – but I have so enjoyed talking to you. I hope you will permit me to do so again?'

'Aye. Mebbe,' he said in the most gracious tone he had used so far. And then, as if irritated by such unusual signs of weakness: 'If I bain't too busy.' And turned once more to the roses.

It was while having lunch that Vanessa first began to take an interest in the interior of the Court and, when they had finished eating, she said, 'Cousin Lilian, should you object if I spent the afternoon going over the house?'

'Not in the least, child,' said her duenna placidly. 'I generally rest in the afternoons. Are you sure *you* shouldn't do so? You were out so long this morning.'

Vanessa shook her head, smiling mischievously. 'No. I feel quite fresh. And I'm not used to being idle for I always ran Penmarne myself, you know.'

'My dear!' said madam, in quick sympathy.

'Please don't feel sorry for me, cousin – there is no need for in many ways I found it enjoyable. There was the house to run, the still-room to oversee – and I even did the farm and mine accounts when Papa was – ' She stopped abruptly, then finished tonelessly, ' – when Papa was indisposed.'

Lilian surveyed her in lively astonishment. Incapable herself of adding a column of figures, she was aghast at the thought of any gently-bred female who could. 'Vanessa,' she said earnestly, 'It's all most admirable, I'm sure – but you must never, never mention it.'

Vanessa roused herself from unwelcome recollections. 'Why not?'

'It would give people an excessively odd notion of you, my dear. Fashionable ladies of birth know nothing of such matters.'

'It seems to me,' sighed Vanessa, 'that there are far too many things I'm not supposed to know – and I can't see the point of it. Surely gentlemen can't really prefer witless *naïveté* – or not the ones who've any brain themselves? And why should I pretend I don't know about their . . . little amusements . . . when I do?

Why,' she finished triumphantly, 'I've even been mistaken for one myself!'

Madam Erskine stared at her with a mixture of bewilderment and dire foreboding. 'I don't understand you in the least – and I don't think I want to,' she announced weakly. 'But don't ever talk like that to Francis!'

Vanessa considered the matter. 'It seems to me that his Grace is the only one who isn't shocked by my frankness. But don't fret, cousin,' she grinned, rising to kiss Lilian's cheek. 'If it will please you, I'll try!' And with that she left the room.

Vanessa began her tour at the top of the house and found the majority of the bedchambers swathed in Holland covers. The ones that were not, were similarly furnished to her own – all that is, except for one particular suite where a wholly feminine boudoir and bedchamber, shrouded but hung with delicately-embroidered brocade, led to another – unshrouded and not feminine at all. Here, magnificent hangings of Nile blue and silver combined with dark mahogany to produce an effect that was at once sombre and exotic. It did not take a genius to guess whose room this was and Vanessa whisked herself hastily back into the corridor without quite knowing why.

She entered the long gallery, her eye drawn to the portraits that hung the entire length of it and she slowed her pace, stopping now and then to look more closely. Most of the Courtenay men were dark and one of them, a buff-coated cavalier, was like enough to the present Duke to cause Vanessa's nerves a briefly unpleasant jerk. Further on she paused in front of a beautiful blonde who must, she decided be the late Duchess. Vanessa observed the disdainful curve of the lovely mouth and concluded that her Grace had probably been as similar to Blanche in character as she undoubtedly was in appearance.

It was the last portrait that interested her most – a recent and faintly uncanny likeness of her guardian. The artist had caught the peculiarly piercing quality of the topaz eyes, the mockery that touched their heavy lids and the derisive curl of the hard mouth; the unnatural pallor was there and the austere, sculpted beauty of cheek and jaw. But Vanessa shivered and hoped she would never see that particular expression outside this piece of painted canvas.

Abstractedly, she went downstairs and in a short time all thought of the Duke had fled and her housewifely instincts were uppermost. Upstairs the lack of thorough cleaning had been less noticeable in rooms seldom used – though she had wondered that the Duke's own room was not kept in better order against his coming; but in those in common use the negligence was undeniably plain. She discovered cabinets of ivory and jade thick with dust, smeared and cloudy chandeliers, fraying curtains and furniture, none of which seemed to have been beeswaxed in living memory. Outraged, Vanessa sent for Jassy and then returned to the south parlour. When Jassy arrived, she jumped nimbly down from the chair she had been standing on to examine the curtains and said curtly, 'What servants does his Grace keep here?'

Jassy blinked. 'Servants? Well, there's Mrs Clayton the cook and Nan the kitchen-maid; then there's James and George the two footmen and . . . three housemaids – Polly, Mary and Ruth.'

Vanessa nodded. 'I see. No housekeeper?'

'No, miss. His Grace never employs one.'

'Then it's time he did. Half these furnishings will soon be beyond repair if they are not dealt with. Look at the curtains – and this table!' She pointed indignantly at these articles. 'Something must be done – so get the maids and bring them here to me.'

'Now?' asked Jassy, stunned.

'Now,' answered Vanessa firmly, shooing her from the room.

Her interview with Polly, Mary and Ruth was brief and direct. She laid no blame but made it plain that all must be put right. Carpets were to be taken up and beaten, curtains brushed and mended and the chandelier was to be dismantled and washed. All the pieces of china and glass were to be cleaned and replaced and the furniture was to be thoroughly polished. The three girls looked at her in frank horror and Vanessa was obliged to laugh.

'It won't kill you,' she said. 'We'll deal with one room at a time – and Jassy and I will help.'

If anything, the girls were even more frightened at the prospect of working side by side with one who was undoubtedly a lady and, seeing that further reassurances were pointless, Vanessa shrugged and hoped that they would soon come to terms with the idea.

'This room first then – ah, and one of you had best see to his Grace's bedchamber. I'm sure you wouldn't wish him to see it as it is at present.' She dismissed the dumbstruck trio and turned to Jassy. 'You will help, won't you? Unless I'm mistaken, those three will need a lot of supervision and direction.'

'Lord, miss – 'course I will. And it seems like *I'd* best mend them curtains. Shouldn't think any of *them* knows which end of a needle to thread,' concluded Jassy scornfully.

Thus began weeks of feverish activity of which the clearing and cleaning of the south parlour was only the start. Despite Vanessa's careful planning it seemed that the entire house was turned upside down. James and George found themselves in constant transit clutching carpets and items of furniture while Vanessa and her handmaidens tripped hither and thither armed with brooms and polishing cloths or priceless pieces of china and glass. And slowly Vanessa's enthusiasm and infectious gaiety communicated itself to her helpers so that their service became less grudging and more cheerful. Two days earned her their respect and within a week they were her willing slaves.

The most surprising conquest of all was Bates. Known to one and all as a 'miserable old devil', it was therefore astonishing when he not only permitted Vanessa to pick any flowers she liked from the bower but actually strode into the hall one day carrying a huge bouquet of his cherished roses.

Madam Erskine could not pretend to approve of Vanessa's housekeeping activities but even she was impressed by Bates' floral tribute. 'You must be a witch, my dear. I distincly recall Blanche telling me that he never permitted her to touch his roses.'

Slowly, the Court came to life and began to wear a more cheerful air. The restoration of the south parlour took nearly a week and, having completed it, Vanessa arranged her precious roses in two large bowls and turned her attention to the dining-room.

So it was that his Grace of Lyndhurst, entering his domain quite unnoticed, came upon her dressed in one of her old gowns and perched upon a stool, energetically rubbing beeswax into the panelling. For a moment he remained by the door watching her until, sensing rather than seeing someone in the room, Vanessa said, still polishing, 'James, ask Mary to get some more wax. This pot's nearly empty.'

'I am desolated to disoblige you,' said the Duke gently, 'but I am not . . . er . . . James.'

At the sound of that soft, drawling voice, Vanessa's head spun round, knocking her off balance. The stool tilted, she reeled and would have fallen but for two strong hands that caught her waist in a seemingly effortless clasp and swung her safely to the floor. Still holding her, Lyndhurst looked down into the flushed face and remarked with his customary languor, 'You lead a perilous life, my child.'

She smiled, eyes alight with pleasure. 'Possibly. But also charmed, I think?'

He released her and nodded slowly. 'Perhaps. Well, my ward – do you have no more fitting greeting for me than to mistake me for the footman? An error which I cannot say appeals to me.'

Vanessa chuckled. 'No. I'm sorry – but it's such a surprise and you can't imagine how pleased I am to see you. I've so much to say that I don't know where to begin!'

He regarded her animation with some amusement. 'I perceive your spirits are much restored. Lyndhurst obviously suits you.'

'How could it not? And now *you* have come – '

'Pray do not feel impelled to rejoice at my coming. It is not one of my requirements, you know.'

'Of course not,' she agreed with disarming simplicity.

The topaz eyes narrowed a fraction but he said nothing. Instead, he lifted his glass and surveyed the depleted room with lazy interest. 'I am at something of a loss to account for all this. It was my impression that spring-cleaning took place in the . . .

er . . . spring and that I employed several housemaids for the purpose.' His brows rose enquiringly.

Vanessa looked down at her hands demurely.

'I didn't expect you so soon,' she explained.

'Evidently. I make no doubt that you have some lengthy explanation to offer me – yes, I thought so.' He sighed in response to her emphatic nod. 'I beg you will reserve it till you have changed your attire. I trust there is at least one room left undisturbed?' She nodded again, laughing a little. 'I think you will find the south parlour quite comfortable. Must I indeed change?'

'Yes. You look a complete urchin and I have my consequence to consider,' he said, waving her away.

In fact, he marvelled at the fact that he had never seen her appear to better advantage. Wayward chestnut curls strayed round flushed cheeks and the grey eyes sparkled with evident pleasure. She was altogether a different being to the one of a fortnight ago and he wondered sardonically what Mr Vaughan would make of the change when he saw it.

As the Duke crossed the hall a footman materialised from the nether regions and froze on the sight of him. 'Your G-Grace!'

'Just so,' purred Lyndhurst. 'I rejoice to see that you have not forgotten me.'

'N-no, your Grace. But we didn't know to expect your Grace today and – '

'It is your place to expect me at all times,' observed the Duke caustically, 'but on this occasion I will strive to overlook the fact. You may serve me wine in the south parlour.' And he walked unconcernedly on, leaving James goggling after him.

In the parlour, Lyndhurst looked searchingly around him, noting the differences of richly glowing wood and gleaming glass. His cabinet of ivory and jade was free from dust and more tastefully arranged than he remembered and the air was heavy with the scent of roses. His Grace smiled faintly to himself.

When James arrived with his wine, Lyndhurst accepted the glass pensively and said, 'Those roses . . . where did they come from?'

'The formal garden, your Grace,' replied James with simple pride. 'Bates cut them himself.'

The blue eyes widened. 'Did he so? How very unlike him.'

'Yes, your Grace. He's taken quite a fancy to Miss Vanessa.'

It was not Lyndhurst's custom to encourage his servants to gossip but he made an exception. 'Indeed?'

'Oh yes, your Grace. It's a real pleasure to serve her, so sweet-natured as she is.' James flushed beneath his master's mocking glance and muttered desperately, 'We all think so.'

'I see.' The smooth voice was expressionless. 'That is all.'

Alone again, he sipped his wine and pondered the intriguing question of how his ward had won the loyalty of his staff whilst initiating so much extra work. He concluded that Vanessa was an exceptional young lady whose effect on society should prove even more entertaining than he had previously supposed.

When Vanessa joined him some ten minutes later she was exquisitely gowned in pale grey tiffany and she swept into the room with a very recognisable imitation of Lady Blanche's most dignified manner. Head held high, she dropped a regal little curtsy and extended one wilting hand.

'It's vastly charming of you to call,' she drawled liltingly.

His Grace received her hand and bowed over it. 'I perceive,' he replied suavely, 'that the obligation is all mine.'

With an arch smile, she glided to a couch and sat down, spreading her skirts. His Grace remained standing and surveyed her with lurking amusement. 'I also perceive that I have deprived the theatre of a talented actress. But you must allow me to point out that my sister never drawls. She has not the patience for it.'

Vanessa grinned and abandoned her role. 'I merely wanted you to know that the "urchin" can display come dignity if the occasion demands it,' she explained.

'I thank you,' responded Lyndhurst politely, 'but I believe we may dispense with that particular species. It does not suit you and I am not at all partial to it. You may be yourself – and therefore original.'

'Original,' she repeated thoughtfully. 'Am I that?'

His shoulders shook in soundless laughter. 'In my experience, which I believe is particularly wide, you are . . . unique.'

The grey eyes rested on his speculatively. 'I'm not sure,' she said, 'that it's a compliment – but I hope you won't enlighten me. Will you tell Cousin Lilian?'

'That you are unique? Can it be that she has failed to remark it?' he asked, deliberately misunderstanding.

'No! Of course she has – Oh!' She broke off, laughing. 'I meant, will you inform her that you don't mind if I say what I think?'

'It seems a rather broad licence. But perhaps my worthy cousin finds you a trifle indiscreet?'

Vanessa nodded mournfully. 'She says it will upset you if I don't guard my tongue and tells me that no well-bred young lady should understand figures or polish the furniture.'

The Duke regarded her through his glass. 'I am constrained, very reluctantly you understand, to agree with her on the matter of the furniture. For the rest, I find your candour in no way discomposing.'

'Then I may speak my mind?'

'To me, child. When you enter the world, however, you will need to employ a little more restraint. *D'accord?*'

'*D'accord,*' sighed Vanessa. And then, reviving, 'Have you noticed this room?'

'I have. You seem to have been busy.'

'You don't mind?'

'Mind? No. I believe I am grateful.'

'There is no need for that. It's better for me to be busy for then I don't . . . think about Papa so much. You understand?' Her face had clouded.

'Perfectly. I am merely surprised that such activity should interest you.'

She shrugged. 'I'm used to it. Mama died when I was quite young and we were never rich so I ran the house myself. But you, your Grace, should employ a housekeeper. The Court is too lovely to be neglected.'

Smiling wryly, Lyndhurst refrained from explaining that his

own finances were in a constant state of fluctuation. Instead, he sat down and said, 'I begin to think I do have a housekeeper.'

She coloured a little. 'I wished to repay your kindness – and later it occurred to me that . . .' She stopped and looked at him uncertainly.

His Grace felt that he had a tolerably exact notion of what was coming next but he gave no sign of it. 'Yes?'

'Well, I – I thought you might prefer to keep me as your housekeeper instead of your ward.' He gazed at her enigmatically. 'Well?' she asked anxiously.

'I should not prefer it at all, child. I find I have become quite set on presenting you as my ward. Amuse yourself with this work by all means, but I cannot allow you to waste your life on it. And, in six months, you will have forgotten you ever wished to.'

Vanessa shook her head but said merely, 'You will at least allow me to discuss the household details with you?'

'I doubt I can prevent you,' he returned drily. 'However, it is only fair to warn you that I leave for Bath in the morning.'

'Oh,' she said disappointedly. 'So soon?'

'Even so. I came only to see how my ward fared – and to bring her a riding habit.'

'Oh!' said Vanessa again, but differently.

'I presume you ride?' She nodded, pink with pleasure. 'Good. In the stables is a bay mare which I judge suitable for you. If you ride beyond the bounds of the estate, you will always do so with a groom in attendance. I pray you remember it.'

'Yes – oh, yes, I will! I don't know how to thank you or how you knew it's the thing I miss most. I am impressed,' she said, peeping at him through her lashes. 'But perhaps you are also unique, your Grace?'

'For which the Lord make us truly thankful,' he quoted lazily. 'And now I suggest you forget your domestic troubles in favour of accompanying me to the stables.'

She laughed. 'I might have known it would be impossible to

make you listen if you didn't want to!' Rising gracefully, she held out her hand with unselfconscious friendliness. 'Very well, sir. I admit the temptation is too great to resist – so let us go.'

Leisurely, his Grace stood and took her hand in his, an odd smile lighting his eyes. 'Being a specialist in temptation, no doubt the devil is always . . . irresistible.'

Enter Mr Joseph Wade

The carriage was occupied by a solitary gentleman who slouched untidily in his seat and gazed moodily out of the window, a frown of palpable irritation on his heavy-featured countenance. He wore a coat of puce-coloured velvet, ill-suited to his high complexion and, though his hair was powdered, one could guess its hue from the sandy brows and lashes. His eyes were small and of a shade so light that they appeared almost opaque and full lips gave hint of a sensual disposition.

Just now he was sadly out of temper. He had always disliked the expense and inconvenience of travelling, but this particular journey he loathed even more than usual. Firstly, he had seen the need to travel fast, which had increased both cost and discomfort, and, secondly, he was annoyed by the belated knowledge that the trip would have been unnecessary had he previously held his tongue.

The coach turned into Gower Street and creaked to a halt before the house in which the gentleman lodged. He descended to the pavement and entered the tall, narrow building. Some half-hour later he emerged again and took a chair to his club where he spent a little time refreshing himself and making certain enquiries. Then he set off for Grosvenor Square.

He gave his card to the butler and was duly shown into the presence of the lady of the house – a proud, cold dame whom the gentleman privately wrote down as hatchet-faced. He smiled at her with a curious mixture of amiability and deference.

'Lady Henley,' he said affably. 'Most kind of you to receive me. I am honoured.'

His bow exhibited a marked lack of finesse and the lady inclined her head but did not smile. She noted that the gentleman's eyes did not meet hers for more than an instant before sliding elsewhere. 'My butler informed me that your business with me was of an urgent nature, Mr Wade.'

'Indeed, ma'am. Indeed.' He rubbed his hands together. 'Most pressing and somewhat delicate, I fear.'

Her brows rose. 'Really? Then you had best be seated, sir.'

He lowered himself cautiously into a gilt chair. 'I had thought that my name could not be unknown to your ladyship.'

'And why should you suppose that, Mr Wade?'

'Because I expected to find my young cousin in your excellent care. She certainly said she would come to you.'

Lady Henley stiffened. 'Your cousin, sir?'

Mr Wade bowed. 'Yes, indeed – and I believe your godchild, madam. I speak of Vanessa Tremaine.' The small eyes watched her closely.

'Be good enough to explain yourself,' ordered her ladyship coldly. He bowed again and smiled ingratiatingly.

'Believing my cousin to be with you, I called in the hope of persuading her to return home, thus relieving you of a troublesome charge. Do I understand that she is not here?'

'She is not.'

'Ah. Then you have not seen her?'

'I did not say so, Mr Wade.'

The mask of cheerful candour slipped a little and he leaned forward saying sharply, 'So she *did* come to you?'

Lady Maria regarded him with dislike and said inflexibly, 'Before I answer you, I feel that I am entitled to an explanation.'

'But of course, madam. Of course,' he replied unctuously. 'You doubtless know of Sir Thomas Tremaine's sudden death. His estate was entailed to the heirs male and therefore passed into my hands. My cousin took it hard and, though I naturally offered her a home, chose to leave in something of a pet.

89

Hearing no word I became concerned for her safety and am come to assure myself of her well-being.'

Lady Henley examined him with a gimlet-like stare and assessed him with shrewd accuracy. 'I see,' was all she said.

'I am most anxious to find her,' continued Mr Wade earnestly. 'If you can help, I beg you to do so, my lady.'

She turned the matter over in her mind for a moment before answering. Finally she decided that if, as she suspected, Mr Wade was no more fond of his cousin than she was herself, it could do no harm to tell him the truth.

'I fear that what I have to say is more likely to distress you than help, sir. Your cousin visited me at the end of June and that was the sole occasion on which we met. She expected me to provide her with a home. I refused.'

A reptilian gleam lit the strange eyes. Then it was gone and he said smoothly, 'Dear lady, I feel sure you had a good reason?'

'I did. How, I know not, but between leaving you and arriving here your cousin fell in with the most notoriously corrupt man in London. They were seen together at a small village inn where it appears they stayed overnight and Mistress Tremaine herself informed me that she spent the following night in this man's house. I drew the obvious conclusions and was naturally reluctant to have so loose a young woman beneath my roof.'

She glanced at Mr Wade and was pleased to see that the effect of her words was all that she had hoped. The jovial smile was wiped from his lips and the thick, sandy brows were drawn fiercely together above narrowed eyes.

'I see you are dismayed, sir. Doubtless you are very fond of your cousin?'

'Very fond,' he confessed, stricken. 'It was the dearest wish of my heart to wed her. I can scarcely believe that she . . .' He broke off, artistically shading his eyes with one hand.

My lady was sceptical but triumphant. 'I almost fear to tell you the name of the man,' she said with spurious sympathy.

By now, Mr Wade was fully aware that the game was one of

mutual pretence. He removed his hand and darted his peculiar lizard glance at her. 'But I must know it – and save her, if it's not too late!'

'And if it is? I hope you would do nothing . . . rash?'

Recognising his cue, Mr Wade replied ardently, 'If I find she is indeed ruined, I shall kill the man responsible – or die in the attempt. But I must have his name!'

'His name, my dear Mr Wade, is Courtenay. He is the Duke of Lyndhurst.'

Mr Wade lost a little of his colour and sat very still. He was not personally acquainted with the Duke but he knew that he would prove no mean adversary and inwardly cursed afresh the ill-judged words that had sent Vanessa flying from Cornwall and into the arms of such a protector.

Lady Maria watched with detached amusement and was rather sorry when she was deprived of further entertainment by the arrival of her son. 'Ah, Carlton,' she said coolly. 'Mr Wade, pray allow me to present my son. This, Carlton, is Mr Joseph Wade – he is Mistress Tremaine's cousin.'

The two men bowed, Wade with his usual faint clumsiness, Carlton with almost effeminate grace and Joseph's eyes conducted a swift appraisal. He saw a willowy young fop, exquisite in lavender satin and complete with elaborate wig and high, red heels.

'Delighted, m'dear fellow,' said Carlton. 'Feeling I've seen you somewhere before. Tom's, was it?'

'Possibly – I am a member there.'

'Mr Wade is seeking his cousin,' interposed her ladyship. 'It has been my painful duty to acquaint him with her conduct.'

'Eh? Oh yes!' Carlton winked and gave his high-pitched laugh.

'It's hardly a matter for levity,' reproved his mama. 'I fear Mr Wade's hopes are sadly dashed.'

The slight edge in her words was lost on her son. He looked at Wade and said, 'Stap me – did you have an eye to the chit?'

Joseph bowed. 'Such is my misfortune, sir.'

'Dashed if I know what's so special about her,' remarked

Carlton carelessly. 'Hardly a beauty, is she? But if you aim to queer Lyndhurst's pitch, you can count on me.'

Wade's quick glance flickered over him, noting the weakness of feature which accorded ill with the malice in Carlton's tone. Then, wringing his hands, he said, 'I'm obliged to you, my lord. It's cheering to know I have some support.'

Carlton giggled again. 'As to that, there's a good many who'd enjoy seeing Lucifer's pride in the dust.'

'Just so,' said Lady Maria quellingly. 'I regret we can offer you no more information, Mr Wade. I can only advise you to call at Lyndhurst House.' She held out her hand in a clear gesture of dismissal.

Joseph bowed over it, offered his rather fulsome thanks and was about to take his leave when Carlton said unexpectedly, 'I'll be at Tom's this evening. Care to join me for a game of piquet?'

Something stirred in the pale eyes. Then, 'I shall be honoured, sir. Honoured. And I shall look forward to it. Until tonight, then?'

After he had gone, Lady Maria looked silently at her son for a moment and then said, 'I rather fancy that there is more to Mr Wade than meets the eye.'

Carlton looked blankly back at her. 'Do you?'

'I do. You will be wise to go carefully for I am not at all sure he is to be trusted. And he is quite certainly not a gentleman.'

He sniggered. 'He ain't, is he? But you needn't worry, ma'am. I shan't say anything I shouldn't.'

'But I do worry, my son. You are possessed of a naturally indiscreet tongue which strong liquor has the effect of loosening.'

'Damn it, I can hold my wine!' he said pettishly.

'That is the boast of every drunkard,' came the glacial reply. 'By all means find out what you can but do not bestow your confidence on that man. And take care at the gaming tables. I am heartily tired of paying for your excesses.'

And, upon this remark, her son shot her the look of one goaded beyond endurance and flung out of the room.

By the time Joseph Wade entered the club that night, Carlton had already won a hundred guineas at hazard and lost two hundred at écarté. He hailed Wade with an air of relief and the two of them settled down at one of the smaller tables with a bottle of brandy. For a time they drank whilst playing a rubber of piquet on which neither appeared to be concentrating. Then they chatted desultorily on general topics. Towards the end of the bottle, Carlton's tongue was wagging freely enough for him to recount a couple of spicy and rather discreditable anecdotes and Mr Wade, still relatively sober, judged it time to raise the subject of their mutual interest. He began by enquiring about Lyndhurst's present whereabouts.

'No idea,' replied Carlton, frowning into his glass. 'Haven't seen the black-hearted scum this age, thanks be.'

'So it's likely he's not in town?'

'Aye.'

'The country then. His estate? Or do you think he'll come to London for the season?'

'Hang it all, I don't know. He makes a cursed habit of popping up where he's least expected – like some damned conjuror.'

Joseph leaned back in his chair and his eyes flickered consideringly over the other man's face. 'You don't like him, do you?'

Carlton expressed his feelings in one long and idiomatic sentence.

Wade nodded slowly. 'Why?'

Carlton regarded him owlishly and then shook his head. 'Not so fast,' he said, his words slurring slightly. 'Fair's fair. I'll tell you if you tell me your interest in that redheaded chit.'

'Done,' said Joseph, holding out his hand. Carlton took it, recoiling slightly at its chill clamminess. 'You first,' prompted Mr Wade, with a sly smile. It would not, he reflected, be particularly difficult to dupe Carlton with some glib excuse; and, just to make certain, he refilled the other man's glass before sitting back to listen.

Carlton's narrative, long and highly coloured, was told the way he was now absolutely convinced that it had happened. This version greatly enhanced his personal charm and courage, showed Lady Blanche as a heartless jade and presented his Grace of Lyndhurst as the devil incarnate. Joseph followed it with some difficulty, realising that it bore scant resemblance to the truth and recognised the violent threats against the Duke for mere bravado born of cowardice. Comtempt for such folly flared in his cold eyes but he murmured sympathetic agreement and made a mental note that, should it ever be necessary to cross Lyndhurst, he would do so from a safe distance. Without thinking, he tossed off his brandy, filled his glass and drained it again.

"S your turn,' mumbled Carlton.

Despite his original intentions, Joseph had been drinking steadily and was now a good deal more inebriated than he knew. He leaned across the table and said flatly, 'Vanessa Tremaine is going to become my wife.'

Carlton goggled at him. '*Wife?* In hell's name, why? It's plain she's not virtuous or she'd not be with Lucifer.'

Wade smiled unpleasantly and Carlton, not normally fanciful, was nastily reminded of an alligator. With a rare flash of insight, he said, 'You don't love her. It's something else.'

Wade nodded, his small, cold eyes openly ruthless. 'Something else . . . yes. The girl herself is nothing.'

Carlton sniggered. 'I wonder if Lucifer agrees with you? He's probably tired of her by now . . . but I *do* hope not.'

'It's immaterial,' shrugged Wade. 'If he has abandoned her, so much the better.'

'What is it you want of her? It must be important.'

'Important? Yes,' replied Wade abstractedly. 'Listen and I'll tell you why. It's possible you may even be able to help.' And leaning one elbow on the table he lowered his voice and began to speak quickly and confidentially.

Concerning the Mysterious Past

After the Duke's visit, Vanessa's days fled by swiftly. The campaign in the house continued but she began to rely more on Jassy and turned her own attention to the still-room and the herb garden. Also, mounted on her mare Sheba, she began to explore the estate and was surprised by the poverty she found among the smaller tenant-farmers. Vanessa was accustomed to poverty. There had been plenty of it at Penmarne where, recently, the mine had hardly paid for the working. But there it was understandable; here it was not.

The land was in poor heart and many cottages stood in urgent need of repair. It was obvious that the estate was in dire need of a vast amount of money and Vanessa was at a loss to know why his Grace did not spend it. The plight of some of the tenants shocked her and she grew angry that the Duke and his brothers should live so extravagantly whilst allowing such a state of affairs to continue. Then she recollected the extortionate figure that she herself was costing and, fuming guiltily, set out to alleviate the worst conditions as best she could.

In particular, the Padgetts needed help for Tom had fallen from his leaking roof and broken his leg. Dr March had set the bone but, when Tom became acutely feverish, had failed to call again. Never one to waste time, Vanessa descended like an Angel of Wrath on the astounded doctor and gave him to understand that he was to attend Tom immediately and could send his bill to his Grace of Lyndhurst. Within two days, Tom was on the road to recovery and the story on everyone's lips.

One afternoon in August, Vanessa rode in a direction she had not before taken and was so deep in thought she quite failed to notice how far she had gone. Emerging from her reverie, she realised that her surroundings were totally unfamiliar and, though this did not alarm her, she was a little disturbed by the thought that she had probably left the estate behind her. Riding on in the hope of finding a signpost, she saw, instead, a horsewoman approaching from the opposite direction. Reining in, she waited, observing that the lady was red-haired and very lovely. As she drew near, she smiled at Vanessa and stopped beside her. Vanessa smiled in response, saying, 'Good day, madam. I'm afraid that I'm hopelessly lost. Could you direct me please?'

The lady's bright hazel gaze sparkled sympathetically. 'Certainly, my dear. I know how easy it is to ride too far – it's a fault I'm often guilty of myself. Where do you wish to go?' Vanessa told her. The sparkle vanished and the beautiful eyes widened suddenly. 'Lyndhurst?' repeated the lady in cold distaste.

Merciful heaven, thought Vanessa, not again. Do I *look* like a courtesan? Aloud, she said coolly, 'Yes, Lyndhurst. I am his Grace's ward.'

The sudden chill evaporated. 'Mistress Tremaine?'

It was Vanessa's turn to be startled. 'How do you know?'

'From Blanche. You see, I am Judith Maynard.'

'Oh,' said Vanessa lamely. 'I see.'

Judith eyed her with a strange blend of wariness and pity. 'Forgive me, my dear, but . . . are you happy?'

'I beg your pardon?'

'Pray humour me, Mistress Tremaine. Are you?'

'Yes, madam. Very happy.'

Judith hesitated and then asked carefully, 'You're not afraid of the Duke? He is kind to you?'

Vanessa's face hardened and she held herself very straight. 'I can't see why it should interest you – but since you ask, I'm not in the least afraid of him and he is kinder than I have any right to expect.'

Judith sighed. 'You must not be angry. It's simply that the Duke is . . . not a good man. And not the person to be trusted with a child like you.'

A spark of anger glowed in Vanessa's eyes. 'I don't wish to be rude,' she said icily, 'but I won't hear his Grace spoken of like that. Not by anyone.'

Strangely, Judith was not offended. 'I beg your pardon,' she said. 'Your loyalty does you credit.'

'It would be better if you could see that it does his Grace credit,' replied Vanessa drily.

'I doubt I shall ever feel so magnanimous,' said Judith quietly. And then, seeing Vanessa's annoyance, continued swiftly, 'But come. I'll show you the way.'

By the time they parted company, their relations were more cordial but Judith was careful to allow Vanessa no opportunity to question her – which was all that was needed to convince Vanessa that some mystery existed. She hoped that her duenna might be able to shed some light on the matter but she was doomed to disappointment for Lilian knew nothing save that his Grace had told her that, since he and the Maynards were not on visiting terms, he did not wish her to take his ward to Audley Vale.

Intrigued, Vanessa continued to consider the matter at odd moments; and then the harvesting of the fruit caused her to push it to the back of her mind. Discovering that she and Nan were the only ones who did not object to the necessary climbing of ladders, Vanessa helped with the picking herself and rather enjoyed it. When she was tired of methodically picking, she hoisted herself on to a convenient branch, as high up as possible, and sat methodically eating instead.

One afternoon she was doing just this when she heard a strange yet faintly familiar voice and, looking down, saw a rakish young gentleman, clad in fashionable riding dress strolling lazily through the orchard. It was with some surprise that she recognised Lord Nicholas Courtenay and, having watched him for a moment, she called down. Nicholas started, swore and turned to look behind him. She laughed. 'Up here.'

He spun back and looked up into the tree, shading his eyes from the sun. 'Blister it, you nearly gave me an apoplexy! What are you doing up there?'

Vanessa grinned and swung her feet. 'Picking apples.' She pointed to the boxes.

His lordship examined them disgustedly. 'It seems to me you've some deuced funny ideas, my girl. Ladies don't pick apples – and, come to that, they don't climb trees either.'

'Why not?' asked Vanessa interestedly.

He wrinkled his brow. 'Burn it – *I* don't know. It's not a ladylike occupation.'

'But I,' announced Vanessa with considerable aplomb, 'am unique.'

'You what?'

'Unique. His Grace said so.'

'Well, he should know,' retorted Nicholas. 'I wish you'd come down. I'm getting a plaguey stiff neck.'

Vanessa chuckled but came obligingly to earth and dropped a graceful curtsy. 'I'm delighted you decided to visit us, my lord. Have you seen your brother?'

'Lord, no!' replied Nicholas with every appearance of loathing. 'Haven't seen him since the day I met you. You don't want him?'

'Yes. I do.'

'Then you've appalling bad taste,' he said firmly. 'I'm staying at Audley Vale for a time so I thought I ought to further my acquaintance with you – m'brother's ward and all that.'

'Thank you. But why not here at the Court?'

His lordship regarded her with a knowing eye. 'Because I've an idea Francis wouldn't like it. Though I should think you could consider me a sort of uncle.'

Vanessa considered him dutifully and then shook her head. 'No, I couldn't. You dont look like an uncle.'

He grinned. 'Mighty nice of you, m'dear. Lilian in the house, is she? No,' forestalling the question, 'I don't want her. She talks too much, always did. I think I'd sooner have you.'

Vanessa raised her brows. 'You can't imagine how flattered I am.'

He frowned. 'Keep talking like that and I've done with you. You sound like Francis – and one of him is more than enough!'

'It's only fair to warn you,' said Vanessa carefully, 'that if you are rude about his Grace we shall quarrel.'

Up went one mobile brow. 'Speaking for myself, I never quarrel.'

'Well I do,' she replied flatly. 'Come into the kitchen garden. I want to talk to you.' She took his hand and tugged it.

Laughing, he allowed himself to be led through the arch and over to a bench. Vanessa seated herself, waited for him to do the same and then came straight to the point. 'I want to know why Judith Maynard dislikes his Grace so much.'

Nicholas looked sideways at her and said cautiously, 'Does she?'

'Yes – and you know it. Do you know why?'

He nodded ruefully. 'I do, but it's not an edifying tale.'

'No? Well I doubt it will shock me.'

'It won't need to if you're to be involved with our family. We're a bad lot and the tragedy is that we're not likely to improve. Only look at the dance Blanche leads poor Laurie!'

'Yes,' she replied single-mindedly. 'And Mr Maynard doesn't like his Grace either.'

'It's a common complaint. I try to avoid him myself.'

'Well that,' said Vanessa crossly, 'is just ridiculous.'

'Devil a bit,' denied his lordship with unimpaired cheerfulness. 'But I'll not tell you anything unless you promise to listen politely.'

Succumbing to this blackmail, Vanessa composed her face into an expression of improbable sanctity and promised to be good.

'Aye, well – remember it, for you'll not like it,' said Nicholas, shaking a finger at her. 'It started about two years ago when Judith Denham, as she was then, first came to town for the season. You've seen her so you can imagine the sensation she caused. She had dozens of suitors but two of 'em had a clear lead over the rest of the field: Charles Maynard and Francis. Myself, I don't think she ever liked Francis above half but there's the title, of course, and he seems to have a certain fascination – charm too, when he wants to use it. And he had to because, apart from the obvious things, no girl in her right mind is going to prefer an impoverished duke to a fellow who might only be the younger son but who has a tidy little fortune and – '

'Just a minute,' interrupted Vanessa, frowning. 'You said impoverished . . . how can he be? The estate – '

'Mortgaged,' said Nicholas with succinct insouciance. 'Not quite to the hilt – but as near as makes no odds. We've not a penny between us except when the dice are lucky.'

Vanessa suddenly understood a lot which had puzzled her but she pushed the knowledge aside for future consideration. 'Go on,' she said. 'You were telling me why Judith should naturally have preferred Mr Maynard.'

'Well anyone would,' replied his lordship reasonably. 'Charles is a good fellow and worth a dozen of Francis. He don't possess a filthy reputation with women or play cards with green youths or peel your skin off in layers with his nasty tongue. And so, when Judith realised that, for all his cleverness, Francis isn't worth a light, she accepted Charles.'

'I see.' Vanessa resolutely repressed a desire to argue. 'But if that's all, it doesn't explain Judith's attitude to his Grace.'

Lord Nicholas laughed. 'All? It's only the beginning! The day after the engagement was announced, Francis abducted her.'

'*He what?*' asked Vanessa faintly.

'Abducted her. He's good at that – didn't you know?'

She closed her eyes and heard a drawling voice saying coolly, *I am forced to admit it is usually necessary to arrange an abduction.* And opened them again to say dizzily, 'Yes. But I didn't believe it.'

'Well, you should have,' observed Nicholas severely. 'Judith wasn't the first and I don't suppose she'll be the last. On the other hand, he don't usually try this sort of thing with ladies.'

'What do you mean – usually? How many have there been?'

'Dozens,' said Nicholas cheerfully. And then, 'Well, three at least.'

Vanessa shut her mouth with a snap. 'Keep to the facts.'

'I always do,' he retorted. 'It was Charles who went after them – he rode all the way from London. Francis had a good start, you see; long enough to – ' He stopped abruptly, remembering who he was talking to. 'Anyway, Charles arrived here at Lyndhurst and they fought. Charles nicked Francis' wrist and Francis pinked Charles in the arm – which should have stopped it if they hadn't both been killing-mad. And that's when Laurie and I came in – five minutes later and Charles would have been a dead man. Not that he isn't a cursed fine swordsman, you understand, but Francis is a master. It's the only good thing to be said for him.'

'Well that,' said Vanessa sarcastically, 'is very generous of you. Go on. You'd got to the bit where his Grace was left gnashing his teeth.'

'As a matter of fact,' responded Nicholas mildly, 'he wasn't. Or not so as you'd notice. He just bound his wrist in a handkerchief, catechised me as to why I was there and asked if we were all staying to dinner.'

Vanessa gave a choke of laughter. 'Superb!'

'Well, in his way, I suppose he is,' he agreed reluctantly. 'No apologies, of course – but you'd say he took it well. I'd say it's easily done when you haven't a heart to be hurt.'

'Oh, Nick!' exploded Vanessa. 'Use your common sense! Why would he want to marry her if he wasn't in love?'

'To get his own way or to spite Randolph,' came the cynical reply. 'Don't mistake him for a man, m'dear. He ain't. In fact, I've a suspicion it's all done with wheels.'

Nicholas visited Lyndhurst almost every day and soon he and Vanessa were fast friends. They talked, rode and laughed together and Vanessa began to learn a great deal about the Courtenays. She also learned of Mistress Sophia Brandon, a hearty damsel who had formed a violent attachment to Lord Nicholas and made them both a standing joke by her determined pursuit. His lordship's gloomy air whilst recounting this information tried Vanessa sorely but she recognised that, for once, he was in deadly earnest and so managed to stifle her laughter.

They quarrelled twice and on both occasions the cause was a flippant remark made by Nicholas concerning his Grace – after which my Lord became more careful; and so the weeks drifted happily by until October came and Nicholas decided that the time had come for him to return to town.

No sooner did it seem that Nicholas was gone than the Duke arrived. This time Vanessa was spruce in white dimity and engaged in practising her music but when she saw him standing in the doorway she flew to his side with rather more speed than grace.

'Such unseemly joy,' he mocked.

She laughed. 'Can you doubt it? I began to think myself forgotten.'

'Impossible! I have come to . . . complete your education.'

Vanessa looked at him suspiciously. 'Education? Not – not *needlework*? I loathe it.'

The hard mouth quivered. 'Hardly, my dear. I'm poor at it myself.'

'What then?'

'The social graces – dancing, deportment and polite conversation. How to use your fan, the correct depth of curtsy to this or that one – and which topics you must not introduce.'

She tilted her head and glanced at him obliquely. 'Well, if you are going to teach me all that, your . . . experience must be even wider than I imagined.'

'It is,' said Lyndhurst with a bow. 'Here endeth the first lesson.'

And so, commanding Madam Erskine to play for them, Lyndhurst taught Vanessa to dance, partnering her himself. He presented her with an elegant brisé fan and showed her how to use it; he spoke of the personalities of the day and made her practise her curtsy to first one and then another of them; and, though compiling a list of forbidden topics, he remained adamant in insisting that she did not try to copy fashionable manners.

He was a stern instructor and praise was not easily won but the days were not all spent in study. Together they walked the

102

long gallery and his Grace identified his ancestors and told her a little of his family history. He taught her to play piquet, invariably beating her without really trying and engaged her over the chessboard where he found his victories less easily won. They talked of books. Lyndhurst was surprised to find her possessed of a familiarity with French and English literature almost equal to his own and Vanessa was intrigued by the breadth of his Grace's scholarship. From six languages he quoted works of history, theology and philosophy; great legends, bawdy comedy and tragic drama. Somewhere along the line, he appeared to have acquired the usual classical education and bettered it, and Vanessa took pleasure in sharpening her wits on his.

They rode together and here at least he was able to find no fault for Vanessa rode well and knew it. And when the Duke realised what feelings she had apparently roused in his tenantry he smiled wryly, well able to guess what thoughts she had harboured of him.

After much consideration, Vanessa came to the reluctant conclusion that she should tell his Grace of her meeting with Judith Maynard and this she did with uncharacteristic hesitancy. The Duke listened in inimical silence and then said sarcastically, 'I deduce that Nicholas was good enough to fill in all the sordid details for you. I hope you were suitably grateful.'

Realising that she should have anticipated this and feeling that she owed his absent lordship some defence, Vanessa said, 'I – I asked him. She holds you in such dislike, I couldn't help noticing.'

'How astute of you,' purred his Grace. 'And no doubt you "could not help" seizing the first opportunity of satisfying your ... curiosity?' There was, of course, no answer to this. Vanessa swallowed and waited uncomfortably. 'No? Or perhaps you sought to perform yet another of your acts of charity? You have reorganised my home and ministered to my tenants – so why not make peace with my neighbours and end your crusade on the pinnacle of my personal reformation?'

She flushed. 'That is neither just nor true.'

'Is it not? Then I have to admit that your reasoning eludes me. Or do I flatter you? Just childish curiosity or a simple taste for delving in gutters, perhaps. Either way, I imagine you found the tale vastly diverting – and am only astonished that you are still here.'

Vanessa's hands were beginning to shake. 'I don't understand.'

He smiled, but not pleasantly. 'Well, well . . . and I had thought you so bright. Very well, my dear. You did not wonder if I might not yet decide to . . . exercise my options? I feel sure my brother – and the lovely Judith – were eager to warn you of your peril.'

Hurt and confused, Vanessa concentrated on keeping her voice steady. 'They had no need. You did it yourself and I told you I trusted you. Have you forgotten?'

'My memory is quite excellent. You said you trusted me as I had given you no cause to do otherwise.'

'And you haven't!'

'True. Yet you evidently considered it worthwhile disinterring the details of my far from blameless past. And having found living proof of my testimony, did you not feel tempted to seek sanctuary elsewhere? No? Well . . . perhaps it's less to do with trust than I thought,' he mocked. 'Doubtless, in the circumstances, you deem the risk well run.'

Vanessa stared at him and saw, sickeningly, the face in the portrait. But though his words bit deep, she detected a note of savage bitterness which she was at a loss to explain; except in one way. Laying diffident fingertips on his arm, she said flatly, 'I'm sorry. I shouldn't have asked Nick but I didn't do it for any of the reasons you suggest. And perhaps it was wrong of me to speak of Madam Maynard . . . but, if I hadn't, it would have been a kind of lie.' She paused and a faint flush stained her skin. 'As for the rest – I thought you knew me better. I thought we were friends.'

Lyndhurst stared down intently at her bowed head. For perhaps a minute neither spoke, then he lifted the small, work-roughened hand from his sleeve and studied it carefully. 'It's time you took better care of your hands,' he said evenly, but with a certain tenseness in his attitude.

She glanced swiftly into his face and, for the first time, was able to interpret what she saw there: evaporating anger, and regret warring with pride. Sighing a little, she smiled and said, 'It's the polishing. Should I soak them in cream?'

He did not reply immediately but his clasp tightened. Then, frowning a little, he spoke abruptly and without his usual drawl. 'You are more generous than I deserve. Gideon once told me that he doubted I knew how to apologise. I think it's time I learned.'

She shook her head. 'It was my own fault.'

'No. It wasn't. I did you less than justice – for which I ask your pardon.'

Vanessa made a tiny inarticulate sound and one hand moved involuntarily towards him, only to be quickly checked. She laughed shakily, unnerved by the impulse and by the bubble of inexplicable comprehension which seemed to have burst within her. 'There is nothing to forgive.'

For a moment he remained silent before saying thoughtfully, 'It is time we left for London.'

'So soon?' She was startled and a shade regretful.

'Does it displease you?'

'No. Not precisely. But I've been so happy here – and I think I'm a little afraid of your world. Also, there is still so much to do here – oh heavens!' One hand flew to her mouth. 'The plums! Mrs Clayton will never forgive me!'

And on this obscure utterance, she hastened from the room leaving Lyndhurst gazing after her out of eyes that were suddenly not enigmatic at all.

In Which Mr Wade meets Apollyon

Lady Alicia waved her parasol to the imminent danger of the passers-by. 'Ha! Vaughan – oh, drat the boy!' She poked her groom in the back. 'Get down – catch Mr Vaughan. Hurry!'

Used to my lady's eccentricities, the man clambered down from his perch and dutifully ran along the crowded pavement in pursuit of his quarry. A few minutes later, Gideon was bowing beside the open carriage.

'My lady,' he smiled. 'What can I do for you?'

Lady Marchant leaned forward eagerly. 'You can tell me about this chit of Lyndhurst's. I understand he's adopted Thomas Tremaine's daughter as his ward. Is it true?'

'Quite true. Surely you've had a card for the ball tomorrow?'

'I have. Sounds to me like utter folly. Francis ain't old enough to be anyone's guardian!'

'He's nearly forty, madam. It's a respectable age.'

'Pshaw! Not a day over thirty-eight! How old's the gal?'

'I believe she is twenty.'

'Is she a beauty?'

'Not exactly. Seen in repose, she is nothing out of the ordinary. But it's not really her appearance one remembers. What she has in abundance is charm – and a disastrously candid tongue.'

'Ah,' breathed Lady Alicia. 'Does she hope to snare him?'

Gideon chuckled. 'Not in the least. I've a notion she regards him in the light of a parent.'

'Nonsense! The gal who could do that ain't born yet. I'll see her.'

He blinked. 'If you attend the ball, you will naturally do so.'

'No – now,' she said with a grin. 'Get in. You can escort me.'

The interior of Lyndhurst House was in a state of apparent chaos, with preparations underway for the first large reception to be held there in ten years. And, in the midst of it all, Jassy was systematically transferring a mound of dress- and hat-boxes from the foot of the staircase to Vanessa's chamber. Lady Marchant sailed forward and accosted her. 'Where is Mistress Tremaine?' she demanded.

Jassy bobbed a flustered curtsy. 'In the library, ma'am.'

My lady nodded and stalked briskly across the hall.

Seated at the escritoire, Vanessa was engaged in sifting a mountain of acceptance cards but she looked up as the door opened and, recognising Gideon, rose and moved swiftly towards him. 'Mr Vaughan – how nice to see you!'

He smiled, bowed over her fingers and realised with a sense of shock that Mistress Tremaine was a good deal more taking than he had remembered. He presented her to Lady Alicia who regarded Vanessa narrowly and then, turning back to him, said ironically, 'You must have high standards, sir! But no matter – you may go away now. We shall do very well without you.'

Gideon accepted his *congé* with relief. 'I take it Francis is at his club?'

Vanessa nodded. 'He was . . . a little put out by all the fuss.'

'I see his point,' observed Gideon feelingly. 'And since I can see I'm not wanted, I'll retreat in good order and join him.'

When he had gone, Lady Alicia seated herself on a sofa and directed Vanessa to sit beside her. Then she said sharply, 'No doubt you're wondering why I'm here?'

'Oh no,' came the placid reply. 'You wish to see for yourself the nature of his Grace's ward. And I don't blame you.'

Her ladyship laughed. 'Well at least you're not a fool. Not that you'd be here if you were. But that don't explain what he's up to now – so what's the answer?' Vanessa smiled, spread expressive hands and said nothing. 'Meaning you don't know either? Hm.' Her ladyship fixed her with a bright stare. 'You take it mighty coolly.'

Vanessa met her eye candidly. 'I didn't – at first. Now I'm not sure it matters. He's been very good to me, you know.'

'Makes a change! So . . . you've some faith in him – and that may be no bad thing. I take it you know what's said of him?'

'Yes. He told me himself.'

'Indeed? I wouldn't have thought he'd take the trouble. And what did you make of it?'

'It's hard to say.' Vanessa's brow creased thoughtfully. 'I believe what he told me but . . . there are times when it's as though he's at war with himself.'

'You're a good gal,' said her ladyship, satisfied. 'I've a kindness for him myself. You'd best tell me about it.'

So Vanessa told her story and, when she had finished, Lady Alicia rose and said decidedly, 'You've more sense than I looked for. Pay no heed to Blanche or that fool Lilian and you'll be the rage within a week. If you want someone to talk to, come to me in Arlington Street.' She chuckled. 'I can't wait to see Maria Henley's face!'

Vanessa laughed and impulsively kissed the wrinkled cheek. 'I'm glad you came, my lady. And you'll attend the ball tomorrow?'

'Wouldn't miss it for worlds. No need to come with me – I'll see myself out. Goodbye, child.' And still laughing to herself, she left the room.

On the following afternoon, Vanessa was practising the steps of the minuet up and down the drawing-room when a footman came to inform her that a gentleman had called to see her. Intrigued by the fact that the gentleman had not given his name, she bade Thomas show him in, sat demurely on a satin-backed chair and resolved to try out her society manners. But when her mysterious visitor crossed the threshold her expression changed to one of wary dislike.

'Joseph!' she said disgustedly. 'What are you doing here?'

Her cousin smiled reprovingly. 'You are not very welcoming, my dear Vanessa,' he said. And, possessing himself of her hand, raised it to his lips.

Vanessa, who had always disliked touching fish, snatched it away. 'It would be marvellous if I were.'

'I had hoped you had forgiven me,' he mourned. 'But since you obviously haven't – I beg you to do so now.' This was unexpected and Vanessa took refuge in silence. 'I am sorry I offended you,' he went on, 'I had no intention of doing so. It was mere clumsiness.'

'Clumsiness! Is that what you call it?'

Mr Wade turned away a little and said with a tolerable assumption of embarrassment, 'Yes. I have always held you in the highest esteem and affection. I knew, of course, that you did not care for me, but I hoped – ' He broke off artistically.

Thoroughly confused, she tried to think of a reply; and failed. 'If you only knew how bitterly I regret those words,' said Joseph with perfect truth, 'how I have longed to unsay them! I have been so anxious, so wretched – you cannot imagine.'

He was right; she could neither imagine nor quite believe it but, being a generous girl, she decided to give him the benefit of the doubt. 'Very well, cousin. We will forget all about it. As for your anxiety – you can see for yourself that it was unnecessary.'

He wheeled to face her. 'Was it? *Is* it?'

Vanessa blinked. 'I beg your pardon?'

'I haven't known a moment's peace since you left Penmarne,' he replied, wringing his hands agitatedly. 'But when I discovered that you had fallen into the hands of Lucifer Courtenay – I was nearly demented!'

Vanessa laughed with resigned exasperation. 'I see. I should have known that you were bound to fall into vulgar error – but I'll endeavour to relieve your mind. His Grace has made me his ward – not his mistress. His cousin is my chaperon and his sister is to present me to society. So, you see, it's all quite respectable.'

This forthright speech had no perceptible effect on her cousin's gloomy countenance. 'I'm glad to hear it,' he said heavily.

'Then smile, Joseph – smile! You should be delighted to know you need have no further concern for me.'

The pale eyes raked her face. 'You have forgiven me?'

'Yes.' She was fast tiring of the conversation.

'Then come back to Penmarne with me.'

'*What?*'

'Come back,' he repeated coaxingly. 'I love you, Vanessa – and I want to marry you.'

Her brows rose in astonishment. 'Do you indeed?'

'I do. I realise that it may not always have seemed so to you – '

'Well that's something at all events!'

'But you must believe me,' he urged.

'I can't think why,' said Vanessa frankly. 'And even if I did . . . it wouldn't change anything for *I* don't love *you*.'

'I know. But in time . . . and you love Penmarne. As my wife you would be its mistress again,' he said temptingly.

She smiled and shook her head. 'It's not a good enough reason for marriage, Joseph. I can't do it.'

He grasped her wrist and his voice lost some of its affecting sadness. 'You must! You can't stay with that man. You'll be the talk of the town – Lady Henley will see to it.'

'Let me go,' snapped Vanessa. 'I don't give two straws for her spiteful gossip – and neither does his Grace.'

Joseph still held her fast. 'Not now, perhaps,' he said slyly, 'but in a few weeks, who can say? You have no claim on him and when he tires of his new toy, as he assuredly will, then – '

'How dare you?' she demanded wrathfully. '*Toy*, indeed!'

Recognising his mistake, Joseph proceeded to make matters worse. 'Forgive me,' he said ardently. 'It's because I love you – '

'Rubbish!'

Feeling that actions might perhaps speak louder than words, Mr Wade caught her in an awkward but passionate embrace.

'Joseph! Release me this instant!' And, managing to get an arm free, Vanessa dealt him a ringing box on the ear.

All signs of lover-like ardour vanished. Furiously, Joseph clamped her arms to her sides and covered her mouth savagely with his own. Still struggling madly, Vanessa felt repulsion turn to nausea. She closed her eyes, trying to overcome the sensation – and found herself suddenly free.

Reeling, she looked for the cause of her miraculous deliverance and saw his Grace, eyes blazing with murderous rage, slowly but effectively choking her cousin with one

110

beautiful, white hand. Mr Wade, his face already alarmingly suffused, clawed unavailingly at the vice-like fingers and emitted horrific, wheezing gasps.

That his Grace was capable, in that instant, of strangling her cousin, Vanessa did not doubt for a second. One glance at his expression had served to convince her of it. Hurling herself forward, she grasped his arm crying frantically, 'Stop! Let him go – *Francis*!'

Her use of his name had the desired effect. His grip relaxed and he looked down at her. Half-conscious, Joseph slid unheeded to the floor. The dangerous glitter faded from the Duke's eyes and he said remotely, 'Is it possible that I misread the situation? I had not thought you would care for his miserable life!'

'I don't,' she replied truthfully. 'But I should care very much if you were arrested for murder.'

For a moment, he gazed intently at her and then, incredibly, laughter claimed him. He said unsteadily, 'They lied – there *is* balm in Gilead. I have a ward after mine own heart.'

'And that,' grinned Vanessa, 'is undoubtedly a compliment.'

Just then, Joseph drew attention to himself by moaning feebly and clutching at his bruised throat. The Duke rang the bell and surveyed him through his glass. 'Who is this person?' he asked coolly.

A small gurgle escaped Vanessa. 'He is my cousin, sir.'

'Your cousin? Ah, yes . . . Mr Wade, I believe?'

She nodded, unable to trust her voice.

His Grace bent and, none too gently, assisted Joseph to his feet as Benson entered the room. 'Ah, Benson. Mr Wade is leaving. I do not know if his own carriage awaits him but, if it does not, it might be a kindness to summon him a chair.'

Benson permitted himself a fleeting but comprehensive glance at Joseph and his countenance became more wooden than ever. 'Very good, your Grace.'

Lyndhurst turned to Mr Wade, who, though able to stand unaided, was still extremely red in the face and plainly incapable of proper speech. He massaged his throat with one hand and his eyes flashed venom.

'You have been undeservedly fortunate,' said the Duke softly, 'and if you cross my path again I would not wager a groat on your chances of another such escape. I pray you remember it.' His eyes seared Wade, whose gaze dropped shiftily away. 'You may show Mr Wade out, Benson. And give orders that he is not to be admitted to this house again.'

Joseph staggered to the door where he turned and managed a sly, disturbing smile. 'You'll regret this,' he croaked. And then allowed Benson to lead him away.

'What do you suppose he meant by that?' asked Vanessa uneasily. His Grace shrugged. 'Absolutely nothing, I imagine. What did he want of you?'

Vanessa sensed an indefinable change in his attitude to her and then it was gone. She eyed him with deliberate blankness. 'It appears he wants to marry me.'

'Does he?' drawled Lyndhurst. 'I wonder why?'

'But for love, of course!'

'Of course! Now . . . why did not I think of that?'

She gave it up, discovering that he was better at the game than she was. 'Because you know perfectly well it's not true. But he gave a very good performance, you know – all humility and remorse.'

'"*The smyler with the knyf under the cloke*"?'

'Exactly.' She hesitated and then asked, 'You would have strangled him, wouldn't you?'

He frowned down at the particularly fine diamond on his finger. 'I am inclined to believe so – and must ask your pardon for making so unpleasant a scene.'

'You were very angry,' she temporised, wishing she could think of a subtle way of asking why.

'I was – but that is no excuse for a deplorable lack of self-control.' He glanced down at her, a gleam of humour appearing in his eyes. 'You, on the other hand, are to be congratulated. Had it been Blanche . . .'

'Had it been Blanche,' finished Vanessa obligingly, 'you would still be trying to calm her hysterics and my horrid cousin would be a corpse.' Her fingers flew to her lips and she said penitently, 'Oh dear – I shouldn't have said that.'

112

'No,' he agreed, urbanely. 'I am persuaded that there is no need to . . . ask you not to speak of this incident?'

'None.'

The topaz eyes gleamed. 'I thought not. And now I desire that you should rest before this evening.'

'But I – '

'Vanessa – you will not argue,' he said firmly.

'No, your Grace.' A roguish glance belied the meek tone. 'And thank you.'

'For what?'

'For giving Joseph the fright of his life. He was always a sly, creeping creature and it's nice to see him taught a lesson.'

His Grace bowed. 'I am glad,' he said ironically, 'that I have succeeded in pleasing you. But do not, I beg, expect me to make a habit of it.'

In Which Vanessa makes her Curtsy to Society

'La, child – for pity's sake be still,' begged Lady Blanche as, clad only in a loose wrapper, hair piled high and thickly powdered, she made the finishing touches to Vanessa's toilet.

'I can't,' said Vanessa flatly. 'I'm too nervous.'

Deftly Blanche pinned two white bud roses to nestle in the curls above the girl's right ear and gave a final twitch to the folds of soft brocade before stepping back to admire the effect. Then she nodded decisively and said, 'It will do. Very well, child, You may look.'

Cautiously, Vanessa stepped over to the long mirror and gasped. Her hair was swept up into a russet mass of carefully ordered curls, just one thick ringlet allowed to fall on to her breast and from the foaming lace fichu her shoulders rose sloping and alabaster pale. More lace frothed at her elbows and on the ruffles of the petticoat, over which deep folds of white brocade gleamed dully. Vanessa gazed and gazed again.

'It's hard to believe it's me,' she said at last. Her ladyship laughed delightedly and Vanessa turned to her with real gratitude. 'Thank you. It's all your doing.'

'Nonsense,' replied Blanche airily, 'Francis chose the gown and one cannot make a silk purse – Heavens! Look at the time! Oh – what now?' This as a knock was heard at the door.

Jassy opened it and returned with a silver-wrapped package which she held out to Vanessa.

'Quick!' said Blanche. 'Open it for I must fly or I shall never be ready in time.'

114

With a hand that was not quite steady, Vanessa opened the box to reveal a triple strand of small but perfectly matched pearls fastened with a diamond clasp. She stared at it, her vision suddenly blurred.

Blanche lifted it out and examined it admiringly. 'It's perfect – and from Francis, of course.'

While Blanche fastened the lovely thing around her throat, Vanessa blinked surreptitiously and picked up the card which had lain beneath the necklet. It said very little – but enough to make Vanessa wish for some quiet retreat where she could howl in earnest. For what, she thought, did one say to a man who, while up to his ears in debt, could casually make such extravagant gestures?

Lady Blanche looked at Vanessa's suspiciously bright eyes and said firmly, 'Now you are not to cry for it will ruin your face. Promise me?'

Vanessa achieved a watery smile. 'I promise.'

'Good. Now – you will wait here. I shall not be long,' and she bustled off to her own chamber.

Impressively, she returned in rather less than twenty minutes clad in a satin gown of her favourite cerulean blue, lavishly trimmed with quantities of silver lace and falling over an enormous hoop. Diamonds sparkled at her wrists and throat and three white plumes nodded in her coiffure.

'You like it? And the shoes?' She exposed a neat ankle to allow a glimpse of diamond studded heels. 'Now, child – you first,' she said, drawing Vanessa from the room to the head of the wide staircase.

Vanessa's heart gave an unpleasant little lurch. 'Must I?'

'Certainly. Off you go – and slowly, mind!'

With sedate grace, Vanessa descended the stairs, pausing instinctively as she rounded the curve. First to notice her, Nicholas gave an appreciative whistle and instantly three other pairs of eyes turned in her direction as she continued her descent. On the lowest step she hesitated again, gazing back at them; at Gideon, elegant in grey velvet, Laurence in claret with gold lacing and Nicholas in blue with an amazingly floral vest;

115

and last of all, her gaze rested on Lyndhurst, resplendent in black silk encrusted with silver and a diamond order glowing fierily on his breast. He moved unhurriedly forward and, smiling, bowed low over her hand.

'You are beautiful, my dear. I am forced to applaud my foresight.'

'Well, Francis?' said his sister. 'Are you pleased?'

'The word is inadequate, my dear.'

Vanessa embraced them all in her smile. 'I think we *all* look very splendid – even Nick!' She looked at the Duke, her fingers stealing to the pearls at her throat. 'The necklet is lovely – and my dress. I'm glad you chose it yourself.' And sinking into her deepest curtsy, she kissed his hand.

Lady Blanche looked sharply at his Grace and at once perceived the odd light in his eyes as they rested on his ward. Gideon and Laurence exchanged glances and Nicholas raised his eyes in mystic communion with the ceiling.

Rising, Vanessa took a couple of gliding steps and pirouetted gracefully. 'You must all dance with me,' she announced.

Gideon smiled and bowed. 'It will be a pleasure.'

'And an honour,' added Laurence gallantly.

'Aye,' said Nicholas heavily. 'Anything that will keep me out of Sophy Brandon's way.'

There was laughter and Vanessa turned expectantly to Lyndhurst.

'Acquit me, child. I never dance.'

The grey eyes widened. 'Yes, you do. It was you who taught me.'

'Well, well,' observed Gideon. 'A dancing master, forsooth!'

Lyndhurst surveyed him languidly, then looked back at Vanessa. 'It is really very kind of you.'

She saw and responded to the laughter in his eyes. 'I know. I hope you are suitably flattered?'

Suddenly the lackeys at the great doors sprang to attention. 'They're arriving,' cried Blanche. 'And where is Lilian?'

'In the ballroom, my dear,' replied her husband calmly.

Vanessa gave the Duke's arm a little shake. '*Please!*'

116

He sighed. 'I suppose I might make an exception. Just this once.'

'Come, child!' urged Blanche taking charge once more. 'At once, if you please. And you too, Francis!' She took Vanessa by the hand and hurried excitedly away.

His Grace turned to the Viscount and regarded him with not unpleasant mockery. 'We are rarely in accord, I know, but I believe that on this occasion I owe you my gratitude.'

Laurence stared at him with suspicion. 'Indeed. Why so?'

'For permitting Blanche to act as my hostess.'

'Oh – that,' said Laurence. 'But candour compels me to admit that I didn't agree to it for your sake.'

Lyndhurst smiled. 'Naturally not. You approve of my ward then?'

'It would be hard not to.'

'Why, so I think.' He made a slight bow and strolled after the ladies.

Nonplussed, Laurence watched him go. 'He is . . . different.'

Nicholas gave a boisterous laugh. 'Blister it – he's almost human! But I'll lay you fifty guineas it don't outlast the evening. Do you take me Laurie?'

Within an hour the house was filled with a fashionable throng and more people continued to arrive. Vanessa began to feel that she had spent a lifetime in smiling and curtsying and was relieved when it was finally time to begin the dancing.

Blanche looked on approvingly. 'March appears taken with her – look, he is laughing! It was a good choice to have him lead her out, Francis.'

His Grace bowed ironically. 'One does one's poor best.'

'Oh Lud! More guests,' said her ladyship, fluttering away as the footman announced, 'The Honourable Derick Crichton, Madam Louisa Crichton, Mistress Jennifer Crichton, Mistress Elizabeth Tierney.'

Falling from nerveless fingers, Gideon's glass shattered on the marble floor. A lackey sprang forward to collect the fragments and his Grace surveyed them with lazy amusement before raising his glass to inspect the new arrivals.

'Not the brunette, I think,' he drawled. 'A trifle too robust, perhaps? The blonde then . . . yes. I feel sure it is the blonde.'

In spite of himself, Gideon laughed. 'You are atrocious, damn you!' Then, frowning anxiously, 'Is Randolph coming tonight?'

'I beg your pardon?'

'Randolph. Your brother Randolph!'

'Ah yes. I really have no idea. One lives in hope, of course, that he will remain notable only for his absence,' replied his Grace coolly. 'Does it matter?'

'To me it does,' retorted Gideon grimly. 'I have developed a veritable fascination for the Colonel's activities.' And he strode off in the direction of the Crichton party.

'Well, well. Now should I not do the same myself?' mused Lyndhurst softly. 'Yes, Blanche. I was talking to myself. A distressing habit. Who is the fair-haired child with the Crichtons?'

She grimaced. 'Some wealthy Cit's daughter. But she is presentable enough and Louisa thought it proper to bring her as the chit is apparently acquainted with Randolph.'

'Ah. How gratifying to have one's surmises so swiftly verified. And I see that Mr Anstey has honoured us. I desire that you will introduce him to Vanessa.'

Lady Blanche opened her eyes very wide. 'You aim high.'

His Grace looked at her cynically. 'I fear you are ahead of me,' he said gently, before turning away to exchange greetings with George Selwyn.

Blanche found Vanessa seated in an alcove drinking negus with March and bore her off to meet Roderick Anstey – an unostentatious gentleman whose countenance was distinguished only by its habitual gravity of expression. Lady Blanche considered him a dull creature but was fully alive to his usefulness to a young lady making her debut, for the Ansteys were extremely wealthy and related by marriage to half the great houses in England. She performed the necessary introduction and then fluttered away. Mr Anstey regarded Vanessa solemnly and offered his arm.

'Will you honour me, madam?'

'Thank you, sir.' Vanessa smiled sunnily at him.

It did not take her long to realise that Mr Anstey's attention was plainly elsewhere and, far from being piqued by this unflattering treatment, Vanessa grew increasingly amused. She tried to determine who it was attracted his gaze and eventually came to the surprising conclusion that it was Nicholas, dancing morosely with a diminutively vivacious brunette.

'Who is the lady dancing with Lord Nicholas Courtenay?' she asked innocently – and thought she heard Mr Anstey grind his teeth.

'That, madam, is Mistress Sophia Brandon.'

Vanessa's eyes widened for, in her opinion, Mistress Brandon did not look at all fearsome – merely young and wilfully high-spirited. Stealing a peep at Mr Anstey, she reached certain swift conclusions and, as the dance ended, could not resist placing a maternal hand on his arm and saying mischievously, 'If I were you, I would ask Mistress Brandon for the gavotte. Lord Nicholas is promised to me.' Upon which she walked away to capture his lordship.

Quite reprehensibly alone in a curtained alcove, Mr Vaughan and Mistress Tierney exchanged urgent words.

'This is impossible!' said Gideon. 'I had no expectation of seeing you here tonight and when I heard your name announced I behaved like an absolute fool.'

Elizabeth smiled. 'Oh?'

'I dropped my glass – yes, it's very well to laugh but Francis was at my side and he guessed instantly.'

Her amusement vanished. 'He can't have done so, surely?'

'Well he did – and by now he's doubtless worked out the rest of it.' He looked at her ruefully. 'You know, Elizabeth, I think it would be best if I told him anyway.'

Mistress Tierney was unconvinced. 'Oh no! Not yet – I thought we had agreed!'

Sighing, Gideon took her hand. 'Yes. We agreed and it shall be as you wish.' He paused. 'I take it that Randolph continues to be assiduous in his attentions?'

She nodded. 'Papa is jubilant. He is certain that a declaration cannot be far off.'

'If he's right, we'll have little choice but to act swiftly,' said Gideon. 'You – you are sure you wish to refuse him?'

Tears filled her eyes. 'How can you ask?'

He gathered her into his arms. 'Forgive me. It's just that I hate the hole-and-corner way in which we are forced to act. And, like the Colonel, I too am a younger son without expectations. I don't even have a title.' He smiled wryly. 'It's not much to offer, is it?'

'Dearest Gideon,' she said, unsteadily. 'It's more than enough – and all I want.'

His arms tightened about her and he gave a tiny laugh which died in his throat as she raised her face for his kiss. Some few minutes later, he said, 'We had best go back to the ballroom before our absence is remarked. When will I see you after tonight?'

'Tomorrow – in the park. I'm walking there with Jenny.'

He nodded wearily. 'So. Another accidental meeting at Rosamund's Pond? Very well, my dear. I'll be there.' He lifted the curtain and glanced swiftly outside. 'Come then,' he said, 'while there are none to see.'

Vanessa discovered that she was enjoying herself very much indeed. She danced again with March and progressed from him to Sir Gareth Merton who recounted several amusing (if carefully censored) anecdotes concerning her guardian. She trod a measure with Viscount Overton and then seized Gideon who, she thought, was looking unusually serious.

From the side of the room, Lady Alicia Marchant observed them indulgently before glancing sharply up at his Grace of Lyndhurst. 'She's a good gal, this ward of yours. I like her.'

'I am so glad,' replied Lyndhurst politely.

Her ladyship ignored this. 'She's a deal of common sense and a broader mind than I'd believed existed in these modern misses. Why are you doing it?'

'I beg your pardon?'

'Don't play the innocent with me – it don't become you. Why go to so much trouble for the chit? To spite Maria Henley?'

120

His Grace sighed. 'I have a number of reasons – though that is certainly one of them.'

'Ha! And you like the child. Admit it!'

'In the recesses of my mind there lies some affection for her, it is true,' he replied resignedly. 'Also, I am inclined to feel that she deserves more than life has so far seen fit to bestow.'

She nodded thoughtfully. 'Yes . . . it's amazing she's come through it so well. You'll be kind to her?'

He raised one mocking brow. 'Don't you think I can?'

The dance ended and Vanessa and Gideon joined them. Her eyes sparkled and she was smiling.

'My lady – I am so glad to see you again!'

'You are enjoying yourself, child?'

'Very much. Everyone is so kind.'

Her ladyship laughed. 'So I've observed. You seem to be quite a success. Who do you dance with next?'

Vanessa cast his Grace an oblique smile. 'With my guardian – if he will have me.' The Duke looked lazily down at her but said nothing. 'You promised!' she reminded him.

'Did I?' And then, smiling, 'Yes. I believe you are right. Come then.'

They made a striking couple and nearly every eye in the room was upon them. His Grace, all black and silver, coolly urbane and apparently oblivious of the attention centred upon them and Vanessa, all in white, her face delicately flushed and radiating intense pleasure. Moreover, they danced well together – almost too well, thought Gideon, a faint current of concern running through his mind. Lady Alicia was also watching closely. She saw Vanessa say something to the Duke whilst glancing sideways at him through her lashes, a habit both fascinating and unconsciously seductive, and she watched his Grace smile back as he replied. Her ladyship drew a deep breath and nodded decisively. 'She'll do.'

'For what?' asked Gideon blankly.

'Why, the next Duchess of Lyndhurst, of course!'

He stared at her open-mouthed and then he laughed. 'Never! He would not ask her – nor she take him.'

121

'You've a lot to learn, my lad,' came the cryptic reply. And then, with a wicked grin, 'But since you're so certain, I'll wager fifty guineas on the outcome.'

'You can't be serious!'

'Ha! Can I not? Come — fifty guineas says she'll be Francis' bride before Christmas. Or aren't you so sure she won't be?'

'Of course I am,' he replied quickly. 'Very well, my lady. It's a bet.' He held out his hand and Lady Alicia put hers into it.

'Done!' she said, with a triumphant laugh.

As the Duke and his ward left the floor they were accosted by Mr Selwyn who demanded an introduction to Vanessa and then dismissed his Grace, saying that he had no intention of being upstaged by any ducal poseur. Then he engaged Vanessa in conversation and soon found himself identifying various persons for her edification.

'Who is the tall lady with his Grace?' she asked.

Mr Selwyn levelled his glass at Lyndhurst's companion, a beauty no longer in the first flush of youth and wearing an extremely daring décolletage. 'Ah. That, my dear, is the latest widow. By name, Lydia Gwynne. By repute, very amusing, very wealthy and very fast.'

'She certainly seems to amuse his Grace,' observed Vanessa with unaccustomed dryness as she watched the Duke (who never danced) lead the dashing widow into the set.

Her attention was claimed by Gideon wearing an air of faint agitation and, after Mr Selwyn had exercised his wit on the subject of persons lacking in tact but blessed with unfair advantages, she walked away on Mr Vaughan's arm and asked him what was wrong.

'I want you to do me a great favour,' he said rapidly. 'I am about to present you to Lord Randolph Courtenay — and the lady who is with him. I will be eternally grateful if you can remove that lady from his orbit.'

Confused but willing, Vanessa said, 'Of course.'

He pressed her hand. 'Bless you, my dear. I'll explain later.'

Clad in rich green brocade, the Colonel was leaning possessively over Elizabeth who shrank distastefully away from him.

'Randolph.' Gideon hailed him smoothly. 'We had begun to despair of your honouring us tonight. Vanessa, allow me to present his Grace's brother, Colonel Lord Randolph Courtenay – and also Mistress Elizabeth Tierney. This is Mistress Tremaine – Francis' ward.'

Randolph cast Gideon a glance of pure irritation but bowed over Vanessa's hand and murmured a conventional greeting. She recognised, beneath the florid heaviness, a resemblance to the Duke and then experienced immediate antipathy as she encountered the inexplicable malice in his eyes.

'So you are the mysterious ward of whom one hears so much?' he drawled with thinly veiled insolence. 'Francis is indeed fortunate.'

Flushing a little, Vanessa raised her brows and said coolly, 'Thank you, my lord. I am sure his Grace will be pleased to know that you think so.' She turned and smiled at Elizabeth. 'I am pleased to meet you, Mistress Tierney.' And, seeing the relief in the other girl's face, decided to waste no time on trying for an original excuse. 'I was about to retire to tidy my hair. Would you care to go with me?'

Elizabeth responded with gratitude. 'Oh yes. Thank you.'

Vanessa swept a dignified curtsy to the gentlemen. 'Pray excuse us,' she said and, taking Elizabeth's hand, led her away.

'You do not like Lord Randolph?' she asked as soon as they were out of earshot.

'No,' sighed Mistress Tierney. 'N-not very much.'

'Neither do I,' came the candid reply. 'But what I can't understand is why Mr Vaughan asked me to help you. He could very well have done so himself by asking you to dance.'

Elizabeth blushed. 'I . . . we have danced twice already and . . . he . . . I . . . that is, we . . .'

Light dawned on Vanessa and she smiled. 'Oh. I *see*.' And watched as the other girl flushed even more fiercely.

Upstairs, Mistress Brandon was critically examining her reflection in the glass. Seeing Vanessa and Elizabeth approaching behind her, she turned to greet them enthusiastically.

'It's Mistress Tremaine, isn't it? You are *so* lucky! Fancy having Lyndhurst as one's guardian – he's terribly attractive. And so formidable! I vow I never know what to say to him. Oh – I'm Sophia Brandon, by the way. But please call me Sophy – everyone does! And you – ' turning to Elizabeth – 'are Mistress Tierney, aren't you? We've never met but Jenny Crichton is one of my dearest friends. What a trio we make!' She drew the other two to the mirror, one on either side of her. 'A blonde, a brunette and a redhead. We must go down together and make an Entrance – I'll wager we'll take the shine out of all the other girls.' She looked appraisingly at Elizabeth. 'I think you are prettier than I am – but, being dark, I have more countenance. And you, of course,' she turned to Vanessa, 'are not only pretty but also charming.'

Laughing, Vanessa managed at last to get a word in. 'Am I indeed?'

'Oh yes. If I have heard one person say it, I must have heard twenty. Even Rod – Mr Anstey, which is amazing because he hardly ever says anything pretty.'

Vanessa glanced searchingly into Sophy's brown eyes. 'Is Mr Anstey a friend of yours?'

Sophy dimpled and nodded. 'Roderick is a dear – but so *dull*. I have known him for ever – their estates march with ours, you know.' She giggled naughtily. 'My mama wishes me to marry him – they are monstrously wealthy – but I do not know that I shall.'

'And Mr Anstey?' prompted Vanessa.

'Oh Roderick is quite devoted to me,' replied Sophy airily, 'and naturally I am fond of him. But he is so pompous and one always knows exactly what he will say. It's a pity he can't be just a little more like . . . well, like Lord Nicholas, for instance,' she finished, becoming rather pink. 'Do you see?'

Vanessa rather thought that she did but prudently refrained from saying so. Together they made their way down to the ballroom and were immediately beseiged by a swarm of gentlemen eager to claim their hands. Elizabeth was led off by Sir Gareth Merton, Sophy by March and Vanessa by Gilly Williams. The festivities continued.

124

Presently, however, people began to call for their coaches and eventually only seven were left in the hall. Lilian retired pleading fatigue but the others remained to discuss the evening's success.

'Lord, what a night!' yawned Nicholas. 'Burgundy, Gideon?'

'The card-room obviously proved exhausting,' remarked his Grace sweetly.

'Aye. It did. And don't lecture me – it was the only way to escape the Brandon chit.'

Lyndhurst moved to where Vanessa sat. 'Tired, my child?'

She nodded. 'A little. But I enjoyed it all so much.'

'I am glad. You were a great success. You agree, Blanche?'

'Naturally,' said her ladyship. 'But, oh Francis! I found her deep in conversation about smuggling – and with Horry Walpole!'

Vanessa gave a little gurgle and smiled wickedly at the Duke. 'It wasn't one of the things you told me *not* to speak of.' Gideon, Nicholas and Laurence dissolved into laughter and his Grace subdued a twitching lip.

'I should have known that you would find some breach in my list,' he sighed. 'It seems I must extend it. Not, of course, that I expected you to be *au fait* with the Trade. My mistake, I suppose?'

'But yes,' said Vanessa laughing. 'It's not a thing you can ignore in Cornwall.'

Gideon looked at her wonderingly. 'You mean you are actually acquainted with persons engaged in it?'

She nodded, eyes twinkling merrily.

Nicholas slapped his thigh and said boisterously, raising his glass, 'It's about the only thing our family's never had a hand in! You're a marvel, m'dear – here's to you. His Unique Grace of Lyndhurst's Unique Ward!' And he put the glass to his lips and drank deeply.

The Duchess of Queensbury's Soirée

As could have been predicted, the Lyndhurst House ball marked the beginning of a nine-day wonder at the core of which was Lucifer Courtenay's latest whim. Rumours began to circulate that Mistress Tremaine had entered his Grace's care in a somewhat unorthodox manner and was in fact his mistress, but few people were inclined to take these tales seriously; and when it was discovered that the rumours had their source in a certain house in Grosvenor Square, those with long memories derived no small amusement from the jest.

On the morning following Vanessa's debut, a number of gentlemen called in St James Square only to be told that Mistress Tremaine was not receiving visitors. Benson accepted their floral tributes with all his usual impassivity and admitted Mr Vaughan without batting an eyelid.

Gideon greeted Vanessa conventionally enough and then said ruefully, 'I owe you an explanation, don't I?'

'No. Not if you prefer not to give it. But it's only fair to tell you that I'm not entirely in the dark. I gather that you and Mistress Tierney are . . . fond of each other.'

He was taken aback. 'She told you?'

Vaness shook her head. 'I guessed.'

'You must think it strange,' said Gideon with difficulty. 'I hope you will believe that the clandestine nature of our . . . friendship . . . is quite repugnant to me but the circumstances –'

'Mr Vaughan, you mustn't tell me anything you don't wish to. And I hope I know better than to think ill of you.'

He coloured a little. 'You are generous – and if it won't weary you, I think I'd like to tell you about it.'

She sat down beside him. 'Of course it won't weary me. I shall be happy to help in any way I can.'

So Gideon explained the complications surrounding his love for Elizabeth while Vanessa listened carefully and without interruptions. When he had done, she said thoughtfully, 'It seems to me that your best plan is to confide in his Grace.'

'Perhaps. But Elizabeth is a little afraid of Francis.'

She frowned. 'That is silly.'

Gideon smiled wryly. 'Mistress Tremaine, you will have to become accustomed to the fact that a great many people share that feeling. I am often amazed that *you* do not.'

The dark grey eyes opened very wide. '*Me?* But you've seen how kind he is to me.'

'My dear, you have perhaps seen the best of him and it's possible you may never see the worst. I hope not. But it would be well to remember that Francis isn't always as you have known him.'

'Would you have me distrust him, Mr Vaughan?'

'It would be better for you if you did. Oh – God knows you've done him a lot of good in a remarkably short space of time and I'm glad of it. Only he knows how to hurt.'

Vanessa smiled cryptically. 'Yes. And practises on himself.' She paused and then went on briskly, 'Now – to return to your difficulties. You won't seek his Grace's help?'

'No. And not solely because of Elizabeth. It also seems wrong to place Francis in the position of having to obstruct Randolph to help me.'

Vanessa nodded thoughtfully. 'Yes. I see that. So what do you propose to do?'

'I wish I knew! Elizabeth says it's useless to approach her father and will only result in more deceit. But if I don't go openly to Alderman Tierney, what can I do when Randolph asks for her hand?'

'It's certain that he will?'

He nodded bitterly. 'He's so deep in debt that this is his only way out.'

127

'I see.' Vanessa eyed him consideringly. 'Then it seems you've only one alternative.'

'And that is?'

'To elope.'

Mr Vaughan shot out of his seat. '*What?* You can't be serious!'

'Yes I can. You don't have much choice, do you?'

Wearily, he passed a hand over his eyes. 'No.'

'I know it's not what you would wish but it may be the only way,' she said logically. 'Think about it and in the meantime I will do what I can to keep Lord Randolph at bay. I imagine I'm better equipped to deal with him than Mistress Tierney.'

After Gideon had gone, Vanessa discovered that he had given her much to ponder on – and not all of it concerned with himself and Mistress Tierney. She contemplated his assertion that she had done his Grace good and found it puzzling but curiously pleasing. Lyndhurst kept the world at a deliberate distance and it was her opinion that he had at some point assumed the mask of cool indifference in order to cloak some hurt. This had obviously been long ago and that mask had now become as much a part of him as his black and silver garments and smoothly caustic tongue.

A little she had learned from Nicholas – enough to be grateful for her own father, despite his addiction to the bottle; but between childhood and the affair of Judith Maynard lay uncharted years of which she knew nothing save that he had, in that time, committed the various acts which had earned him the appellation 'Lucifer'. She wondered for perhaps the hundredth time what had made him go to so much trouble and expense on her behalf but could find no reason. She sighed, wise enough to realise that in all probablity she would never fully understand him should she spend a lifetime in the attempt. And on this philosophic but oddly depressing thought, she forced herself half-heartedly back to her music practice.

By the evening of the Queensbury soirée, Vanessa was becoming quite used to society and had acquired a few devoted admirers of whom, it seemed, Mr Anstey was one. He had come to regard her as the most conversible female of his acquaintance – a remark which he was ill-advised enough to utter at his club and which was the subsequent source of much ribaldry and merrymaking.

To attend the soirée, Vanessa wore another gown selected by her guardian, a bewitching creation of pale peach-coloured satin ornamented with seed pearls and échelle of silver ribbon. Lady Blanche was accompanied by her husband and together with his Grace they arrived in good time at Queensbury House – Blanche having insisted that on this occasion it was quite ineligible for Francis to make one of his customary late entrances.

The Duchess greeted them with affectionate raillery and separated them in the same manner by passing Mistress Tremaine to her son and carrying Blanche away with her to converse with Dolly Cavendish. March grinned engagingly at Vanessa and bore her off to the other salon where some of the guests were engaged in composing sonnets. As they entered, Tom Wickham concluded his reading amidst a roar of critical teasing. Vanessa caught sight of Mr Anstey sitting aloof from the group and asked March if Mistress Brandon was likely to be present that evening.

'*Sophy* – at a *soirée*? Never!' laughed his lordship. 'Can you imagine her listening to Horry Walpole's essays or Mistress Norton's infernal harp?'

Vanessa was bound to admit that she could not. Then, struck by a brilliant idea, she said impulsively, 'My Lord, I'd like to sing this evening. Can you arrange it?'

He blinked but replied gallantly, 'Why, certainly – it is my privilege.' And then, cautiously, 'Forgive my curiosity, but . . . does Francis know?'

Her smile was deceptively demure. 'No. I thought it might be nice to surprise him.'

March eyed her with dawning admiration and drew a long breath. 'Yes. It might at that.'

She had just time to thank him before they were drawn into

the high-spirited, poetically-minded group and were soon laughing with the rest at the dire quality of their rhymes. After a while, Vanessa read out her latest attempt, heard it greeted with goodnatured derision and withdrew to sit beside the palpably depressed Mr Anstey. They conversed for a few moments on general topics and then she said, 'Mr Anstey – you must not be offended if I say it's a mistake to take Mistress Brandon's capriciousness too seriously.'

Mr Anstey jumped. 'Am I to understand,' he asked ponderously, 'that you are not unaware of the esteem in which I hold Mistress Brandon?'

She nodded and, colouring faintly, he said, 'Then I will not trouble to deny it. May I ask how you know?'

'I guessed, sir. It wasn't difficult. I'm afraid Sophy's present predilection for Lord Nicholas is universally known.'

'I see.' He stared across the room in gloomy silence.

Vanessa laid a tentative hand on his arm. 'She is very young and it's only natural she should wish to flutter her wings a little.'

'Why, so I believed,' he answered heavily. 'We have known each other most of our lives and I had thought we had an understanding.'

'And that was?' prompted Vanessa, reflecting that advising lovelorn gentlemen was becoming a habit.

'That she would have her season but that our engagement should be announced at the end of it.'

'Oh.' Nothing in Sophy's artless confidences had hinted at this. 'Yes. I see.'

'I do not wonder at your surprise,' continued Mr Anstey grimly. 'Until she met Lord Nicholas, I had no doubts of her feelings – but since that day she has behaved outrageously. She refuses to heed my admonitions or even to admit my right to question her conduct.'

Vanessa drew a deep breath. 'Does she indeed? But I hope . . . I hope you didn't try to scold her?'

'Hardly that, madam,' he replied huffily. 'I merely asked her to desist from behaviour which can only make her appear foolish.'

'Oh. Is that all?' But amusement was banished by the hurt she saw on his face and she said maternally, 'Mr Anstey, I think you must try to remember that Sophy is not a little girl any more. That tone may well have been effective once but now she has seen a little of the world and listened to many pretty speeches, it would be marvellous if she didn't hope for something a thought more romantic from you.' She paused and regarded him pensively. 'Forgive me – but do you love her?'

Mr Anstey fought with himself. Then, stiffly, 'Certainly I do.'

'And have you told her so? Ah – I see you haven't. You should, you know. It's quite likely she feels you take her for granted and wishes to make you jealous – hence Lord Nicholas.'

'Jealous! *I?*'

She rose, smiling. 'Yes, sir – you. And now, if you will escort me, I've a mind to hear some of the readings.'

Mr Anstey offered his arm but they did not get far. In the doorway, her face freezing into an expression of affronted dislike, stood Lady Henley. Vanessa stopped abruptly and made a tiny, almost mocking, curtsy.

'Good evening, my lady,' she said coolly.

Too angry to conceal her emotion, Lady Maria replied with open malice, 'Enjoy your triumph while you may, Miss. I assure you that it will be but brief.'

Vanessa smiled slowly. 'Pray do your worst, madam. As you see, I still live.' And, nipping Mr Anstey's arm with urgent fingers, they moved on.

He looked at her, puzzled. 'It seems she does not like you.'

'You are too mild, sir,' said Vanessa with a wry laugh. 'She is my godmama. Didn't you know?'

'Your godmother! Then why – ?'

'Because she has a gutter-mind,' responded Vanessa, calmly forestalling the question, 'and refused to accept me. Oh, hush! My Selwyn is about to read.'

After Selwyn's neat and highly-acclaimed verses, the floor was taken by a small, effeminate gentleman in rose-pink brocade who proceeded to read an essay on Love.

'Good God!' Vanessa's gaze rested appreciatively on the

nip-waisted figure as she listened to fulsome passages rendered even more absurd by a lisping voice. Then, involuntarily, her eyes sought her guardian and found him beside the Duchess of Devonshire, inspecting the reader through his glass with an expression of pained boredom. As if aware of her scrutiny, he lowered the glass and turned to look at her, languidly raising one ironic brow. Their eyes met in a moment of mutual understanding and Vanessa was forced to stifle a giggle.

As the dainty gentleman concluded his epic amidst tepidly polite applause, March stepped briskly forward and withered a possible encore in the bud. He said, 'And now we have a very special pleasure. I have persuaded Mistress Tremaine to sing for us.' And, offering his arm to Vanessa, led her to the harpsichord through a rustle of speculative gossip. Lyndhurst remained quite still. A smile lurked in his eyes but he made no comment and this time Vanessa was careful not to look his way.

She seated herself at the instrument, waited calmly till the room fell silent and only then did she raise her hands to the keys, play the introduction to the beautiful aria from Handel's *Serse* and at last begin to sing. Controlled and wistful, her pure soprano filled the room, holding her audience captive by its sweetness so that every eye in the room was fixed upon her. And when the last, haunting note faded away, there was a moment of profound stillness before the applause broke out, spontaneous and enthusiastic. Shyly smiling, Vanessa rose and made a graceful curtsy. She was besieged by requests to sing again but these she turned modestly aside whilst searching the throng for one special face.

The Duchess of Devonshire looked into Lyndhurst's veiled gaze and said lightly, 'She is talented, this ward of yours.'

'It would appear so.'

She rapped his arm with her fan. 'You had best have a care, my friend. If I didn't know you better, I might be tempted to believe a little of what I hear.'

'My dear Dolly! But, as you say – you know me better.'

She nodded. 'There is, however, a first time for everything. And there are enough rumours concerning the two of you –

from those poor fools who think her your mistress to the ones saying that she is Maria Henley's goddaughter.'

'Such lurid imagination,' he complained fastidiously.

'So it's all untrue?'

His Grace sighed. 'All save that Lady Henley is indeed Vanessa's godmama. Does that content you, Dolly?'

'Not in the least. But I will hold my peace till I can confound you with my observations.' And she strolled away laughing.

Frowning slightly, Lyndhurst moved across to Vanessa and, at his approach, the remaining enthusiasts melted away to leave her to meet enigmatic silence with speculative mischief. And then, seeing that no comment was forthcoming, she tried mock reproof.

'Well, sir? Have you nothing to say?'

'Such as what, *ma fille?*'

'Such as a word of congratulation . . . as my guardian.'

'Ah. Well, you see . . . as your guardian, I consider too much approbation dangerous,' he explained suavely.

'And so you are withholding yours?'

'Possibly. Or I might be maintaining a tactful silence.'

'Because you hated every minute of it? And did you?'

Laughter gleamed in his eyes. 'No. I think you cannot need me to tell you that you have a particularly lovely voice.'

It took her by surprise and she flushed. 'Perhaps not. But it was for you that I sang – to prove a point and in the hope of astonishing you.'

The heavy lids were raised suddenly, revealing an unguarded expression that vanished before she could interpret it. Then he said evenly, *'Mignonne,* I can say with perfect truth that you never cease to astonish me. One wonders what the notoriously correct Mr Anstey makes of you?'

Vanessa gave a rippling laugh. 'I doubt he knows, sir.'

'Yet he appears to seek your company.'

'Does he?' She repressed a temptation to relate the gist of Mr Anstey's conversation. 'I had not noticed it.'

Sir Gareth Merton strolled up to them. 'One feels that there should be legislation to deal with guardians who monopolise

133

their ward's attention,' he remarked plaintively, taking Vanessa's hand and drawing it through his arm. 'Do go away, Lucifer, like a good fellow.'

The Duke made a profound (if rather ironic) bow and walked away to flush the lisping poet from Madam Gwynne's side and devote himself exclusively to her for the next half-hour – an interesting fact which did not pass unnoticed.

On the opposite side of the room sat Madam Julia Anstey in conversation with Lady Henley. It had always been one of Lady Maria's greatest ambitions to rank as a close friend of the socially influential Mrs Anstey and, fearing that her goddaughter might forever blight these hopes, she had wasted no time in pouring a catalogue of Vanessa's supposed iniquities into that lady's ear. 'And you have only to watch her, my dear ma'am. So pushing and brassy! Only see the way she is making an exhibition of herself tonight.'

Julia Anstey, astutely intelligent despite her air of languid elegance, looked at her ladyship from beneath raised brows. 'I do not consider it an exhibition,' she said quietly. 'On the contrary, I found her performance quite charming.'

'Indeed!' said Lady Henley, annoyed. 'And have you met her yet?'

'No, but I intend to ask Roderick to present her to me. I have a certain regard for his judgement and he assures me that she is a young lady of unusual wit.' She surveyed her ladyship keenly and with an element of distaste. 'I hesitate to mention it but I understand that Mistress Tremaine is, in fact, your godchild?'

Lady Maria's colour rose. 'She is indeed. You may imagine then my dismay on discovering that she was apparently under the protection of Francis Courtenay!'

'That she is in his *care* is beyond dispute,' replied Madam Anstey coolly. 'But though I am the first to admit that Lyndhurst has many faults, I have yet to find him guilty of compromising his sister by making her party to one of his affairs. He has always been most careful of her good name – as you, my lady, should surely realise.'

Lady Henley gasped at this pointed snub and her colour

deepened alarmingly but Madam Anstey seemed oblivious to it as she rose and glanced across to where his Grace flirted gently with Lydia Gwynne. Turning back to Lady Maria, she said, 'It seems to me that his interest lies in that direction – one hears that he visits her. And I have seen no sign of any romantic attatchment to his ward. Nor do I expect to do so. I am sure that Madam Gwynne is very much more to his taste.'

'He wishes us to think so, certainly,' said my lady waspishly.

Madam Anstey sighed. 'Possibly. But, in all likelihood he has assumed your responsibilities purely to annoy you – no more and no less. And now, if you will excuse me, I wish to speak to my son.' Upon which she moved thankfully away, leaving Lady Maria to fume impotently at her retreating back.

Under cover of his light *badinage* with the dashing widow, Lyndhurst observed Lady Henley's discomfiture and presently he also saw Roderick Anstey introduce Vanessa to his mother. His Grace noted that Madam Anstey spent some minutes with his ward and gave every appearance of approving her. Contentedly, he restored his attention to his fair companion.

The Disappearance of His Grace of Lyndhurst

As the weeks passed, Vanessa's growing friendship with Elizabeth Tierney and Gideon Vaughan was directly responsible for making her an implacable enemy. Quick to perceive her interference in his plans, Colonel Lord Randolph soon realised that there was a good deal more to it than mere girlish meddling; and when it eventually dawned on him that Mistress Tremaine was also contriving to aid Mr Vaughan, he was very angry indeed.

It was at Lady Carlyle's rout party that matters came to a head for the Colonel had manoeuvred Elizabeth into an alcove and was fast moving towards a declaration when Vanessa espied them as she strolled by with Lord Nicholas. She stopped abruptly, her hand gripping his arm.

'Rot it!' his lordship expostulated mildly. 'D'you have to ruin my coat?'

'What?' asked Vanessa absently, frowning at the alcove.

'My coat! Dash it – it's the first time on and here you are crushing the sleeve,' he said, prising her fingers from the cherished garment. He smoothed down the blue satin and inspected the damage. 'Plague take it – it's creased!'

'Oh, bother your coat!' said Vanessa impatiently. 'There are more important things to think of.'

'Devil a bit! You don't know my tailor's charges.'

'Do you?' retorted Vanessa wickedly. 'When did you last pay a bill?'

'Can't remember,' he replied, frankly careless. 'But that ain't the point, Mistress Impertinence.'

Glancing again at the two in the alcove, she caught his hand in an urgent clasp. 'Nick – I want you to ask Mistress Tierney to dance.'

Withdrawing his hand, his lordship folded his arms and regarded her sardonically. 'Do you, by Gad? And, setting aside the fact that I hardly know her, is there anything else you'd like me to do?'

'No.' She smiled innocently. 'But it's kind of you to ask.' His lordship pulled a face. 'Please come. There is a reason, but I can't explain it just now.'

Muttering protests, Nicholas allowed himself to be led off. When he saw that he was expected to remove Mistress Tierney from under the nose of his brother, his jaw dropped a little and he shot a fulminating glance at Vanessa who pretended not to notice and attacked the Colonel with alarming vivacity.

'My lord! How delightful to see you again. And Mistress Tierney – I believe you know Lord Nicholas, do you not?'

'Indeed I do,' smiled Elizabeth, dipping a grateful curtsy.

'Well, Nicholas,' drawled the Colonel. 'Charmed though I am to see you, I find you a trifle . . . unexpected.'

Though well aware of his brother's meaning, Nicholas thought it best to feign ignorance. 'Can't think why you should, m'dear fellow. Laurie ratted and I was appointed chief substitute. Lord, Randolph, but you should know Blanche by now!'

'I do, of course,' agreed Lord Randolph sweetly. 'As well, in fact, as I know you.'

Nicholas' blue eyes sparkled as the humour of the situation began to strike him. Taking the Colonel's coat between a thumb and forefinger, he said confidentially, 'You're in a devilish queer mood, Randy. Dashed if I don't think you're liverish. Nothing worse than the liver for making you bilious. You need one of Dr James' powders – set you to rights in no time!'

Lord Randolph was not amused. 'What I need, Nicholas, is for you to remove yourself – and your infantile wit – from my hearing.'

137

'Well I will,' replied Nicholas, unabashed. 'Mistress Tierney – will you abandon this ill-tempered fellow and honour me?'

With a smile and a nod, Elizabeth placed her hand on his sleeve and they walked away. Watching them go, Vanessa remarked provocatively that they made a handsome couple and heard the breath hiss between the Colonel's teeth.

'I suppose,' he enquired softly, 'that this is your doing?'

Her brows rose haughtily. 'Sir?'

'Come, mistress – I think you understand me very well. For some reason I cannot fathom, it pleases you to obstruct my courtship of Mistress Tierney and you are becoming a nuisance. It would be as well if you refrained from meddling in my affairs. I trust I make myself clear?'

Vanessa smiled. 'Perfectly. There is just one small thing . . .'

'And that is?'

'Are you attracted to Mistress Tierney – or her father's money?'

His face darkened and his hand clenched tight on his snuff-box. 'I fail to see what concern it is of yours,' he snapped. 'And it is scarcely flattering to the lady.'

'So you love her?'

'*En despère.*'

'Then I see no difficulty, my lord. For if you love her, you will undoubtedly place her happiness above your own and cease distressing her with your attentions.'

For perhaps twenty seconds Vanessa held his gaze and was glad that they were in a crowded ballroom. Then he said gratingly, 'Vastly affecting, mistress. One wonders where you acquired such romantic notions. I'll swear it wasn't from Francis – though I imagine he is proud of his protegée. But I suggest you have a care. My brother is not overly fond of petticoat management – nor of . . . curtain lectures.'

Her eyes flashed but she said lightly, 'No? And how fond do you expect him to be of Elizabeth's parentage?'

'You are clever,' acknowledged the Colonel savagely, 'but not clever enough, I fear. You think to wed him, do you not? But you are doomed to disappointment. Lucifer is fickle, my dear – and proud. Soiled goods may serve to pass a dull hour or two but they won't tempt him to matrimony.'

Vanessa's colour fled but she had herself well in hand. 'Then that at least should please you, sir – for you may continue to live in hopes of succeeding him.'

'I – beg – your – pardon?' he demanded furiously.

'And not before time,' she smiled. And walked calmly away.

At about the same time, his Grace and Mr Vaughan were strolling down St James Street on their way to the Cocoa Tree.

'She is quite a success,' Gideon was saying. 'And deservedly so, for she has much more than mere beauty.'

'Oh much more,' agreed the Duke urbanely.

'And her smile is absolutely ravishing,' Gideon persevered, trying to read his Grace's expression.

'Absolutely.'

Abandoning subtlety, Mr Vaughan stopped dead and grasped his friend's arm. 'Francis – are you in love with her?'

'How strange,' drawled his Grace. 'I was about to ask you the same question.'

Gideon choked. 'Really I – '

'But fortunately I know better. You are *épris* with the soulful blonde. Let me see . . . ah, yes. Mistress Tierney, is it not?'

Recovering himself, Gideon refused to be diverted. 'That's beside the point. What of Vanessa?'

Lyndhurst sighed. 'I believe I have mentioned before my dislike of being manhandled in the street – or, indeed, at all.'

Snorting with disgust, Mr Vaughan released him. 'I suppose you've realised that she will eventually marry?'

There was a second's hesitation and then, 'Naturally. It is . . . "*a consumation devoutly to be wished*".'

'And it won't have escaped your attention that Anstey appears very taken with her?' This time his Grace said nothing at all. 'It's very convenient,' observed Gideon. 'You couldn't have found a *parti* more calculated to enrage Maria Henley if you'd tried. Or did you?'

'That is what you think?'

'What else?'

'What else indeed? But I do not quite see your objections. He is probably the best match in town. You are not, I imagine, of the opinion that I should marry her myself?'

'Hardly!'

'No, I thought not.'

Lyndhurst walked on and Gideon followed, saying thoughtfully, 'There are those who predict your marriage to Lydia Gwynne.'

A gleam of humour reappeared in the topaz eyes. 'And what do you think of that? She is much more my style, you know.'

'Yes. I know,' agreed Gideon drily. 'But you'd be making a big mistake.'

'Oh? Why so?'

'Because you don't love her. With you it's the money – and she has a fancy to become a duchess.'

'How uncomplimentary of you,' complained the Duke. 'I believe my self-esteem is quite wounded.'

'Impossible,' said Gideon, not even trying to resist this opening. 'You're the only man I know with an armour-plated ego.'

Lyndhurst's laugh held genuine amusement. 'Pique, repique and capot! I asked for that.'

'Yes.' Mr Vaughan was taken aback. 'Well, as I was saying, it's no reason for marriage.'

'My dear Gideon – I thought you wanted me to take a wife?'

'I do. But – '

'Then you really must cease cavilling at every possibility or I shall never do so.'

'Yes – but a real marriage, Francis. Not some bloodless union of self-interest.'

His Grace paused on the steps of the club and when he spoke the soft voice held a curious flatness. 'You are advocating a lovematch. But I, unfortunately, do not know what love means. You have told me so yourself. Frequently.'

'Lucifer! Just the man we need!' announced Wickham.

'What? Not worshipping at the shrine of the Goddess Lydia?' laughed Sir Gareth Merton. 'You don't deserve your good fortune!'

'Aye. Would that I had it!' said Mr Drew in mock-despondency.

His Grace surveyed them languidly through his glass. 'Dear me! I really had no idea you were all so . . . interested.'

They laughed and Sir Gareth said protestingly, 'But how can we help it? You conjure up the most captivating little witch imaginable and, while we languish at her feet, steal the affections of the town's richest and most beautiful widow! It's too much – though, for myself, I'm inclined to prefer your ward.'

The Duke's black brows rose. 'My dear Gareth . . . can this be a declaration?'

This provoked more laughter and noisy ribaldry.

'Alas, no. She can't seem to take me seriously . . . and I fear her heart lies elsewhere,' came the deliberately light reply.

'Ah.' His Grace reached impassively for his snuff-box. 'And whom do you deem the . . . er . . . fortunate one?'

'Why, Anstey!' cried Wickham boisterously. 'Who else?'

'We were debating the likelihood of his making her an offer,' said Mr Drew. 'What's your opinion, Gideon?'

'It's a possibility,' agreed Mr Vaughan quietly.

'More than that,' averred Wickham. 'What do you think, Lucifer?'

Lyndhurst's mind appeared to have wandered. Following the direction of his gaze, Gideon saw that it was centred upon Carlton Henley and the somewhat uncouth-looking individual sitting with him. The Duke restored his attention to Wickham. 'I think,' he replied silkily, 'that I would very much . . . object . . . to the involvement of my ward's name in any club-room wager.'

Wickham's mouth fell open and Sir Gareth and Gideon both glanced sharply at Lyndhurst's impenetrable countenance. Mr Drew laughed. 'Very proper – though a thought surprising. You take your responsibilities seriously, then?'

'I believe so,' admitted his Grace, his apparent languor belied by the uncompromising line of his mouth. He glanced fleetingly across the room and then his shoulders shook in soundless laughter. 'Yes . . . I believe so.'

Jospeh Wade saw the glance and subsequent laughter. Flushing, he scowled angrily at Carlton and said, 'Arrogant fool! We'll see if he can laugh when I'm done with him.'

Carlton sniggered. 'It'll take more than you've managed so far to stop him.'

The scowl deepened and Wade's reptilian glance flickered unlovingly over his companion. 'Perhaps. But I don't take defeat as easily as you.'

The smile was wiped from Carlton's face and he too flushed. 'Have a care! I vow you will need my help in the end.'

It occurred to Joseph to wonder of what possible use Carlton's assistance was likely to be but, knowing the weakness of his cards, he saw the wisdom of holding close to them all till the time came to play. For aught he knew at this stage, Carlton might prove an ace after all so he summoned up a jovial smile and said, 'Come, man – a joke. Nothing more. I've no wish to quarrel with you.'

'No, for you've too much at stake!'

'And you stand to gain something more than Lyndhurst's discomfiture yourself,' snapped Wade irritably. 'I've said you'll not be the loser, haven't I?'

'Aye. But I'm damned if I know how we're to do it.'

'Nor I yet – but I'll find a way. So far I've not been able to get near her since that day . . . but it can't last. And if you can get me invitations to some of the parties she's likely to attend it might help.'

Carlton nodded. 'Very well. But I don't see what you expect to achieve by it. That approach has already failed.'

Wade frowned at the memory. 'Yes . . . but if it's true Lucifer's out to wed the rich widow, she may feel differently now. Only I'll have to see her before this Anstey declares himself – as they all seem to think he will.' He jerked his head at the vociferous group across the room.

Carlton leaned back in his chair. 'Does she know about the st – ' he checked himself swiftly, 'of the reason for your interest?'

'No. Old Tremaine would never speak of his wife after she died. As for Culver – he said nothing at the time and now he don't know where to find her.'

Carlton giggled. 'It's a good jest, stap me if it's not! When all's done, Lucifer will be double sorry he let her slip through his fingers,' he remarked, carelessly letting his voice rise on a tide of growing hilarity.

Wade grabbed his wrist in a crushing grip while darting a glance at Lyndhurst, now sitting with Mr Vaughan at a table not far distant. 'Be silent, you fool! If he hears you it will ruin everything!'

The Duke looked thoughtfully at Mr Vaughan, a faint frown creasing his brow. 'Now what, I wonder, should one make of that?'

'Of what?' asked Gideon, bewildered.

'You overheard nothing?'

'No.'

'Ah.' His Grace inspected the whiteness of his hands through the folds of black lace which fell over them. "*Now the plot thickens very much upon us.*" I wonder... yes. One might almost infer that there is something of which I am lamentably ignorant.' He smiled at the palpably confused Gideon. 'You are amazed. But even I cannot know everything.'

'Not amazed,' retorted Gideon with a grin. 'Bemused!'

His Grace nodded slowly. 'I think... I really think I must go out of town for a few days.'

'Out of town! In God's name, where? And why?'

'I am afraid I cannot tell you... yet. I may be quite wrong. Who knows?'

'Not I, certainly! How long do you expect to be away?'

'A fortnight perhaps, possibly less. I really have no idea.'

'Then it's some distance you're going?'

His Grace bowed ironically but did not answer, saying merely, 'I shall be in your debt if you will keep an eye on my ward during my absence.'

Mr Vaughan looked searchingly at him and then shrugged. 'Both of them, if you like.'

'It should not be necessary. She has Lilian and Blanche . . . and Laurence. But it might be no bad thing if you devoted your other eye to our puce-clad friend over there. His name, by the way, is Wade and he is Vanessa's cousin.'

'Her *cousin?*'

'Softly, my dear,' warned Lyndhurst. 'Yes, her cousin. She is not partial to him and I . . . mistrust him.'

'Is that all you intend to tell me?'

'At present there is nothing further that I can tell you – with any certainty. And I prefer not to guess.'

'When will you leave?'

'At first light.' The Duke picked up the cards and shuffled them with easy expertise. 'We have time, I think, for another game. Will you cut?'

Mr Vaughan's Hand is Forced

Vanessa ran her fingers idly up and down the keys of the harpsichord, feeling oddly listless and a little bored; which, she thought, was both stupid and illogical in a girl whose past week had consisted of three balls, two rout parties and a visit to Drury Lane to see Garrick's Abel Drugger. Irritably, she sat down before the instrument, her hands moving automatically through her favourite passages of the *Messiah* and became so absorbed that Nicholas was beside her before she knew it. Stopping abruptly, she looked up and was obliged to laugh at his expression of profound revulsion.

'Lord, what dismal stuff – it's enough to make you suicidal! Don't know how the fellow does it.'

'But it's Handel!' she protested.

His lorship threw himself into a chair and sank his chin on his chest. 'It would be. If you ask me, the man's a modern Torquemada.'

Vanessa grinned and gave up. 'You've no soul, Nick. None.'

'Agreed. Where's Lilian?'

'Purchasing a bonnet.' She hesitated a moment. 'Have . . . have you heard from his Grace at all?'

'Devil a word, m'dear. Wouldn't expect to.'

'No,' she sighed. 'I suppose not. But it's a week since he left and Mr Vaughan says he may be gone two. And although I've a shrewd idea he knows where he is, he won't tell me anything.'

My lord gave a snort of amusement. 'Devilish discreet of him!'

Vanessa regarded him with sudden and flattering interest. 'What do you mean?'

Nicholas shook his head, blue eyes dancing mischievously. 'Oh no! You'll repeat it, sure as check – and probably to Francis himself.'

'I promise I won't. Please?'

He looked at her for a moment and then gave in with a fatalistic shrug. 'It's only conjecture, of course, but it seems that the dashing widow is also out of town at present.'

Vanessa did not immediately grasp his meaning but then understanding dawned. She stiffened. 'You mean that his Grace and Madam Gwynne are . . . together?'

He nodded carelessly. 'It's a possibility.'

It was a long moment before she replied. 'I had no notion that they were so . . . friendly.'

'Lord, yes! These last weeks Francis has paid her no little attention – and I've seen him coming out of her house myself. They're laying bets as to whether she'll catch him.'

'Marriage?' The thought came as a shock and she wondered why.

'Aye. I don't say he will, mind you, but there is no denying she's deuced attractive. And there's always the money. God knows he needs a rich wife.'

'That,' said Vanessa, revolted, 'is the very last thing he needs. You can't want him to do such a horrible thing?'

'Why not? He doesn't possess a heart – so why not a marriage of convenience as well as any other?'

'Because it would make him all the things you think he is! But you're wrong, Nick – I'm certain of it.'

Nicholas laughed and shook his head. 'You don't know him. The woman who marries him because she has a fancy to be a duchess will suit him very well, mark my words. Not that I know it's the case with Lydia Gwynne for he appears very taken with her.'

Vanessa looked down at her hands. 'Mr Selwyn says she's very amusing,' she remarked in hollow accents.

An unpalatable and sobering thought occurred to Nicholas. 'Oh Lord,' he said ruefully. 'What it is to have a loose tongue like mine. I talk too much – always did. It's only gossip, you know, so forget I told you.'

Her chin came up. 'Oh I don't believe it. It's just I can't help . . . wondering a little.'

Luckily, he was spared the necessity of making any reply to this as the door opened and Benson announced Mistress Tierney. Entering hard on the heels of the butler, it spoke volumes for Elizabeth's sate of mind that she appeared not to notice his lordship's presence but went directly to Vanessa.

'I'm sorry to disturb you like this,' she said breathlessly, 'but I didn't know what else to do. I must see Gideon and I thought if I came here you could . . . he might . . .'

Vanessa looked back at her, frowning a little. 'I take it Lord Randolph has asked for your hand?'

Elizabeth nodded. 'Yesterday.'

'Randolph has *proposed* to you?' asked Nicholas incredulously. '*My brother Randolph?* Plague take it – I had no idea!'

'No,' agreed Vanessa drily. 'I rather think that Colonel Courtenay has been careful to conceal his intentions – particularly from his Grace. And he's chosen his moment well. Doubtless he has discovered that his Grace is out of town.'

'Yes,' sighed Mistress Tierney. 'I believe, till yesterday, he did not know it.'

'Then he has wasted no time,' observed Vanessa.

Nicholas looked from one to the other of them, unsuccessfully trying to follow the conversation. 'Rabbit it – I wish you would explain. Why should Francis not know – and what has Gideon to do with it? It's like a Chinese puzzle!'

Vanessa smiled perfunctorily and then glanced enquiringly at Elizabeth who gestured hopelessly and nodded. 'Briefly, Nick, Mistress Tierney's father is a merchant and rich – and Randolph is heavily in debt.'

'Lord, yes,' admitted Nicholas casually. 'He always is. It's quite normal in our family.'

Vanessa sighed. 'Well it seems his affairs are more pressing than usual for he has decided on marriage as a means of settling them. He knows that his Grace won't approve – hence the secrecy.'

'Oh. But I'm dashed if I know what he thinks Francis can do. It's true he can be filthy unpleasant, but – '

'It's not that,' she interrupted. 'His Grace would intervene because Mistress Tierney is in love with Mr Vaughan – and he with her.'

Up flew the mobile brows. 'Good Gad! Gideon is it? Who'd have thought it?'

'Quite,' said Vanessa firmly. 'And now you know all about it, I think the time has come for you to go and fetch Mr Vaughan.'

He grinned engagingly and swept a flourishing bow. 'Behold me – Cupid's messenger!'

Vanessa laughed. 'You are impossible – and I don't wish to behold you at all. It's *urgent*, Nick!'

He saluted. 'Yes, ma'am!' And went.

'He is very kind, isn't he?' said Elizabeth as the door closed behind him.

Vanessa nodded. 'Very kind – and probably the most goodnatured person you'll ever meet. It's impossible not to be fond of him.'

While they waited, Vanessa talked almost continuously to prevent Elizabeth from brooding. What she said, she could never afterwards remember but it seemed that she discoursed on everything from the latest fashion in trimmings to the recent signing of the peace at Aix-la-Chapelle and, by the time Nicholas reappeared, her tongue was beginning to cleave to the roof of her mouth.

As Gideon entered the room, Elizabeth ran to him, hands outstretched. He took them and said steadily, 'So, my dear – it has come. What did your father say?'

'He is delighted,' she replied bitterly. 'Mama too. It's not that they wish to force me, but I can't make them see that I truly do not desire it.'

Catching Nicholas' eye, Vanessa rose and attempted to make a tactful exit but Gideon prevented her. 'No – don't go. There is no need and you may be able to help.'

'I don't see how,' said Nicholas.

'Well, let's start by sitting down,' suggested Vanessa, 'and then we can discuss what is best to be done.'

They sat and fell silent until, gazing round at them all,

148

Nicholas said, 'I'm dashed if I know why we're all thinking so devilish hard for it seems to me there's only one way out.'

'And that is?' asked Gideon, not noticeably hopeful.

'You'll have to run away with her, my dear fellow!'

Vanessa smiled brilliantly at him. 'That is exactly what I said weeks ago.' She turned to Gideon. 'Have you considered it?'

'Not really. I confess that I've been hoping for some alternative to present itself – and, of course, it hasn't.'

'There is always an alternative,' Vanessa announced. 'Elizabeth can simply refuse to wed the Colonel. But it would subject her to weeks of unpleasantness and there is still no guarantee that Alderman Tierney would consent to her wedding you.'

Gideon looked at Elizabeth. 'What do you think of that, my dear?'

'It's as Vanessa says,' she replied listlessly. 'Papa doesn't mean to be unkind but he is ambitious and he's never understood that I'm not like him. And it's two years before I shall be of age.'

'Then that settles it,' said Nicholas. 'Plague take it, you're too respectable, Gideon – and it sticks in your gullet to make it a runaway match. Admit it!'

Gideon smiled reluctantly. 'It's true enough. And I don't want to place Elizabeth in such an equivocal position.'

'Surely that is for Elizabeth to decide?' asked Vanessa logically.

Elizabeth flushed and a tiny spark glowed in her eyes, making her suddenly beautiful. 'I would not mind . . . not at all.'

'You are sure?' asked Gideon, very low.

She smiled. 'Quite sure?'

He drew a deep breath. 'Then so be it.'

'A chaise-and-four to Gretna?' Nicholas was bubbling with mirth.

Gideon frowned. 'No. It will have to be by special licence. I imagine tht it will mean falsifying a detail or two – but, given that, it should be possible.'

'Needs must when the devil drives,' said Nicholas philosophically. 'When do we set it for?'

Gideon took Elizabeth's hand. 'Will the day after tomorrow suit you, my love?'

She said nothing but her fingers tightened on his and she nodded, shyly smiling.

'Can you pack some things and have them brought here?' asked Vanessa.

'Yes . . . I think so. My maid will see to it – she seems quite devoted to me. I had no idea till today. And – and you will come to the wedding, won't you? And you, Lord Nicholas?'

'Thank you,' said Vanessa smiling. 'I shall be delighted.'

'And I,' grinned his lordship. 'Wouldn't miss it for worlds! And Lord Nicholas be damned – it's Nick, if it please you.'

Elizabeth laughed. 'Nick then – and thank you.'

'Think nothing of it, m'dear.' He laughed, hugely enjoying himself. 'Lord, but who'd have thought it? The Honourable Gideon Vaughan making a secret marriage – and with a bride snatched from beneath the very nose of Colonel Lord Randolph Courtenay. Oh, I beg your pardon, Gideon – but you have to own it's a splendid jest! Even Francis will be amazed and you'll agree it's not an effect easy to achieve. Rot it, but I can scarcely wait to see his face!'

The wedding of the Honourable Gideon Vaughan and Mistress Elizabeth Tierney was accomplished without the arrival at the church of either the bride's irate parents or her spurned military suitor and when the ceremony was over, Lord Nicholas (having performed his part as groomsman with nonchalant grace) ushered them all to the carriage where he produced champagne and insisted on drinking a toast to the happy couple.

It had been decided that the newly-married pair should leave immediately for the country and Elizabeth had left a note for her mama which she had every confidence would not be discovered until they were well on their way. Her maid was to accompany them along with Mr Vaughan's valet.

Vanessa and Nicholas waved till the couple were out of sight and then, feeling immoderately pleased with themselves, drove back to Lyndhurst House where their jubilation fled before the sound of a stridently angry voice emanating from the library. Vanessa smiled wryly at Nicholas. 'Oh dear. Do you think . . . ?'

'Aye,' he replied darkly. 'Come on. If we're quick, they'll never know we were here.' He turned and would have made a precipitate exit but that two capable, feminine hands closed about his arm.

'You don't want to cry craven?' asked Vanessa, shocked.

'Yes, I do. Damn it, *I* don't want to face some noisy Cit!'

'Oh? You'd let me do it alone?'

His lordship regarded her from sardonic blue eyes. 'You'll not get round me like that, my girl!' Vanessa said nothing but a smile flickered into being and her lordship discovered himself less armoured than he had thought. 'Oh hell!' He looked resignedly at the ceiling. 'All right. Come on.'

She gave a little trill of laughter. 'Thank you. You are very good.'

'I know,' came the martyred reply. 'But why is it no female can ever do anything without leaving a deuced note behind?'

Serenade with Variations

The scene in the library held an element of farce. Vinaigrette in hand, Lilian Erskine was prostrate on a sofa beneath the ebullience of a forceful person who could only be the Alderman while, on the other side of the fireplace, Colonel Lord Randolph Courtenay had plainly reached the nadir of irritation. In vociferous exhortation with him was a stout lady in purple armazine whose ornate coiffure supported a hat of dynamic originality and whose expression of vivid affront closely resembled that of a startled dromedary. Vanessa stole a glance at Nicholas and was forced to stifle a giggle.

First to notice them, the Colonel cut short his companion's verbosity, saying, 'Well, well. My little brother and the busy Mistress Tremaine. I should have known you would be involved in this, Nicholas. It's just about your level after all.'

'Vanessa – thank God!' said Madam Erskine in devout but failing accents. 'Dear child, where have you been – and who *are* these people? I understand nothing – *nothing*!'

'Now see here, Miss,' rapped Mr Tierney. 'It seems to me you've a deal of explaining to do so – '

'All in good time, sir.' Vanessa walked composedly past him to kneel beside her duenna. 'Cousin Lilian, this need not concern you. Wouldn't you be better lying on your bed?'

'I daresay I should,' came the fretful reply, 'but my place is with you, so here I stay.'

The Alderman could contain himself no longer. 'I demand an answer, madam! *Where is my daughter?*'

152

'I really have no idea,' responded Vanessa truthfully.

'*No idea?* No – damn it, Miss, wasn't it you who fostered this whole farrago of nonsense from the beginning?'

'Yes. But it's hardly my fault, you know.'

The purple-clad vision sailed across the floor like a ship under full canvas. 'I vow all this was never my little Lizzie's idea. She would never act so sly without someone put the notion into her head.'

Vanessa raised her brows with deliberate hauteur. 'We have not been introduced, ma'am, but I must presume you to be Elizabeth's mama. I am Vanessa Tremaine – his Grace of Lyndhurst's ward – and I am delighted to make your acquaintance.'

This ploy summoned all Madam Tierney's refinement. She dropped a reluctant curtsy and, producing her handkerchief, dabbed artistically at her eyes. 'Likewise, I'm sure! But I vow my heart is quite broke! Such plans as I had – and all my schemes for a grand wedding breakfast wasted. I – '

'Oh have done, Rachel!' commanded her husband in exasperation. 'I'm still waiting to hear where Lizzie is got to.'

Realising she could not prevaricate much longer, Vanessa said tranquilly, 'She is travelling to the country with her husband – the Honourable Gideon Vaughan.'

'Married!' snapped Lord Randolph, entering the fray. 'They are married?'

She nodded distantly. 'This morning at St Margaret's, Westminster.'

'Damn you, then!' he hissed. 'Damn you for the interfering adventuress that you are!'

Cousin Lilian closed her eyes and moaned feebly.

'Blister it, Randolph, that's enough!' expostulated Nicholas. 'I'm not surprised you're vexed – but you've no right to speak to Vanessa like that.'

Lord Randolph fixed his brother with a glittering stare. 'The so-noble protector!' he sneered. 'Tell me, my bantam – are you man enough to do more than spout at me?'

Nicholas paled but he held himself very straight and looked

the Colonel in the eye. 'Yes. If I have to,' he said with a crisp dignity that Vanessa privately thought suited him very well but that made her hasten to intervene.

Elizabeth's parents, meanwhile, were simultaneously voicing their own views and, as Vanessa turned back to them, Mr Tierney thundered, 'I'll have it set aside – see if I don't! Lizzie ain't of age and the marriage of a minor ain't legal!'

'And what good will that do?' demanded Vanessa sensibly. 'All you will achieve is to make your daughter's name a byword and then, even if Lord Randolph still wanted to wed her, I imagine his Grace would have something to say.'

'It makes no odds what he says!' sniffed Madam Tierney.

'It's clear,' said Vanessa, with a disquieting smile, 'that you don't know his Grace.'

'No – and he doesn't know me!' boomed the Alderman. 'I'm a plain man, young lady, and a direct one – but I'm one as gets my way. That's how I've become one of the warmest men in the City – and what use is money if it don't buy me what I want?'

Lilian shuddered at such frank vulgarity. 'My dear, sir,' she entreated, 'I pray you will not talk so loud. My nerves are in shreds.'

Oddly touched by the merchant's honesty, Vanessa spoke more gently. 'Mr Tierney, please listen a moment. It's true that Mr Vaughan has no title but he is a gentleman of good family and excellent reputation. He loves Elizabeth and cares nothing for her expectations. He – '

'Then he's a fool,' said the Alderman bluntly, 'and that don't make it any better.'

'Then think of your daughter's happiness, sir. You can't wish to – '

'I'll thank you to leave Lizzie's happiness to us,' said Madam Tierney huffily. 'Everything we did was for her good.'

'Then it seems you've a very odd idea of what that may be,' remarked Vanessa drily.

This was unfortunate as it again provoked both husband and wife into simultaneous and lengthy justifications. Vanessa raised a hand to her head, feeling suddenly helpless. She looked

154

towards Nicholas but, as he was still arguing hotly with his brother, it was plain she could expect no support from him. And then, as Babel reached its pinnacle, help arrived in its most improbable form.

The doors were flung open and his Grace of Lyndhurst stood on the threshold. For a fleeting second, Vanessa thought her mind was playing tricks. Then, across the battlefield that was the library, she encountered a pair of topaz eyes, agleam with mocking laughter; and was too shaken to notice the silence when it came.

His Grace walked slowly into the centre of the room and, sweeping a comprehensive glance around him said in his inimitable way, 'Dear me! Such an exhilarating reception. I am quite overcome. Or do I take it that I was not, in fact, expected?'

Mr Tierney examined him beneath lowered brows. 'And who in Hades are you?' he demanded irately.

The Duke raised his glass and levelled it with practised insolence. At length he said languidly, 'I believe you might call me its founder member. Or so they say.'

Understanding dawned upon the Alderman. 'You are Lyndhurst?'

His Grace bowed slightly. 'I have that honour . . . but I fear you have the advantage of me. Vanessa . . . will you not present your . . . er . . . friends?'

Amusement at his tactics had restored Vanessa's self-possession and, demurely, she made the introductions. The Alderman bowed stiffly and his wife made a curtsy so deep he had to assist her to rise from it. Then she said simperingly, 'La, your Grace, I am vastly delighted to meet you – though never did I think it would be like this.' The handkerchief came into play again. 'We are in such trouble! My poor little Lizzie (and a sweeter, more innocent girl there never was) who should have become your Grace's sister – '

'Oh stop it, woman!' snapped her spouse. 'This ain't the time for senseless maunderings. I knew I shouldn't have brought you!'

155

The Duke stared in apparent fascination and then turned, lifting one enquiring brow at Vanessa.

'I don't think you have met Mistress Tierney,' she supplied, trying not to laugh. 'But four days ago Colonel Courtenay asked for her hand in marriage.'

Lyndhurst glanced mockingly at his brother. 'Well, well . . . I suppose I need hardly ask if Mistress Tierney is handsomely dowered? But I interrupt you . . .' He smiled at Vanessa and flicked open his snuff-box. 'I am agog to hear of Gideon's role in all this.'

The grey eyes widened and then filled with resignation. 'Viva Nostradamus. I should have guessed.' She paused and then said casually, 'Ah well. His role is that of bridegroom.'

The Duke's hand checked in mid-air; then, after an infinitesimal pause, he calmly inhaled the snuff and said pensively, 'Now that *is* surprising. Gideon has risen in my estimation. What a pity I missed it.'

'You're damned flippant, sir!' accused Mr Tierney fiercely.

'Why not? It's done – and your best course is to accept it gracefully. Your daughter has contracted a very eligible alliance – a good deal more so than the one you had planned for her.'

The Alderman was somewhat nonplussed. '*You* say that?'

'Certainly. Gideon will never lose several thousand guineas in a night's play . . . nor set up a mistress and lavish expensive gifts upon her. Randolph would undoubtedly have done so.'

This was more than the Colonel was prepared to tolerate in silence. 'And how, precisely, do my habits differ from your own?' he asked sweetly.

'In the examples I have cited, scarcely at all,' replied his Grace placidly. 'But happily it is not my morals which concern Mr Tierney.'

The merchant appeared much struck by this logic. He pursed his lips thoughtfully. 'Hm! Gaming is one thing – I expected that and money's no object, never was. But women is something else again . . . I'd not have my girl made miserable by that sort of thing – and, damn it, it ain't respectable! It may do in your family, your Grace, but it don't in mine!'

156

There was a potentially dangerous silence and then, 'It not only ... er ... "does" ... but is something of a tradition,' replied Lyndhurst with careful gravity. He moved to the door and opened it. 'I suggest that you go home and count your blessings – of which marriage with my family was not likely to have been one.'

It was not to be expected that either the Alderman or his wife had said their last word on the subject but the Duke's adroitly gentle dismissiveness was hard to withstand and within a very few minutes they took their leave. Thankful to see them go, Vanessa smiled gratefully at her guardian.

'Thank God you came when you did or we should never have been rid of them.'

'Aye,' agreed Nicholas. 'Take it all in all, we managed pretty well on our own, but it's plain there's none to beat you when it comes to routing a Savage Cit!'

His Grace bowed with mild irony. 'I am overjoyed to have been of some small assistance.'

Madam Erskine arose from her sofa and tottered towards the door, weakly announcing her intention to nurse her splitting head in the privacy of her bedchamber. Nicholas cast a sapient glance at the Colonel and decided to remove himself before the inevitable explosion. Grinning impudently at Vanessa, he bade a casual farewell to the Duke and left. After he had gone, Lyndhurst remained quite still, gazing enigmatically at his brother.

'Well, Randolph? If you have something to say, I pray you will make haste with it.'

'I will do so. Your time, of course, is too precious to be wasted on so trivial a matter,' returned the Colonel with heavy sarcasm.

'You really should strive to perfect your sneer,' observed the Duke dispassionately. 'It is dramatically overstated.'

'Damn you! Don't you care that we've said goodbye to a fortune owing to the infernal meddling of this – this *cocotte* whom you are pleased to call your ward?'

Lyndhurst did not move but the heavy lids were raised

suddenly and there was that in his eyes that forced Randolph to restrain the impulse to step back a pace.

'You will leave us, Vanessa.'

The tone, though new to her, was instantly recognisable and she was swift to do as she was bidden.

Left alone with his brother, Lyndhurst said softly, 'Understand this well, Randolph, for I shall not repeat myself. The child is my ward and nothing more. If you refer to her in such terms again – in my hearing or out of it – my objections will inevitably become more . . . pointed.'

The Colonel's face lost some of its colour but he laughed shortly. 'You think to challenge me?'

'Hardly. But pray do not deceive yourself that sentiment would prevent me if I wished to do so. I deplore the necessity of making crude threats . . . but I believe you to be encumbered with certain pressing obligations which I imagine you will be hard put to settle without my assistance?' The Duke paused delicately and this time his lordship found nothing to say. 'Just so. I trust I have made myself clear?'

'Admirably.' Lord Randolph's knuckles gleamed white.

'Then, since there is no more to be said, I will not detain you,' concluded Lyndhurst, politely holding open the door.

The Colonel departed without a word.

The last course having been cleared away, his Grace sat back sipping his port and lazily contemplated his ward. Gowned in amber and old lace, elbows resting reprehensibly on the polished table, she toyed absently with a piece of marchpane and described Gideon's clandestine marriage. Lyndhurst's eyes were drawn to the delicate grace of her wrists and hands; from time to time, they gestured expressively and such was their fascination that he eventually realised that he had heard very little of what she had said.

' . . . and then they set off to visit Mr Vaughan's mama. The rest you know.' She hesitated a little and then said, 'What did you say to Colonel Courtenay?'

Something altered in his face leaving it rather stern. 'Very little. I merely corrected his . . . misconceptions. He need not concern you.'

'He doesn't. You have a way of succeeding – and, since my reputation matters to you, I know it's safe.'

He smiled wryly. 'I feel impelled to point out that I am not God.'

'No, sir. So you said this afternoon.'

The ironic twist left his lips. He refilled his glass and stood up, motioning for her to come to him. Willingly, she crossed to his side and laid a hand on his arm.

'The library?' she asked, smiling up at him.

'I think . . . the drawing-room. I hoped I might persuade you to sing for me.'

A faint flush stained her skin. 'You have no need to persuade – it is my pleasure.'

He bowed and together they progressed to the parlour. Vanessa sat before the harpsichord and the Duke in a large wing-chair nearby. She began by playing a stately pavane and the hour, tranquil save for the music decorating it like a jewel, was suddenly bewitched. As the last chord died away, grey eyes were raised to vivid topaz ones and, 'Sing, my bird,' he commanded softly.

So Vanessa sang while Lyndhurst allowed himself to drift, suspended in a web of silken sound; and though, in some dim corner of his mind, the voice of reason apostrophised him as a fool, he silenced it. No pressing need to speak of his discoveries tonight, no harm in a small measure of self-indulgence. And it seemed a pity to shatter the evening's fragile spell – a nameless content that, God knew, was rare enough. He closed his eyes and floated in pleasant abandonment along the liquid cascade of notes.

When at last she stopped, there seemed no need for words and, leaving the instrument, she sank down upon a footstool beside his chair. For a few minutes she stared, dreaming, into the flickering fire and then, without turning round, remarked, 'I am glad you came back today.'

'Dare I hope I was missed?' he asked, his fingers straying involuntarily to the bright curls so close to his knee.

'Of course – though I did not know it at first. Everything was the same – yet different.' She stirred, smiling a little. 'And I believe I am guiltily glad of poor Lilian's headache. I'm fond of her, of course, but if she were here we couldn't be like this.'

'You think she would be shocked?'

'I know she would.' She fell silent for a moment. And then, 'It's strange, isn't it? When I left Penmarne, I thought I'd lost all the things that matter – only it's not so because others have come to replace them. I suppose that always happens . . . if you let it.'

'And if you do not?'

'Then you take to port,' she said flatly.

His fingers stilled and the silence lapped the air like a living thing. Then he said, 'Tell me about it.'

'There's little to tell. Mama died when I was eight and Papa never got over it. Or not enough to stay sober. Fortunately, the estate was small and Mr Renfrew, the mine manager, ran Wheal Betty. Not that it's shown a profit for months and I'm afraid Joseph will close it.' She paused and then said lightly, 'And that's enough of that. Won't you tell me about some of the things *you* have done?'

His hand left her hair and she turned to look enquiringly at him. His mouth twisted sardonically. 'I think not.'

The grey eyes met his hard stare unflinchingly and with a good deal of understanding. 'You can't have spent your whole life doing things too shocking to mention?'

'Most of it, I promise you. It is . . . the tale told by the idiot.'

'Won't you let me judge for myself?'

His smile was bitter. 'No. And that, my dear, is final.'

'Very well.' She settled back against his chair. 'Your barriers are effective, aren't they?'

There was a long pause. And then, 'You are very . . . perceptive.'

'No. Just not fool enough to believe that, because the facade is sensational, it's all there is.' She turned again, an odd little smile trembling about her mouth. 'You don't deny it, I see?'

The topaz eyes gazed back enigmatically. 'No. But neither do I intend to discuss it. I really cannot allow you to shatter my mystique. I believe it to be my principal attraction.'

'Your mistake, then.'

He smiled but refused to be drawn and led her, instead, to an account of her days in his absence. It was natural that Lord Nicholas' name should feature largely in this and, when she had done, he said, 'You appear to find Nicholas amusing.'

'Yes I do. But it's more than that. He was a warm heart and I'm fond of him – and I think it's a great pity the two of you exist in such a fog of mutual injustice.'

'I see,' remarked Lyndhurst, expressionlessly. 'Are you in love with him?'

Vanessa started a little and then gave way to laughter. 'In *love* with him? With Nick?'

'That is what I asked.'

'Of course I'm not! Good God – whatever made you think that? There's never been anything in the least romantic in our relationship – far from it – and I'm glad of it. Nick is my very dear friend, the brother I never had and I value him more highly than you do. But it's ridiculous to suppose I might fall in love with him. How could I? I l –' She broke off abruptly, gasping at the enormity of what she had so nearly said and the simultaneous dizzy knowledge of a hitherto unsuspected truth. Her horrified eyes flew to his suddenly intent ones and then the lashes fluttered down while a slow flush stained her cheeks.

His Grace frowned at her, puzzled. 'Yes?'

'It's n-nothing,' she stammered, rising swiftly from her stool. 'I – am foolish this evening.'

Lyndhurst also rose and, possessing himself of her hand, found it cold to the touch. 'Too much excitement, *mignonne?*'

She nodded, grateful for the excuse. 'I am a little tired. If you will excuse me, I think I will go to bed.' She glanced fleetingly into his face. The frown was still there. 'I . . . enjoyed tonight,' she offered, striving for her usual tone.

'And I.' He bowed very low and kissed her hand. 'Good night, my dear. Sleep well.'

She curtsied uncertainly. 'Thank you. Good night.'

Leaving the room hurriedly, she ran up to her chamber where she found Jassy waiting to undress her. For once, Vanessa did not encourage her to linger and soon she was alone, to lie open-eyed with her discovery. And when the first shock waves had subsided, she was left with a single, fundamental truth, earthshaking only in its familiarity.

'I love him. And it is not new – for when did I not?' Then, like the stirrings of a malignant creature, another thought was born and the breath caught in her throat. 'How stupid I am. He does not feel the same. Why should he? He is kind, he may even like me a little – but that's all. He thinks of me as the child he so often calls me. And, put beside Lydia Gwynne, it's what I am. She is seductive without even trying; I wouldn't know where to begin. And supposing Nick is right; suppose he is in love with her?'

Eyes wide open, she stared up at the silk tester, fitfully illuminated by the flickering fire. 'If he is, I imagine I shall be somewhat in the way. And worse, he will guess how I feel. He is too clever.' The concept brought agonising anxiety in its wake. At best, just an unreturned affection; at worst, an unattainable one to be met, perhaps, with indulgent amusement.

Her thoughts ran this way and that, growing ever more confused. And finally, irrevocably facing stalemate, she drifted into restless, uneasy sleep.

Concerning Certain Proposals of Marriage

Mistress Brandon was feeling decidely irritable. Why it was she knew not, but Mr Anstey was quite failing to respond in the desired manner to any of her strategems. Instead of becoming violently jealous or romantically masterful, he merely grew increasingly stiff and censorious. He lectured where he should have commanded and retired when he should have pressed his advances. It was all most unsatisfactory and the situation was rapidly getting out of hand.

By the night of the Vanes' masked ball, she had almost abandoned hope but, seeing her Roderick enter the ballroom arm in arm with Horry Walpole, she determined on one final attempt. Not without difficulty, she entrapped Lord Nicholas and virtually dragged him into the gavotte where she proceeded to laugh and chatter outrageously whilst contriving to keep a watchful eye on Mr Anstey.

Quick to perceive Mistress Brandon's animated progress round the floor, Mr Anstey affected total oblivion but, as the dance ended, he courteously excused himself from Mr Walpole and managed to encounter Sophy, apparently by chance, beside a huge tub of hothouse blooms.

'Why, Roderick,' she said carelessly. 'I'd no notion I should see you here tonight.'

'No? But then, my movements hold but little interest for you,' came the involuntary reply.

Her eyes widened. 'I'm afraid I don't understand you.'

'That, madam, I can readily believe.' For a man of such

163

measured temperament, Mr Anstey was uncommonly angry. 'But if you will do me the honour of according me a few moments in private, I will try to make myself more plain.'

Too surprised to argue, Sophy had laid her hand on his sleeve before she well knew what she was about. Mr Anstey led her to a small adjoining room and turned to face her with a sternness that occasioned her a tiny and entirely pleasurable shiver.

'I think it's time we put an end to this comedy, don't you?'

Sophy stiffened. 'Comedy?'

'Yes – though I confess it's not one which amuses me. You, however, doubtless feel differently since you are the one who began it.'

'*I*, sir? You talk in riddles.'

His teeth came together with a snap. 'On the contrary, madam, you are wilfully obtuse. But if you desire it, I will make my meaning unmistakable. I refer to your foolish pursuit of Lord Nicholas Courtenay – to which, as you will recall, I have made repeated objections.'

'Oh!' said Sophy, flushing. 'I do not pursue him!'

'No? What do you call it, then?'

There was no answer to this and the fact only served to aggravate her temper. 'How dare you speak to me so – you have no right!'

Mr Anstey scowled. 'Have I not? I had thought that, as your future husband, I had every right but, since I no longer know where I stand, I ask you plainly, Mistress Brandon – will you be my wife?'

By now, Sophy was as angry as he and she had no intention of accepting so ungraceful a proposal. 'I think it unlikely, sir, if you do not mend your manners! I suggest that you remember that if *you* cannot make a pretty speech, there are others who can!'

'Such as Lord Nicholas, no doubt?'

She tossed her head. 'Jealous, Mr Anstey?'

'Hardly!' he retorted, nettled. 'I hope I have more sense than to harbour such a futile emotion.'

'I begin to doubt that you harbour any emotion!' announced Sophy, hurt and determined to make him eat his words.

'Indeed?' was all he said.

'Indeed! I tell you frankly, sir, I've no mind to so cold a marriage.' She waited hopefully.

A quiver crossed his face and he grew rather pale. 'And I've no mind to a wife who is either naturally flirtatious or imbued with a childish desire to make me jealous.'

Sophy gasped and felt suddenly rather faint as she perceived to what end her scheming had led her. Her head felt hot and the palms of her hands grew clammy but she pulled her scarlet domino more closely around her and said the only thing that seemed left to her. 'Then it's fortunate we discovered our error in time.'

Mr Anstey assumed an attitude of equal dignity. 'I can only agree with you and beg you will henceforth regard yourself as quite free to dispose of your hand as you wish.'

'Thank you. I will do so – and, no doubt, you will quickly find a lady more to your taste than I.' She made a brief, jerky curtsy and swept out of the room.

Her parting words seemed to hang on the air and Mr Anstey stood quite still for a moment, staring after her out of hurt and bewildered brown eyes.

Vanessa also stood alone at the edge of the ballroom, her gaze resting on his Grace and Madam Gwynne and a dull ache of unhappiness in her throat. The last few days had been difficult but she had got through them by avoiding him – a thing in itself suspicious but on which he had so far made no comment. Sighing, she wondered how long she could maintain it.

'Sighing, Mistress Tremaine?' Colonel Courtenay raised his glass in the direction of her gaze. 'Can it be that you are facing the ruin of your hopes?'

This remark plucked at her nerves and she flushed. 'You have a vivid imagination, my lord,' she replied, trying to speak lightly.

'Oh, I think not. But my brother's attachment to the lovely widow can scarcely be a surprise to you – it has been most extensively remarked upon these last weeks. And Francis is so palpably *épris!* One would imgine that he is waiting for you to contract an eligible alliance. I doubt even *his* address is

165

sufficient to persuade Madam Gwynne into marriage whilst you are still on his hands.'

She tried to dismiss his words but they sounded all too plausible and a chill crept into her stomach. 'I don't believe you,' she managed to say.

He smiled mockingly, 'Don't you? You should. My noble brother took you into his care to irk Maria Henley – and what could irk her more than to see her repudiated godchild become the daughter of the lady she most desires to impress? I refer, of course, to Julia Anstey.'

Vanessa grew white. This was something new and he spoke with the confidence of one who had received incontrovertible information. She thought back: *I merely corrected his misconceptions*. And, feeling suddenly sick, gripped her fingers until the knuckles gleamed white. 'It's a lie.'

He laughed triumphantly. 'Ask Francis – or Blanche.' And he strolled away.

Vanessa stood quite still. There was nothing discreditable in Lord Randolph's disclosures; he had said only that his Grace wished her to make a good marriage and was contemplating doing the same himself. It was reasonable, it was possibly true – and it struck her like a death knell. Seeing Lady Blanche, she hurried to her side and, bluntly, but with as much composure as she could muster, asked if it were true that his Grace hoped to see her wed to Mr Anstey.

Blanche was surprised. 'Why, I believe it's possible. Mr Anstey is highly eligible, you know and it would grossly offend your godmama. La! Only look at that puce gown and lilac domino!' Her mind in the grip of a nightmare, Vanessa turned to gaze again at Lyndhurst. Lady Blanche gave her a sudden curious glance. 'Lud, child – you've gone quite pale! What *can* you be looking at?' And then, thoughtfully, 'Oh – Lydia Gwynne . . . well, I am not partial to her myself and I was certain Francis' interest lay elsewhere – but one can never tell.' She looked sideways at Vanessa. 'You really do not look at all well, my dear. Shall I get Nicholas to take you home?'

Vanessa thought that nothing could suit her better than the

privacy of her bedchamber but had no wish to face the inevitable questions if the Duke discovered her to have left early with Nick. She shook her head.

'Then pinch your cheeks to put some colour in them,' Blanche advised. And, with that, she fluttered away.

Dumbly, Vanessa watched her go, her mind occupied in sifting her confused thoughts. The Duke had never hidden his dislike of Lady Maria but never in her wildest dreams had she imagined tht he might settle his differences by means of her own marriage. She was startled to find a tall, elegant gentleman bowing before her.

'Mistress Tremaine?' he enquired in a pleasant, musical voice.

'I . . . yes.' She tried to concentrate.

'You must forgive my presumption in presenting myself,' he said and behind the mask blue eyes gleamed with a particularly sweet smile that disarmed reproof, 'but my brother told me you were not the lady to object to such unconventional behaviour. In truth, he has told me so much about you that I could not find it in me to leave town without having made your acquaintance.'

'Your brother?' There was something faintly familiar about the gentleman but his mask baffled her.

'Yes, madam – my brother,' he replied, removing the mask. 'Laurence.'

Vanessa no longer needed the information for the likeness was very pronounced. So this was the universally popular Charles Maynard. She had often hoped she might meet him but was too preoccupied tonight to appreciate it. She curtsied and managed a smile. 'I am very happy to know you, sir. Is your wife here with you?'

'Unfortunately, I am here alone – and that but briefly. A pity, for I know Judith would have liked to further her acquaintance with you.' He hesitated and then said a little stiffly, 'As you may be aware, his Grace and I do not visit.'

'Yes, I know. And I beg you will convey my apologies to your wife for any disrespect I may have shown her. I . . . did not quite understand her concern for me.'

The blue eyes surveyed her keenly. 'And now you do?'

She nodded. 'Nick explained it to me.'

Up went Mr Maynard's brows. 'But you would not otherwise have discovered it? Forgive me – but you don't look quite happy.'

Vanessa knew a bitter desire to laugh. He was clearly thinking that his Grace was pressing unwelcome attentions on her when the real truth was that they would not be unwelcome but that he was bestowing them elsewhere. 'It's just that I have the headache,' she prevaricated.

Charles saw the muscles of her throat tighten and caught a note of pain in the low voice. Frowning a little, he was about to enquire further when they were interrupted by Mr Anstey who greeted him tersely and immediately asked Vanessa to dance.

She had no wish to do so but saw the wisdom of leaving Mr Maynard before she betrayed herself. Laying her hand on Mr Anstey's arm, she said candidly, 'Sir, I am glad that you introduced yourself for I had hoped to meet you – but I fear I am poor company just now and so I will leave you before you decide I am a dull creature.'

Charles laughed and bowed very low. 'Mistress Tremaine, I am maligned for I am not such a scurvy fellow. I shall hope to meet you again.'

About to join the dance, Vanessa saw that Lyndhurst was making one of his rare appearances on the floor, partnering Madam Gwynne. Pain welled up inside her and her fingers tightened on Mr Anstey's, making him wince. 'I can't! That is, I – I don't wish to dance, sir,' she said unevenly. 'I – my head aches – please take me somewhere quiet.'

Surprised but submerged deep in his own miseries, he made no demur, merely leading the way to the small room where he had confronted Mistress Brandon. Vanessa sank down on a small sofa, pressing her fingers to her temples where a bona fide headache was just beginning. She said, 'I'm sorry. I am not myself tonight.'

'No,' agreed Mr Anstey gravely. 'I do not wish to intrude but if you would care to confide in me . . . ?'

'Thank you. But there is nothing you can do.'

He sat beside her, smiling bitterly. 'Then we are in similar case for *I* was intending to confide my troubles in *you* – yet there is nothing you can do either.'

'Oh?'

'Yes, indeed. But now I see how wrong I was to think of burdening you with my woes.'

'It's no burden, sir. And I'd rather listen to you than brood on myself.'

He nodded thoughtfully. 'There is much in what you say. Perhaps it would be no bad thing if we shared our problems. It's said talking helps – and it would be fair exchange after all. I assure you that you may rely on my discretion.'

'I know it, sir.' Vanessa hesitated for a moment and then said, 'Very well. But I beg you will go first.'

So Mr Anstey described the catastrophic results of his interview with Sophy and it was plain to Vanessa, preoccupied as she was, that he was not only deeply hurt but also angry and bitter. Her own part in the bargain she fulfilled as simply and quickly as possible, omitting only all mention of his Grace's expectations regarding her marriage. And when she had finished, Mr Anstey remained silent for a long time and then said slowly, 'Odd as it may seem, I think it possible for each of us to offer the other a solution.'

'How?' asked Vanessa, hovering between hope and despair.

'It occurs to me that, as we neither of us have any future with those to whom our hearts are given, we could do a good deal worse than to wed each other,' he announced seriously.

She stared at him and then the irony of the situation struck her and she began to laugh helplessly.

Offended, Mr Anstey regarded her disapprovingly. 'I fear I cannot see the humour of it,' he said stiffly.

Vanessa managed to check her mirth. 'I beg your pardon. But though I am honoured, you must see it's quite impossible.'

'I beg leave to contradict you. *You* must find it painful to remain in St James Square but have no other home; *I* wish to forget Mistress Brandon in the shortest possible time. Marriage

169

would remove you from Lyndhurst House and give me intelligent companionship. An ideal solution!'

'But . . . Sophy may change her mind.'

'That will be her misfortune,' he said with sulky stubbornness. 'I have no wish to be accepted as an after-thought.'

Vanessa continued to protest but, finally she said wearily, 'I do not deny, sir, that your generous offer would help me but I can't believe that all is over between you and Sophy. I should not even consider your proposal but I am at my wits' end and I *do* consider it. With your permission, I should like to speak to Sophy before I give you my reply.'

'Please do so,' he begged. 'And I assure you that if you feel able to become my wife, I shall consider myself fortunate. My heart is another's, it is true, but I respect and admire you more than any other lady of my acquaintance.'

Rising, Vanessa smiled bleakly at him. 'I thank you, sir. I am . . . very grateful to you and will not keep you waiting long.'

Mistress Brandon was easily found at the centre of a noisily excited group of young people where she was busily engaged in making herself the life and soul of the party. If her laugh was a trifle forced and her gaiety a little feverish, no one noticed it; and if her eyes were over-bright and her cheeks hectically flushed, there was more than one young gentleman who thought her quite in her best looks. Vanessa had some difficulty in removing her from the others but eventually accomplished it and came directly to the point by asking if it were indeed true and all was at an end between her and Mr Anstey.

'Oh – utterly!' said Sophy carelessly. 'And you can't imagine how glad I am! *He* told you, I suppose?'

'Yes. Are you *sure*, Sophy? It wasn't just another quarrel?'

Mistress Brandon smiled brightly. 'Not *just* another quarrel – the *last*, I am happy to say!'

'But I was convinced that you were fond of him,' said Vanessa, troubled.

'Oh I daresay I was – once.' Sophy shrugged and twisted her handkerchief in fingers that were not quite steady. 'But he is so very dull that I am glad to be free. He lectures one so and has no

170

notion of how to say anything pretty. Indeed, I can't conceive how I ever came to fancy myself in love with him.'

A little less perceptive than usual, Vanessa was deceived. 'Well, I can only hope you do not live to regret it.'

'Thank you – but it's most unlikely, I assure you. We should never have suited. I daresay I shall marry someone very different – Tom Knightley or dear Merton.' This remark surprised Vanessa almost as much as it would have surprised the two gentlemen had they been privileged to hear it. 'And now,' continued Sophy, 'I am quite tired of discussing it. Indeed, I believe I promised this dance to Sir Gareth – yes, there he is!' She waved gaily.

Sighing, Vanessa gave up and walked slowly out of the ballroom and into a deserted corridor where she found a small sofa, hidden between a pair of extravagantly foliaged potted plants. Here she sat and tried to make sense of her thoughts. This was not a success for the only fact which had any meaning was that she could not remain with Lyndhurst and beside this nothing seemed to matter very much.

A gentleman in a virulently blue domino was walking along the corridor towards her. Vanessa observed him with scant interest. It was not until he stopped in front of her and spoke that she realised who was behind the mask.

'Well, my dear. I'd begun to despair of ever finding you alone.'

'Since we have nothing to say, Joseph, I can't imagine why you should wish to do so,' she replied indifferently.

Mr Wade smiled. 'Still so cold?'

'I'm not likely to change – so you might as well go away. I am in no mood to be plagued by you.'

The little eyes flickered unlovingly over her but the smile on his lips did not waver. 'That is not kind. I have no wish to plague you – simply to assure you of my humble devotion and to say that if you change your mind – '

'Which I never shall.'

Mr Wade shook his head reprovingly. 'You are very hasty, aren't you? I think you may be glad to accept me . . . in the end.'

171

Vanessa could not help reflecting that for whatever reason, she was at least rich in suitors. 'What do you mean?'

'Only that when your fine guardian weds Lydia Gwynne, you may find yourself somewhat . . . delicately placed,' he suggested, rubbing his hands in apparent satisfaction.

Abruptly, Vanessa stood up. 'Happily, my delicate position is no concern of yours. And, since it's plain that your love for me is about equal to mine for you, I'm intrigued to know why you are so persistent – but I doubt you intend to enlighten me, so I see no point in pursuing this conversation.'

As she brushed scornfully past him, he seized her wrist, saying, 'Not so fast, cousin – I haven't finished.'

Much of Vanessa's icy dignity deserted her and she turned on him wrathfully. 'Take your hands off me!'

His fingers tightened cruelly. 'Where is your gratitude, Vanessa? I doubt there are many men who would take Lyndhurst's leavings to wife.'

Contempt flared in the grey eyes and she said deliberately, 'I would not marry you if I was starving in a gutter.'

'Forgive my intrusion,' said a crisp voice, 'but it seems this gentleman is inconveniencing you, Mistress Tremaine.' Charles Maynard stood a few paces away, regarding Mr Wade with cool distaste.

Joseph uttered an oath and let Vanessa go. Thankfully, she stepped back, rubbing her bruised wrist. 'Yes, sir. He is.'

Wade's lizard glance darted venomously at each of them in turn and then he made to walk away. Mr Maynard prevented him. 'One moment. I believe you owe this lady an apology.'

Joseph ground his teeth. And then, 'I beg your pardon,' he muttered ungraciously.

She nodded coldly and Mr Maynard stepped aside, allowing him to pass. When he was gone, Vanessa said, 'I am grateful, sir. You saved me a lot of unpleasantness.'

He smiled and, placing her hand on his arm, led her slowly back towards the ballroom. 'It was less than nothing. No doubt he has drunk a little too much wine. He didn't frighten you?'

'No. He is a paltry creature. He merely made me angry.'

Charles laughed. 'So I saw. And Nick tells me that you have a temper worthy of respect.'

She smiled. 'Does he? Well, it's true. But only when people are rude about – ' She stopped, the brief spell of forgetfulness over.

He looked quizzically down. 'When people are rude about Lyndhurst? Yes I know. Nick told me that too. He said you are the Duke's fiercest defender. Lucifer's champion, he called you – which, for Nick, is rather neat. And talking of the devil . . .'

She looked up to see his Grace approaching them.

'My dear Charles,' he drawled, bowing profoundly. 'What an unexpected pleasure . . . and I see you have made the acquaintance of my ward.'

Mr Maynard also bowed. 'As you say,' he replied coolly. 'I was about to restore her to you. Some oaf in a blue domino was making a fool of himself. It seems Blanche is a poor chaperon.'

Lyndhurst frowned and looked questioningly at Vanessa. 'Wade?'

'Yes.'

'Ah.' He turned and said less frostily, 'I am grateful, Charles.'

Mr Maynard nodded and then kissed Vanessa's hand. 'Goodbye, Mistress Tremaine. You should avoid lonely corridors, you know. One meets the strangest company! Servant, Courtenay.' And he walked swiftly away.

The Duke gazed thoughtfully at his ward. 'He is right, of course. Blanche is no duenna . . . and you should not be here. Why are you?'

'I – I have the headache,' she faltered.

He continued to survey her for a long and trying moment before placing her hand on his arm and strolling back down the corridor. 'You have had it for some few days, I think,' he remarked. 'In fact, since the day after I came home.' She said nothing and kept her eyes on the carpet. 'Is something troubling you, child?'

'N-no. What should there be?'

He stopped and lifted her chin with an imperious yet coaxing hand. 'Look at me, Vanessa.' Slowly, reluctantly, she raised her

173

eyes. 'I thought we agreed that you would always speak your mind to me.'

'We did.'

'Then do so now.'

'I – I can't!' she cried, turning away.

Softly, he asked, 'Don't you trust me?'

'Yes! But I can't explain and I won't lie to you.'

He looked, frowning, at her averted head and, laying one flawless hand on her shoulder, said, 'Very well. But if you change your mind, I am always ready to listen.'

A tremor ran through her body. God knew she wished nothing better than to lean back against him and say 'I love you', and be done with the whole dreadful charade – but it was not possible.

'Thank you,' she replied huskily. 'I know.'

'I hope so.' His hand left her shoulder and she felt bereft. 'I may be quite wrong, of course, but I am inclined to believe that you have perhaps . . . lost your heart . . . to one of your admirers,' he said expressionlessly.

Vanessa's heart demonstrated its presence by seeming to jump into her throat. 'Oh?' she asked painfully. 'Why so?'

'For a number of reasons. Am I wrong?'

She hesitated for a long time before finally whispering, 'No.'

'Ah.' The hard mouth tightened but he went on in the same tone, 'Well, there is nothing tragic in that. My guardianship was ever a temporary measure and, though I shall be sorry to lose my ward, it is right and natural she should marry.'

'Is it, sir?'

'Yes.' He frowned down at his snuff-box. 'Is it Anstey?'

Vanessa smiled bitterly to herself. 'And if it is?'

'It . . . would be a good match.'

'And vastly displeasing to my godmama.' She faced him.

The topaz eyes widened fractionally. 'Indisputably. But that need not concern you. Anstey is the stuff of which good husbands are made . . . unlike, for want of better examples, men such as your cousin – and myself.'

'I doubt Madam Gwynne agrees with you,' Vanessa heard herself say.

He smiled oddly. 'That is quite another matter.'

'She is very lovely.'

'Very.'

'And she amuses you?'

'You might say so. She is a very amusing lady.'

'I am glad,' she said in a tight little voice. She had not known that misery could cause a physical pain and, in that minute, decision was born and she said, 'Mr Anstey has this evening done me the honour of asking me to be his wife.'

His Grace's expression did not alter but a muscle moved in his cheek. 'And you have accepted him?'

'Not yet. But . . . I shall do so,' she replied steadily. And then, 'Unless you wish it otherwise?'

Quite without warning, his composure seemed to desert him. '*I?* Good God, what right have I?' he snapped.

'Every right. But for you he would not have proposed to me,' said Vanessa, deliberately ambiguous. 'I thought it would please you.'

'Please me?' he repeated absently. Then, 'Yes. Of course.'

'Then I am . . . content.' She spread her fan and started to move away. 'I must go. He is waiting.'

His Grace said nothing but let her go. He did not glance after her but stood quite still, staring down at his hands; and in his eyes was a mixture of mockery and bitter desolation.

Repercussions

It seemed to Vanessa that the days following the announcement of her betrothal passed in an enshrouding mist through which she received the felicitations of her friends with a polite smile and a sense of utter detachment. It had been agreed that the wedding should take place three weeks after the ball given by Roderick's mama to mark their engagement and, though aware that such haste was as unseemly as it was unusual, Vanessa was eager to put an end to the strain under which she was living. Fear of betraying herself made every moment in Lyndhurst's company one fraught with pitfalls; and yet, if he noticed her constraint, he made no remark upon it, seeming content to let her avoid him. Vanessa could only assume him happy to be relieved of his charge; and when, on the day after the Anstey ball, he stated his intention of departing forthwith for Bath, she was sure of it.

His servants saw him go with a sigh of relief since, in the last few days, his tongue had achieved an edge like a razor which caused Lord Nicholas to remark that, after Francis' uncustomary benevolence of the past few weeks, the poor fellow was bound to suffer a chronic relapse.

Amidst the hectic arrangements for her wedding, Vanessa found Nicholas her sole comfort for he took to haunting the house and considerably helped to lighten her spirits. Quick to notice her unusually subdued manner, he observed wickedly that Anstey was enough to depress anyone and that, in his opinion, Vanessa was out of her mind to marry a man with no sense of humour. Vanessa smiled wryly but did not take his lordship into her confidence.

A week after the Anstey ball, Lady Blanche held a rout party and, having been escorted to Great Jermyn Street by Nicholas, it was to him that Vanessa returned after completing the first dance with her betrothed.

'Enough is as good as a feast, eh?' he asked sympathetically.

'Don't be rude, Nick,' she replied, without heat. 'Roderick is a sensible man with a well-informed mind.'

'I know. Devilish dull, too. And it ain't as though you loved him, is it?'

'Why do you say that?' asked Vanessa warily.

His lordship regarded her with a knowing eye. 'Plain as a pikestaff, m'girl. You may respect him – like him, even – but you don't love the man! If I said Francis was a cold devil with as much humanity in him as an iceberg, you'd give me a rare trimming; but if I tell you Anstey is a tedious fellow who'll bore you to death in a twelve-month, you calmly say I'm wrong. The truth is he don't inspire you to any emotion whatever. I'd give a lot to know why you're doing it – but, since you ain't going to tell me, I can only hope it don't turn out to be a terrible mistake. The fellow would drive *me* to drink!'

Lady Blanche bustled up and laid a magisterial hand on her brother's arm. 'Nicky, what are you doing? You know I depended on you to help entertain.'

'Not me! I see the Brandon chit's here tonight and I've no mind to fall into her clutches. I'm for the card-room.'

Vanessa glanced across the room to see Sophy, most surprisingly, in conversation with Mr Anstey.

Blanche regarded Nicholas with disapproval. 'You had much better dance,' she argued. 'I have at least three young ladies without partners.'

'Oh, *have* you? And all of 'em butter-toothed or squinty, I'll be bound!'

'Certainly not,' said Blanche primly. 'They are all charming girls.'

'Then they'll have no difficulty finding partners without the

177

aid of yours truly,' retorted her brother. And he walked obstinately away.

Lady Blanche looked after him, pouting. 'He is quite impossible – and monstrously disobliging. I daresay he has never been the least use to anyone.'

Vanessa smiled. 'He was very helpful to Mr Vaughan.'

'Oh – that.' Blanche shrugged. 'Well, it was just like him, after all. He doubtless enjoyed fooling Randolph. The story has got about, by the way. Any number of people have spoken of it to me.'

'That's a pity,' frowned Vanessa. 'And if it's Lord Randolph who has let it out, he should beware in case his own part becomes kown. I doubt if he would enjoy that!'

Blanche's eyes widened. 'You don't like Randolph?'

'No. Not at all,' replied Vanessa coolly.

Her ladyship squeezed her hand. 'No more do I. He is like Francis – yet very unlike. For sure, he isn't half so amusing.'

'Nor half so honest. In fact, he is scarcely like him at all,' rejoined Vanessa, who found herself disliking the turn the conversation had taken. 'I pray you will excuse me – I am promised to Sir Gareth for the gavotte.' And she walked away, leaving her ladyship prey to interesting speculation.

Mistress Brandon had approached Mr Anstey solely with the intention of offering her congratulations in such a dignified way as would leave him in no doubt as to her indifference to the event. This had seemed very simple when she rehearsed in the privacy of her bedchamber but, by the time she had witnessed his progress in the minuet with Vanessa, she was feeling far less composed.

'Good evening, Mr Anstey,' she said, curtsying. 'You must allow me to felicitate you on your betrothal. I wish you *very* happy.' This speech was beautifully delivered and Sophy was pardonably pleased with it.

Mr Anstey bowed, his face very stern. 'I thank you, madam. I believe that Mistress Tremaine and I will deal admirably together.'

'Yes, indeed! She is so charming that one can scarcely be

surprised that your affections could be so swiftly transferred. It's comforting to know you are not wearing the willow for me.'

Mr Anstey looked at her sharply. 'As to that, you left me in so little doubt as to the nature of your own feelings that the entertaining of further hopes seemed entirely without point.' Sophy's eyes flew to meet his, an unspoken question in them. Mr Anstey declined to answer it. 'And what of you, Mistress Brandon? May we expect to hear shortly of your own betrothal – to Lord Nicholas, perhaps?'

Rather shaken, Sophy forgot her role and said truthfully, 'You may not. I don't care a fig for him – nor he for me.'

'Oh? You appear to have been long in discovering it.'

'No. It never – I was – it was never serious.'

'I see. And whose heart will you choose to play with next, I wonder?' he enquired bitterly. 'Though I'll admit that his lordship seems to have emerged unscathed from your toils.'

She gasped, hardly able to believe that this cold, rather frightening stranger was her own Roderick with whom she had grown up. 'I . . . you are unkind.'

'If I am, madam, it was you who taught me how,' he retorted.

The shock of this remark stopped her breath for a moment and then, bravely acknowledging the justice of it, she inclined her head. 'I know and . . . I am sorry. But it can't matter to you, can it? Your betrothal shows how little you cared for me.'

'You think so?'

Mr Anstey was prey to conflicting emotions. The die was already cast and his initial sense of joyful optimism was swiftly tempered by irritation at the thought that, even if Sophy really did love him, she had wantonly destroyed their happiness.

'For whatever satisfaction it may be to you,' he said grimly, 'the truth of the matter is that Mistress Tremaine and I have decided on a marriage of convenience. I need hardly ask, however, that you will not repeat it. I consider myself most fortunate and see no need for the world to be privy to our reasons.'

Sophy had grown rather pale. 'Then . . . you don't love her?'

179

'I do not. But in time I hope my respect and liking may ripen into that happy state.'

'Oh.' A tear trembled on her lashes and she brushed it aside with a defiant gesture. 'Then did you . . . were you – '

'In love with you? Yes, Mistress Brandon, I was,' he replied angrily. 'But you knew that – and cared very little for it! I am but a dull, cold fellow whom you are happy to be free of.'

She turned away and whispered. 'I didn't mean it. I was young and silly and I thought – I thought that I should prefer you to be . . . romantic . . . and jealous.' Mr Anstey ground his teeth. 'I'm sorry.' The dark head drooped. 'It was foolish of me. Can . . . can you forgive me?'

His hurt wrath suddenly deserted him and he took her hand. 'Oh, Sophy – Sophy, my dear! If I forgave you a thousand times it could make no difference. It's too late.'

Quicksands moved beneath Sophy's feet. 'No! No, it can't be! Vanessa is kind and she'll understand. She – '

He shook his head. 'It's you who doesn't understand, Sophy. I daresay Vanessa would release me from our engagement – but I cannot ask it of her.'

'Why not?' came the anguished question.

'My dear, I am not at liberty to explain it all to you. But I am not, I hope, so dishonourable as to go back on my word and so expose her to the unpleasant gossip which would result from it.'

'But in these circumstances – ?'

'Particularly in these circumstances, Sophy. The suggestion was mine and I persuaded her to it. I cannot now excuse myself. I wish you had been open with me before but it's done now and no good can come of whining.' He gazed at her firmly but with a certain tenderness. 'You must try to understand. There is no choice.'

From her chair at the edge of the ballroom, Lady Alicia Marchant beckoned imperiously to Vanessa who smiled and was prompt in obeying the summons.

'My lady – it seems an age since I last saw you.'

'It's a month or more. I've been visiting my youngest granddaughter – she's just given Knightley an heir,' replied

Lady Alicia. 'But that ain't what I wanted to say to you. Sit down. I want to know the truth of this nonsense I hear about you and young Anstey. Do I understand you're betrothed to him?'

Having a profound respect for her ladyship's intelligence, Vanessa was careful to keep her tone light.

'I am indeed. It was announced a week ago.'

'Well I hope you don't expect me to felicitate you,' said my lady sharply. 'Utter foolishness! What made you do it?'

Vanessa smiled. 'It's a good match, I believe – and I must marry someone, after all.'

Her ladyship snorted in disgust. 'Don't act like the fool you're not! If I read you aright, it would take more than the prospect of wealth and position to tempt you to marriage – and don't try to flummery me with talk of love for I shan't believe it!'

'Then perhaps I had best remain silent.'

'Ha! Well that's more like you, at all events. Anstey does well for himself. They tell me the wedding is in two weeks. What's your hurry? One would think the devil were at your heels!' She regarded the girl with a knowing eye and watched a telltale flush stain her cheeks. 'So *that's* it – I thought as much! You've discovered yourself in love with Francis – no, don't trouble to deny it! But why that needs must make you rush headlong into matrimony with the first man who offers, I don't know. Don't you *want* to be Duchess of Lyndhurst?'

Vanessa's insides seemed to recoil. 'I think you must be – teasing me, madam. There can be no possibility of such a thing. I had not thought of it.'

'That's no answer,' came the acid reply. 'Well?'

Vanessa toyed with her fan, tracing it's pattern with one slender finger. When she spoke her voice was very low. 'There is nothing I want more.'

Her ladyship nodded in brisk satisfaction. 'Then where is your patience, child? All you had to do was wait – so why this silly engagement?'

'You don't understand,' said Vanessa wearily. 'I am almost sure he contemplates a marriage with Madam Gwynne. I am just his ward . . . and it's his desire that I wed Mr Anstey.'

My lady frowned. 'I never heard such a farrago of nonsense! Who told you this rubbish?'

'Any number of people. And he himself admitted he found Lydia Gwynne beautiful and witty – and said he'd be pleased if I accepted Mr Anstey,' replied Vanessa flatly.

'And you believed him? I thought you had more sense.'

'What else am I to believe? It's true he has been good to me but he's never give any indication that he thinks of me in any way other than as his ward.'

Lady Alicia tapped her fan against her knee. 'Where is he?'

'In Bath. He left the day after our betrothal was announced.'

'Did he so? Drat the boy!' She turned back to Vanessa and fixed her with a sharp stare. 'I begin to think I should have stayed in town. Unless I'm mistaken, Francis is head over ears in love with you – and it's my belief there's no truth in this talk of Lydia Gwynne. As to Anstey – I don't know. It may be that Francis thinks you in love with him, though one would suppose him to know better. But remember this: he's complicated, this man you've lost your heart to and in such a case, love ain't enough. Think about it.'

She walked away leaving Vanessa torn between the undeniable lure of budding hope and that part of her nature which forced her to face things realistically. She gazed around the room, suddenly aware of its noise and artificial brilliance and, out of the blue, an idea was born. Without further ado, she went in search of Lord Nicholas and, finding him in the card-room, said, 'Nick, I want to go to Lyndhurst. Will you take me there?'

Amidst a legion of well-wishers, there were two who regarded Vanessa's betrothal with acute displeasure. Lady Henley received the tidings firstly with a sense of deep chagrin and then, when her hopes that Mrs Anstey might look disfavourably on the alliance were dashed, with implacable resentment.

Her nature was such that she had to speak of her grievance and thus nourish its growth and in this his Grace was not spared for she exhumed the forgotten, twenty-year-old tale of a callow youth's first love and its ridiculous conclusion. This enjoyed some measure of success for Lyndhurst was a man whom many either feared or disliked but her ladyship found few inclined to listen to her slander of Vanessa. The world indeed began to talk and then to laugh – but not at Mistress Tremaine.

The other ill-disposed personage was, of course, Mr Wade. His rage on first hearing of his cousin's betrothal was extreme in its ferocity. He called down a plague of curses on Mr Anstey, Lyndhurst and on the masked gentleman whom he had discovered to be the Honourable Charles Maynard. Most of all, he entertained a series of vicious and satisfying thoughts of what he would do if he were ever fortunate enough to lay his hands on Vanessa; and when the first blaze of fury had diminished, it was these very thoughts that brought a new turn to his calculating mind.

He began by engaging the services of a sly but plausible rogue by the name of Hick whom he set to watch the comings and goings at Lyndhurst House and, if possible, to ingratiate himself with one of the maidservants. This measure bore immediate fruit with the tidings that the Duke had left for Bath with the intention of remaining there until the wedding. Joseph rubbed his hands together and paid his hireling almost cheerfully, but the following days passed with slow uneventfulness. Mr Wade's frown deepened along with his impatience. And then, at the end of a week. Hick informed him that Mistress Tremaine had that morning departed quite suddenly for Lyndhurst, accompanied only by her maid and Lord Nicholas Courtenay.

It was the moment for which Joseph had waited. Jubilantly, he paid off Hick and sat down to lay his plans. Then he went cheerily to Grosvenor Square and sought out Carlton Henley.

Of Valour and Villainy

Rain beat incessantly against the windows and although it was early in the afternoon the light was almost gone. Pausing in his occupation of casting dice, right hand against left, Lord Nicholas Courtenay looked gloomily out across the stone terrace awash with puddles and the vivid green of the sodden lawn and then turned back to the dice with something less than his usual good humour. Even in the finest weather he could not be said to love the country but in this steady downpour he felt the stirrings of a positive resentment. Worse still, Vanessa was passing the time at the harpsichord with airs by Gluck and Handel. It was more than Nicholas thought a man should have to bear.

'Plague take it, can't you play something more cheerful?'

The doleful melody ceased abruptly. 'No,' said Vanessa flatly. 'I don't *feel* cheerful.'

'No more do I. But those dirges don't make me feel any better.'

She laughed wryly and got up. 'I suppose not. I'm sorry, Nick – I shouldn't have dragged you here. But there's no need for you to stay, you know. I'll only depress you.'

Nicholas' ill temper deserted him and he smiled ruefully. 'Well, it's true you're devilish quiet but that ain't it. It's this cursed rain. I need a good gallop to shake out the fidgets but I've no business taking it out on you.'

Vanessa joined him at the window and gazed out mournfully. 'It would be nice to ride,' she agreed, sighing. 'Tomorrow, perhaps. It must stop by then.'

184

'Belike Noah thought the same! In the meantime, do you play piquet? Dicing against oneself ain't the most enlivening pastime I know, and it strikes me you need some diversion yourself.'

Vanessa stood on tiptoe to plant a kiss on his cheek. 'Yes. Thank you.'

Laughing, his lordship put his arm round her waist and gave her a quick hug. 'Sixpence a rubber – or shall we live dangerously and make it a shilling?'

His preference being for dice, Lord Nicholas was an indifferent card-player and so it was, by dinnertime, that Vanessa found herself several shillings to the good. Nick eyed her with misgiving.

'Cleaned out – and by a chit of a girl! Who taught you?'

'Your brother.'

'*Francis?* Oh Lord!' He leaned his head upon his arms and gave way to helpless laughter. 'I should have guessed it! Small wonder you're too good for me.'

By mutual consent they forebore to change their dress for dinner but sat down to it as they were. The meal passed happily enough and, when they had finished eating, they visited the kitchen to pay their compliments to Mrs Clayton with whom it transpired Lord Nicholas was an especial favourite. Then they returned to the south parlour and debated various way of passing the evening. His lordship strongly vetoed Vanessa's suggestion that they play cards, pointing out that he was neither fool enough nor rich enough to be fleeced twice in one day. 'In fact,' he concluded firmly, 'I'd as soon read a book!'

'Well, that would be no bad thing.' She crossed to a small bookcase and, pulling out a volume at random, began to read.

> '"*Worthy Wytys in all this Werd Wyde*
> *Be Wylde Wode Wonys and every Weye-went*
> *Precyous Prinse, Preckyd in Pride*
> *Thorwe this Propyr Pleyn Place in Pes be bent!*"'

She stopped to grin at Nicholas' patent revulsion. 'Well? What do you think?'

'I think,' replied his lordship in a tone of utter disgust, 'that the fellow who wrote that stuff ought to be shot.'

Vanessa gave a gurgle of laughter. 'It's a bit late for that. He's already dead.'

'Is he? Well that,' came the unequivocal reply, 'is the best news I've heard today. And, if you take my advice, you'll use his rotten verses to stoke the fire.'

The following day dawned overcast but dry. Eager to ride, Lord Nicholas tried to persuade Vanessa to set off with him directly after breakfast but, as she insisted on first visiting the garden to seek out Bates and then going to the lodge with a basket of tempting morsels for the gatekeeper's wife, he was forced to set off alone and agreed to meet her in the vicinity of the Padgetts' cottage.

Vanessa spent a pleasant hour with Bates, delivered her delicacies at the lodge and then picked her way down the treacherously muddy lane on her mare Sheba. She expected to find Nicholas already waiting where the lane joined the road to the village but when she got there she saw no sign of him. Instead, she was mildly surprised to see a travelling carriage and four horses drawn up at the side of the road.

No premonition warned of impending danger and Vanessa rode serenely on. As she drew level with the equipage, the door opened and her eyes widened and then grew dark with anger as her cousin Joseph stepped down from it.

'*You!*' she said, in accents of loathing.

'Yes, my dear Vanessa. *I!*' he replied, smiling. 'It seems that luck favours me this round. I hardly expected to encounter you so soon.'

'Oh Lord – not again!' said Vanessa in exasperation. 'Need you pursue me even here?' And, gathering her reins, she urged Sheba on.

Mr Wade seized her bridle and gave it a vicious tug. Vanessa replied by striking out furiously with her crop and left a deep wheal on his cheek. Swearing, Joseph caught the crop in his free hand and, wrenching it from her, hurled it into the hedge. Then, grasping her arm above the elbow, he dragged her out of the saddle.

Stumbling heavily, Vanessa landed on the road, one foot tangled in the trailing folds of her habit. But she recovered quickly and in one fluid movement ground her heel upon his instep whilst tearing herself from his momentarily loosened hold. She snatched up her skirts and, turning to run, saw a familiar blue-coated figure approaching across the fields.

'*Nick!* Nick – help me!' she cried.

Hardly had the words left her lips when she was seized from behind. A heavy hand clamped down over her mouth and dragged her back towards the coach. Savagely, she dug her teeth into it and, wrenching her head round, managed to call again to Nicholas.

On hearing that first cry, his lordship had looked up, startled, and, over the low hedge, was just able to see Vanessa struggling frantically in the grip of one who was a total stranger to him. 'Hell and devil confound it!' he swore, hurriedly setting spurs to his horse and charging across the meadow to clear the hedge with feet to spare.

Mr Wade, engaged in forcing Vanessa to the carriage, perceived the unexpected arrival of his lordship with an oath and a swift order to his hitherto unseen accomplice. 'Bestir yourself, man! *Do* something!'

Blue eyes blazing, Lord Nicholas had flung himself from the saddle and was storming down upon them.

Carlton Henley leaned out of the carriage window, stupefaction yielding to fright. And before anyone had the remotest idea of his intention, he pulled a small, gold-mounted pistol from his pocket, aimed and fired it. The report made Vanessa cease her struggles and gaze horrified at Nicholas who had dropped abruptly to his knees, one hand pressed to his shoulder where an ominous red stain was already growing.

'You damned fool!' raged Mr Wade. 'Hurry! Help me get her into the chaise. We've got to get moving.'

Together they bundled Vanessa roughly into the coach and were moving before the door had closed. Still kneeling in the road, fingers clamped to the burning, stabbing agony that was his shoulder, Lord Nicholas watched them go. 'Burn it, blister

187

it and rot it!' he gasped savagely. 'What the hell am I going to do?'

There seeming little point in aught else, Vanessa leaned back in her seat and reserved her strength for a time when it might be of some use. She glanced contemptuously at her companions and by dint of rigid control managed to keep her voice light as she said derisively, 'Surely you don't imagine that you will get away with this?'

'But I do,' replied Joseph smoothly. 'Take it all in all, we have done remarkably well so far.'

'Oh remarkably,' she agreed, ironically. 'No doubt the shooting of Lord Nicholas was an integral part of your plan.'

His expression darkened and Carlton shifted uncomfortably in his seat. Tilting her chin, Vanessa rested her head against the upholstered squabs. 'No? Well, you should be praying he isn't badly hurt. For if he is you are dead men.' Carlton paled and glanced nervously at Mr Wade. Vanessa's smile held a confidence she was far from feeling. 'Have your forgotten, *dear* Joseph, how closely you courted death once before? His Grace nearly strangled him, Lord Henley – and all for a kiss. Did my cousin neglect to mention it?'

'Be silent, damn you!' snarled Mr Wade. Vanessa merely raised her brows a little and said chidingly, 'I think you should have told him, you know.' Carlton thought so too and he swallowed uneasily.

Mr Wade snorted irritably. 'Oh calm yourself, man! There's nothing to send you into a panic. Lyndhurst is in Bath, remember, and there's no way he can overtake us in time.'

Vanessa's heart sank. It was plainly useless to try intimidating them with threats of his Grace's vengeance. She got a grip of her failing courage and began to wonder what else she might do. She recognised that the most important thing was to keep her head and, with this in mind, she said, 'Why are you doing this, Joseph? If you hope to force Lyndhurst to pay for my safe return, I fear you are doomed to disappointment. I imagine he will see you damned first.'

Mr Wade smiled. 'But I have no such intention, dear cousin. I assure you the end I have in view is a good deal more certain to produce results.'

'Indeed? And may I ask what it is?'

'Why, certainly, my dear. I plan to marry you.'

Her eyes opened very wide and then she laughed insultingly. 'Then you are sadly optimistic. I shall never marry you.'

His expression did not alter but the pale eyes travelled appraisingly over her. 'Oh I think you will. In the end.'

Something in his tone sent a shiver of apprehension down her spine and nameless terrors crowded suddenly close. 'I doubt it,' she replied with apparent calm. 'But to what do I owe this somewhat dubious honour? I don't somehow see you as Paris to my Helen.'

'Hardly.' He paused and sat rhythmically rubbing his hands. 'You never consulted Culver about your mother's will, did you?'

'You must know that I did not.'

'I do, of course, and your ignorance has been of inestimable value to me. It was convenient that no one suspected what an eligible *partie* you are.'

Vanessa frowned. 'What are you talking about?'

Mr Wade smiled thinly and his hands resumed their contortions. 'She left you a set of emeralds, my dear. Ah, that surprises you, doesn't it? I thought it might.'

It certainly did and for a full minute Vanessa was inclined to deny its possibility. 'I don't understand,' she said at last. 'How could Mama own such things?'

'That is not important. She never wore the stones and locked them in the vaults of the bank in Truro. They were left to you – but only on the occasion of your marriage.'

Vanessa was quick to perceive the flaw in this arrangement. 'But that's silly! How could Mama be sure I *would* marry? And what happens to the emeralds if I don't?'

'That is also unimportant. On the day of your marriage they become yours – absolutely. And, as your husband, I shall have the right to dispose of your property in any way I choose.'

'I see.' Her eyes rested on him with soul-hacking contempt. 'I

189

always knew you were despicable, Joseph, but I never till now realised that you have the mind and morals of gutter-scum.'

His reply was to lean forward and strike her, calmly and forcibly, with the back of his hand. Bells rang in Vanessa's head but she managed a mocking smile. 'You won't subdue me that way,' she taunted.

'Perhaps not, cousin. But there are others – many others.'

Carlton giggled and again Vanessa felt that prickle of fear. She wondered how long she could feign indifference for already she was forced to keep her fingers clasped tightly together so her captors might not see how they trembled.

'You are so crude,' she sighed. 'I imagine his Grace could teach you a little of how to carry out an abduction. I understand him to be an expert in such matters – which is why he will undoubtedly catch up with you sooner or later.'

Once more Carlton giggled. 'An expert, is he? Well he needs to be since his address don't serve to make his women go to him willingly. Haven't you heard about him and Hetty Wentworth?'

Vanessa regarded him disinterestedly. 'No. Nor do I wish to.'

'You must learn to mind your manners,' said Mr Wade, gently onimous. 'I find them sadly lacking.'

'Do you? I suit them to my company,' she retorted.

For an instant she wondered if he would hit her again but he merely threw himself into his corner and Carlton, determined not to miss an opportunity of performing before a captive audience, embarked on his tale.

'It was while the old Duke was alive – some twenty years ago. Courtenay was still Marquis of Sulgrave then and new on the town.' Vanessa's heart gave a little lurch and she started to listen attentively. 'He fell in love with Lady Henrietta Wentworth – wife to old George Wentworth. They say she was the loveliest woman in London and with a wit to match her face.'

'How old was she?' asked Vanessa, deceptively casual.

'Eh? Oh, twenty-six or so. Well, Courtenay made himself the talk of London. He followed her everywhere, haunted her house, never danced unless it was with her and eventually asked her to run off with him. Of course, everyone knew she was only amusing herself – probably thought he needed a lesson. At all events, she told her husband the whole story. He passed it on to Courtenay's father and between 'em it was fixed up that Wentworth should issue his challenge. They met and half the men in town turned up to see the fun – it's even rumoured that Lady Hetty watched secretly from within a closed carriage. Even the old Duke was there. Wentworth was a devilish fine swordsman by all accounts. He played with Courtenay – made a complete fool of him – and, when it was over, the Duke said, "Your manner of dalliance and your fencing are likewise lacking in finesse. Pray see that you mend them." Then he went off with the rest of them to breakfast.'

Looking down at her clasped hands, Vanessa said nothing. With disgusted and bitter anger, she reflected that it was not difficult to see how Francis Courtenay's nature had been warped into suppression. Between them, the Wentworths and the late Duke had blighted whatever warmth and trust he had possessed and left him maimed and incomplete. She looked across at Carlton and said quietly, 'Thank you. I'm in your debt.'

Taken aback, he gazed at her blankly and then glanced questioningly at Mr Wade who shrugged but made no reply.

Vanessa leaned back in her seat and stared through the window. Resolutely dismissing his Grace from her mind, she pondered the various ways in which she might slow down their progress. Then an idea presented itself and, closing her eyes, she groaned faintly.

'I rather think,' she announced weakly, 'that I'm going to be sick.'

In Which History is seen to Repeat Itself

'Good God! What happened to you?'

The Honourable Charles Maynard, having received an urgent but mysterious summons to Lyndhurst, stared down at the sofa where Nicholas, surrounded by bowls of reddened water and bloodstained cloths was stripped to the waist and engaged in pressing a thick pad to his wounded shoulder. His face was alarmingly pale and he grimaced expressively as he tried to sit up.

'Happened? I've been shot, damn it! And Vanessa's been kidnapped!'

Charles stiffened. 'By whom?'

Nicholas gave a short laugh and winced. 'By Carlton Henley.'

'*Henley?* You're sure?'

'Well I'm damned sure he shot me,' replied Nicholas irascibly, 'but it was the other villain who had his filthy hands on Vanessa and let him only wait till I catch up with him! I'll – '

'That's the last thing he's likely to do,' interrupted Charles drily. 'Did you recognise him?'

'No.' He frowned fretfully. 'Deuce take this shoulder of mine – it hurts like Hades! I can't go after 'em and Francis is in Bath, rot him!'

'So you want me to go? Very well. Which road did they take?'

'Through the village. After that I haven't a clue.'

'South, then . . . or west. Not to London, certainly.' Charles looked searchingly at Nicholas. 'Have you sent for old Harvey? That bullet needs to come out as soon as possible.'

'He'll be on his way. But it's Vanessa I'm worried about. She – ' He broke off, hearing sounds of arrival and the next moment the doors opened to reveal his Grace of Lyndhurst. Nicholas gaped and Charles coloured with embarrassment at being caught in what felt like *flagrante delicto*.

The Duke's brows rose slightly but he walked forward in his usual manner and said calmly, 'Dear me! I appear to have missed some excitement. How very distressing.' He bowed to Mr Maynard. 'My dear Charles ... what an unexpected honour. Well, Nicholas ... how did it happen? And where, by the way, is Vanessa?'

Nick sank back, eyes closed. 'Oh Lord! You don't know then?'

'I do not. I am but now arrived from Bath and here I find Bates occupying my hallway, armed with a pitchfork and you bleeding copiously in my drawing-room. So far I have received no word of explanation and am fast losing patience.'

The blue eyes opened again. 'Then why *did* you come?'

'I came, Nicholas, because I received a largely unintelligible missive from Lilian – from which I understood her to believe that you had eloped with my ward,' replied his Grace with biting rapidity. 'I need hardly say that I placed no reliance on her views but came to see why Vanessa is not where she should be.'

At this point, Mr Maynard decided that it was time to intervene. He turned to Lyndhurst. 'Mistess Vanessa has been abducted and Nick was shot trying to prevent it.'

The heavy lids were suddenly raised and Lyndhurst drew a swift, harsh breath. Then, 'Who?' he asked.

'Carlton Henley and one other.' It was Charles who answered.

The Duke turned away a little, staring down at his clasped hands. His face showed none of the more dramatic signs of emotion and, save for the rigidly controlled breathing, he might have been considering some move at chess. Then, in a voice not quite his own, he said, 'Wade. I should have guessed.'

'The blue domino!' said Charles, suddenly understanding. 'Her cousin, I believe?'

'What cousin? And why has he run off with her?' Nicholas was becoming feverishly flushed.

His Grace crossed to lay a hand on his good shoulder. 'Easy, child. It is this. Sir Thomas Tremaine's estate was entailed to the male heirs and so was inherited by Vanessa's cousin, Joseph Wade. But the tin mine is failing, the land produces no profit and Wade cannot afford such a millstone. But he has discovered the precise nature of Vanessa's personal legacy from her mother. Elizabeth Tremaine was born a Castellan. An only child, she married Tremaine against her father's wishes and he swore never to see her again. On his deathbed, he repented of his decision and made amends in the only way he knew. He bequeathed her the pride of his house – the Castellan emeralds.'

Charles' eyes widened. 'But they're quite famous! I never saw them myself but I remember my father saying that, as a set, they were past price.'

His Grace nodded. 'And although she does not know it, they are left to Vanessa – but only on the day of her marriage. Otherwise they revert to the Castellan family. A singularly foolish arrangement, as you will doubtless perceive.'

'So this Wade will force her to the altar,' asked Nicholas.

'He will try.'

'If Vanessa is ignorant of this, how did you discover it?' enquired Charles, thoughtfully.

'Certain things aroused my suspicions so I went to Truro last month to consult Tremaine's man-of-law.' Uncharacteristically, he hesitated and then concluded briskly. 'And now, if you are satisfied, I will set off.'

'Aye,' approved Nicholas. 'I never thought I'd be glad to see you, Francis – but the thought of Vanessa in the hands of those two bastards curdles my blood – what's left of it. But they've over two hours' start and we don't know where they are going.'

His Grace picked up his gloves. 'They are going to Cornwall,' he said, moving towards the door. 'Just one more thing, Nicholas . . . which of them shot you?'

'Henley – and I'll see he regrets it, too!'

'I think not,' purred Lyndhurst, subtly menacing. 'You see . . . I am before you in the lists.'

He laid his hand on the catch but, before he could lift it, Mr Maynard called after him. 'One moment. There are two of them so it seems you could perhaps use a second. I should like to offer my services.'

Silence, interminable and suffocating, filled the room as cool blue eyes met faintly incredulous topaz ones. Then Lyndhurst bowed.

'You are . . . generous. Shall we go?'

'Aye – do,' urged Nicholas. 'You'll never catch 'em else.'

His Grace smiled, but not pleasantly. 'Trust me, child. I shall overtake them – with luck, tonight. And when I do . . .' The hard mouth tightened and the smile became graceless with malice. 'And when I do, it will be well for them if they have not harmed her. Otherwise . . . I believe I may well kill them.'

Over the fields they went, towards the road leading to the west and, though dull and cool, the day mercifully remained dry for the going was soft enough from the previous day's rain. Charles' mare, Dolly, was fresh and eager and he was content to let her have her head but his Grace's long-tailed grey was restive and Lyndhurst had to check his pace until, eventually, Sultan matched his stride with Dolly's.

On reaching the far side of the village, they reined in and proceeded at a canter for a little way.

'I think we must follow the road,' said Lyndhurst. 'It's safe to assume they will take the most direct route and with all possible speed but some mishap may force them to stop – or Vanessa may do so.' He gave the ghost of a smile. 'She is a very resourceful child.'

'So I understand.'

The smile faded. 'They will undoubtedly put up for the night . . . it grows dark before five . . . yes . . . somewhere between Shaftesbury and Sherborne, I should think.'

Charles calculated rapidly and nodded his agreement. 'If

195

they travel for five hours, we might do it in three. All things being equal, we should come up with them at about six.'

'With luck, yes.'

Again they increased their speed. Once they caught and overtook the lumbering mailcoach. Lyndhurst scarcely saw it, but aware of the gruelling test ahead, slackened his pace and forced Sultan to a trot. Charles did likewise and so they went on in silence for perhaps another half-hour.

Then away again, flying down the road in swift, easy strides; a sedate trot through Salisbury, then on to Wilton. The miles rushed by but the Duke was conscious of every passing second for in another hour it would be dark and then, or soon after, the coach would stop. He was vaguely surprised to discover within himself a tremor of fear and doubt; yet he could not escape the sardonic reflection that this was history repeating itself with twisted vengeance. Only the hand of Nemesis could devise a plot so cunning that it sent him riding *ventre à terre* in an effort to save his ward from the fate he had once planned for the lady who was now his companion's wife. The situation was undeniably piquant and he wondered why he was unable to derive more amusement from it. Dimly, he heard Charles call to him to slow down and, with an effort, forced himself to do so.

'*Nihil esse grate animo honestius*. This is ironic, don't you think?' he asked with a touch of mordant humour. 'Why did you come?' said Lyndhurst.

Charles shrugged. 'Not for your sake.'

His Grace smiled crookedly. 'I see. Nevertheless, I am grateful. I – she is . . . dear to me.'

'Is she? You will forgive my scepticism, I hope?'

A slight flush stained Lyndhurst's cheek. 'Naturally. Can Apollyon do aught else? One might argue, of course, that though I indulge in this particular melodrama myself from time to time, my motives are by far the purer . . . but, on the other hand, my experience and versatility are undeniably superior. No. I doubt my equal exists this side of Hades. And you would be surprised to know what a comforting thought I find that – just at present.'

Charles was surprised, less by the sentiment than by the note of stark bitterness in the smooth voice. He was inescapably reminded of his own ride to Lyndhurst on a similar errand and saw the wisdom of postponing judgement for a more suitable occasion. 'The horses are rested,' he said briefly. 'Let us on!'

All too fast, the cloud-hidden sun sank and the light began to fade. By the time Shaftesbury was reached the darkness was almost complete and the Duke's mask of calm impassivity was beginning to crumble. It was, of course, unlikely that Mr Wade would elect to spend the night less than three hours' ride from Lyndhurst but it was equally possible that some accident might have forced his hand. At the first inn they drew a blank but at the Crown they were more fortunate. The landlord was able to tell them that the coach they sought had left little more than an hour since.

Further enquiry elicited the information that the young lady had seemed quite well at first but, on the party's preparing to quit the inn, had succumbed to a sudden, deep swoon which had delayed their departure by some fifteen minutes and from which it had taken quantities of burnt feathers to revive her.

Charles expected these tidings to alarm his Grace but, instead, as they mounted their horses and left the town behind them, he discovered that the Duke was actually laughing.

'Did I not say that she had infinite resource?' came the soft voice through the darkness.

'I take it that you don't believe in that "sudden swoon", then?'

'Hardly. But I confess that I should like to have seen her withstanding the feathers.'

They cantered on for perhaps another mile before breaking into a gallop. The horses were tiring now and the darkness slowed them still further for the road was badly pitted. Only short bursts of speed were possible if necessity decreed that they must go as far as Sherborne and beyond that, his Grace dared not think.

In Henstridge they gave the horses a well-earned rest while they combed the hostelries for signs of the fugitives. It was half-past five and the Duke could not rid himself of the thought that Wade might have deemed it advisable to leave the main

197

road and put up for the night at some remote tavern. Hope lay in the facts that this could only lose them time and that, believing him in Bath, they would probably consider themselves safe from pursuit.

He was not reassured when they found no trace of their quarry but he pinned his faith on Sherborne and on they went. Only five more miles but the horses were nearly spent. Their sides heaved pantingly and sweat rolled from their skin. Lyndhurst and Charles dismounted and walked them for perhaps half an hour. Then up again and one last spurt till the lights of the town were in sight. It was half-past six.

With the gathering dusk Vanessa's self-possession had begun to desert her. Her cousin had fallen asleep soon after their brief halt at Shaftesbury but Carlton had remained wakeful and kept up a flow of vapid conversation from which she had learned that they planned to sleep only in turn. It was then that her courage began to fail and she realised at last in exactly what danger she stood.

They drove into Sherborne at half-past five and Carlton duly awoke Mr Wade to inform him of these facts. Some minutes later they drew up outside a small inn on the furthermost outskirts of the town and, stiffly, Vanessa allowed herself to be handed from the carriage and led inside. Mr Wade pushed her into a high-backed settle and there she stayed, watching while a grubby housemaid ineptly kindled a fire.

Tired, cold and frightened, Vanessa stretched out her hands to the pitiful blaze and tried to face the facts of her situation. The possibility of rescue was remote indeed and her chances of escape scarcely less so. The one man who could save her was far away and she must shift for herself as best she could. For it's certain that Joseph intends to ravish me, she thought, her skin crawling, and so I suppose I ought to look for something to use as a weapon.

By the time the landlord appeared to announce the arrival of their dinner, Vanessa had observed that the only suitable objects were the poker at her feet and a heavy brass candlestick on the table. Both of these seemed equally useless since they were too large to hide and as she took her seat at the table her eye fell upon the large and lethal-looking carving knife, the very thought of which made her shudder.

The meal was neither imaginative nor very well cooked but Mr Wade made a hearty repast while downing quantities of wine. Vanessa remained silent and concentrated on forcing herself to eat – a difficult task, since the food seemed to stick in her throat. She managed to drink a glass of wine, however, and, dreading the time when the servants would leave them alone, tried to postpone it by toying delicately with some fruit. Eventually, Mr Wade grew impatient and tersely commanded the maid to clear the board and be quick about it. With a sinking heart, Vanessa watched the dishes gradually disappear and the door close behind the girl for the last time.

Joseph smiled at her with the air of a cat who knows the mouse is all but caught and indicated the settle. 'Come and sit here,' he said. 'We've a number of things to discuss.'

'There is no point. I am content where I am.'

In two strides he was beside her and, roughly seizing her arm, dragged her to the settle and pushed her into it. 'You'll learn not to defy me, my dear.' He sat down at her side. 'It's a quality I find misplaced in my women.' Her breathing swift and shallow, Vanessa found nothing to say. Joseph nodded approvingly. 'You learn fast, cousin. That is good. As I have said, I plan to wed you. I have a licence in my pocket and the ceremony can take place as soon as you give your consent.'

'Which I never shall.'

'Oh, I think you will,' he continued silkily. 'You may give me your promise now or you may put me to the trouble of forcing you. It matters little to me which you choose.'

'No. Do as you please – but I'll never marry you.'

'Think, my dear. There are five days and nights between us and our destination. Much may happen in that time. You give me leave to do as I will. That is all very well *now* – but don't you think that tomorrow you may not regret it?' He took her chin in his hand and made her look up at him. Vanessa held herself rigid but she could not disguise the fear in her eyes. Joseph observed it, smiling. 'The night is long, cousin – and we have all of it before us. Your refusal can only hurt yourself for I swear I shall have some pleasure in my . . . persuasions.'

Very white, Vanessa wrenched herself away and darted towards the door but, before she reached the table, he had caught her. 'Let me go!' she cried, her nerves at breaking point. Joseph twisted her hands behind her to hold her trapped against him. Struggling frantically, she panted, 'His Grace will come! You dare not touch me. He – '

'He will not come. And if he did it would be too late.'

'So much the worse for you, then!'

Mr Wade merely laughed. He could see the despair in her face and it pleased him. Carefully, he imprisoned her wrists in one hand and, with the other, began to stroke her cheek with slow and deliberate intent. Vanessa shuddered and turned her face away but he grabbed a handful of her hair and dragged her back to him. Dimly, she heard Carlton giggling and then a deadly faintness assailed her as Joseph pressed his mouth to hers. She felt as though she were being sucked into some dark and suffocating pit and when he raised his head bitter fluid rose in her throat. Unsteadily, she said, 'Joseph . . . for pity's sake . . . if it's just the money let me go and you shall have it. When I marry Mr Anstey the emeralds will be mine to dispose of and I will pay you.'

He surveyed her dispassionately. Her hair was falling down her back and her eyes were like black flowers in the paleness of her face. She had never looked more appealing but he was not impressed. 'A clever notion, my dear, but I really don't think I can rely on your word. It's encouraging, however. You're plainly becoming more tractable – don't you think so, Carlton?'

'Not a doubt of it,' sniggered his friend. 'By morning, I swear she'll be an eager bride, won't you, m'dear?'

'No – never,' she whispered. But her control was in shreds and all three of them knew it.

Joseph still had her hands fast and she was quite helpless. No chance now to reach the poker or anything else. She looked, mesmerized, into the pale eyes and again he began to caress her face and then her neck. Desperately, she writhed to be free but he caught hold of her gown and the material gave with a dry, tearing sound. In the grip of terror the like of which she had never known, Vanessa fought with fresh vigour. She tried to kick him but found he was too close for it to be effective and then, once more, his mouth sought hers. She wrenched her head round, sobbing a brief, unthinking invocation.

'Oh God . . . *Francis!*'

'You are wasting your breath, cousin. He ain't likely to hear you from Bath,' sneered Mr Wade.

But even as he spoke, the impossible happened. The door was thrown open and from the threshold came a voice – soft, drawling and deadly.

'*Ring the bells backwards* . . . my cue and your mistake, Mr Wade.'

Lucifer Plays the Hero

The effect was electric. Framed in the doorway, with black hair windswept and a smile like a bane, the man they called Lucifer appeared suddenly as infernal as his name. And then, tearing herself from Joseph's slackened grip, Vanessa half ran, half stumbled across the room to fling herself against his chest.

His arms closed tight about her and his lips brushed her hair. '*Mignonne* – you knew I should come, surely?' he asked unsteadily.

'I – I thought you c-could not know.'

'I always know. Is it not my custom?'

She laughed shakily, her face still hidden against his shoulder and, over her head, death looked at Mr Wade out of bright topaz eyes.

It was Charles, entering in Lyndhurst's wake, who saw Carlton's hand sliding slyly into his pocket and, swiftly drawing his own pistol he levelled it. 'Stand!' he ordered calmly. 'And lay it gently on the table.'

Shaking, Carlton did as he was bidden and retired to the shadows while Charles picked up the pistol and dropped it into his pocket. Then he closed the door and leant nonchalantly against it.

Lyndhurst was still holding Vanessa. Gently, he took her by the shoulders and stepped back, eyes narrowing as he observed her dishevelled state. Very softly his fingers touched the bruise on her cheek as he asked, in a voice oddly unlike his own, 'They have hurt you?'

A smile trembled into being. 'A little. It's nothing.'

He smiled back, but grimly, and then turned to Charles. 'This is no place for her. There must be some other room.'

Mr Maynard nodded and gestured contemptuously at Carlton. 'Him too, I think. I doubt he'd hesitate to strike from behind.'

Vanessa looked from one to the other, suddenly tense. She grasped the Duke's arm and said flatly, 'You're going to fight him, aren't you?'

He did not reply and she shook his arm. 'You must not. There is no need.'

'I am sorry it distresses you, child, but there is every need.' His tone was firm. 'I shall be quite safe, I promise you. And you are ruining my coat.' He covered her hands with his own and detached them. 'Go now.'

She shook her head. 'I won't. If you *must* do this thing, I shall stay – as a witness. It's the custom, isn't it?'

His Grace looked at her with a mixture of helplessness and amusement.

Behind him, Charles laughed. 'She undoubtedly has a point,' he said. 'And I must own a desire to see our friend here taught a lesson.'

There was a pause and then, abruptly, Lyndhurst capitulated and began to divest himself of his coat and heavy riding boots. He tucked up his ruffled, unbuckled his scabbard and withdrew his sword from it.

Mr Wade, meanwhile, stood motionless, his colour alarmingly high and his eyes flickering from one face to another. Carlton was now a broken reed and the game, it seemed, was all but up.

His Grace rested the point of his sword on the floor and gazed mockingly at him. '"*Whoso diggeth a pit shall fall therein.*" I perceive that you wear a sword, Mr Wade. All that remains is to see if you know how to use it. I await your convenience.'

Furiously, Joseph tore off his coat and scabbard and hurled them at Carlton. 'Damn you to hell!' he said.

'Certainly,' agreed the Duke, calmly. 'On guard!'

Wade opened with a wide thrust in tierce which the Duke

parried easily and followed with a lightning riposte en quinte. Jospeh countered just in time but clumsily and the blades slithered together before he found himself disengaging over Lyndhurst's supple wrist.

From her position behind the settle whither Charles had pushed her to be out of harm's way, Vanessa watched anxiously. She had never before seen any fencing but even to her inexperienced eye there was a world of difference between her cousin's insane violence and his Grace's neat restraint. Several times she held her breath, expecting to hear the thud of Joseph's body as it fell but, by some miracle, he always managed to counter. She began to wonder why the Duke did not finish it and then a glance at his face told her. He was intent on administering punishment; and he was enjoying it.

Wade started to tire. His breath came noisily and, knowing he could not survive a long encounter, his play became more vicious. His Grace fought on seemingly tireless; a faint smile bracketed his mouth but it seemed to Mr Wade that the devil looked out of the ice-cold eyes. Lyndhurst feinted inside the arm and, as Wade sought to take advantage of what he deemed an opening, he saw his adversary's blade flash towards him in a flanconnade opposing his left hand. With a gasp, Joseph whipped up his guard and forte met foible. Hearing the Duke laugh, his rage boiled over and, with a savage twist, he disengaged so that his blade glanced down Lyndhurst's arm leaving a long gash that began to bleed steadily. Charles' brows snapped together and Vanessa gave a tiny cry, quickly checked.

'You will have to do better than that,' remarked his Grace, critically. And cold and sleek as his own steel, opened an immediate and suddenly relentless attack. The gems on the wrought-gold hilt of his sword gleamed fitfully and the light seemed to play on the jewelled arm of Lyndhurst.

Joseph's arm was aching from shoulder to wrist and his heart felt as though it would burst. In one last desperate move, he lunged ferociously in quinte. His Grace parried and riposted with a straight thrust above the other's guard. With unhesitating precision, his blade bit deep into Wade's right shoulder. Slowly, very slowly, Joseph crumpled where he stood and lay still. His Grace stood over him, leaning on his sword, his breath coming quickly. He smiled still but his eyes were hard and pitiless.

And then the door burst open and the landlord flew in.

'Out, man, out,' said Charles, taking him firmly by the arm. 'No one is dead so make haste and fetch the doctor – and some hot water and cloths.' Having got rid of mine host, he bent over Wade's body and then, seizing the tablecloth, he ripped it up to make a pad to staunch the bleeding.

Unable to wait any longer, Vanessa whisked herself from behind the settle, sparing no glance for her cousin nor even noticing that her skirts brushed his prostrate form. She saw nothing but his Grace and, though he neither moved nor spoke, his gaze met hers and it was enough. Filled with a calm, sweet expectancy, she waited for him to take her in his arms. He did not do so and, slowly, she saw his expression change to one of bitter recollection. Then the heavy lids were lowered and his countenance was enigmatic as ever.

Rising from his position beside Wade, Charles moved to the door, saying tactfully, 'I'll go and check on the horses. I doubt the ostlers here are to be relied on.'

Neither answered and he doubted they had heard him. Smiling to himself, he slipped out quietly, having quite forgotten the silent and quivering occupant of the corner chair.

Somewhat shyly, Vanessa removed the sword from the Duke's unresisting grasp and laid it on the table. Then she took his hand and led him to the settle. The door opened again to admit the landlord bearing a bowl of water and some white cloths and bandages. These Vanessa took and, setting them down beside the settle, knelt at Lyndhurst's feet and began rolling back his blood-soaked sleeve.

'It's nothing,' he protested, trying to pull away. 'A scratch – nothing more.'

Undeterred, Vanessa dipped a piece of cloth in the water and wrung it out. 'Be still,' she said placidly. 'I won't hurt you.'

His lips quivered at that but he yielded meekly to her ministrations and leant his head back to regard her between

205

half-closed lids. 'Your performance at Shaftesbury must have been impressive.'

She looked up, grimacing expressively. 'Ugh! The smell of burned feathers would raise the dead!' She began to bandage his arm. And then, keeping her eyes on her work, 'Joseph spoke of some emeralds left to me by my mother.'

'Yes, child. I know.'

Startled, she looked up. 'You do? But how?'

'My suspicions and inquisitive nature. Whilst you were busy arranging Gideon's elopement, I went to Truro to consult Mr Culver.'

'Oh! So you weren't – ' She stopped, flushing with mingled embarrassment and pleasure. 'But why didn't you tell me?'

He did not reply immediately and then said slowly, 'I meant to. But some change occurred on the evening of my return and after that . . . there seemed no opportunity.'

'Oh,' she said again, resuming her bandaging. 'And . . . today? I thought you were in Bath.'

'And I thought you were in London,' was the swift rejoinder.

Carlton, meanwhile, began to edge his way through the shadows towards the door, praying he would be unnoticed. So violent was the knocking of his heart, he half-expected them to hear it and his mouth was dry with fright. Wade was still unconscious but Carlton had no compunction in leaving him. There was nothing he could do now except preserve his own skin and there was little chance of doing so while he remained within reach of Lyndhurst. He skirted the wall till he stood beside the door and, scarcely daring to breathe, turned the knob. Only when he was out of the room did he take to his heels.

He need not have worried. It was perhaps the first time in his life that Francis Courtenay had allowed any point of importance to escape him, but just then Carlton might have danced a hornpipe across the room without provoking any undue attention.

'And what of Nick?' Vanessa asked, securing the bandage.

'In a few weeks he will be good as new. Ah yes . . . that reminds me . . .' He looked up and glanced across the room.

Catching his thought, Vanessa did the same and then exclaimed, 'Why he's gone! Now how did he manage that?'

His Grace leaned calmly back in his seat. 'No matter.'

She sighed and asked wistfully, 'Must you find him?'

'I am afraid so. I . . . er . . . promised Nicholas, you see.' His shoulders shook in soundless laughter. 'Indeed, our precious pair might have fared worse for I imagine Bates' reprisals would have been considerably less . . . civilised.'

'Bates?' she echoed blankly.

'Just so. He was on the point of giving chase brandishing a pitchfork before he was reluctantly persuaded to leave the business to me.' He paused and then said pensively, 'It's a lowering thought, but I cannot dismiss the notion that Bates holds me in very poor esteem. And having allowed Carlton to elude me, I begin to think he may have reason. I am not usually so careless.'

'Not careless at all,' replied Vanessa with an odd little smile as she raised the injured hand to her lips.

Because she was distracted by a groan from her cousin, she did not see the way the Duke froze at her gesture. Rising, she walked to Joseph's side and remarked dispassionately that he was still bleeding. No sooner had the words left her mouth than Mr Maynard came back followed closely by a small man carrying a black bag.

'Your patient, sir,' said Charles, indicating Mr Wade.

The doctor knelt and removed the makeshift pad. His eye brightened and he nodded approvingly. 'A good, clean wound,' he announced cheerfully. 'Deep – but no vital spot is touched. A very neat thrust, upon my word. Yours, sir?' He beamed at Charles who laughed and disclaimed. The little doctor glanced across the room to where his Grace was engaged in letting down his ruffles. 'Then it was you, sir?' Lyndhurst nodded distantly. 'Ah! Allow me to congratulate you. A very fine wound, sir. A very fine wound indeed! I shall have much pleasure in dressing it.'

The Duke rose and reached for his coat. 'I rejoice to hear it. Doubtless you will wish to do so upstairs.' He pulled open the door and the landlord was precipitated into the room. 'Such efficiency,' marvelled his Grace. 'Pray be so good as to assist the doctor to remove this . . . this gentleman to a bedchamber.'

With a ripple of instructions, the little doctor succeeded with the aid of mine host in raising Mr Wade from the prone to the vertical. As they were about to pass the Duke, he detained them with a movement of one white hand.

'Once again you have been undeservedly fortunate,' he told Joseph softly. 'Had you . . . harmed her, I should have killed you. As it is, I do not wish to see your face again. I trust I make myself clear?' His piercing gaze held Wade's. 'Well?'

Joseph's eyes dropped defeatedly away. 'Aye.'

'See you remember it. You may proceed, Doctor.' Lyndhurst closed the door behind then and turned to Charles. 'I must own to having mislaid Carlton.'

Mr Maynard smiled wickedly. 'Indeed? How so?'

'I'm afraid,' said Vanessa guiltily, 'that we were deep in conversation.'

'I see,' said Charles gravely.

Frowning a little, his Grace picked up a discarded cloth and began to clean the blade of his sword. 'I think that we must spend the night in this hovel,' he said haughtily. 'It is not what I would wish but I see no help for it.'

'And tomorrow we go home?' asked Vanessa. 'I want to see Nick.'

The frown deepened and he continued polishing his rapier. 'I ride to London.'

'Oh?' There was no mistaking her disappointment.

He looked up and met Charles' gaze. 'I have no right to impose on you further, but if you will escort Vanessa to Lyndhurst and arrange for her to journey on to town with her maid and baggage, I should be glad.'

Puzzled, Mr Maynard said, 'Of course.'

'Thank you,' said his Grace, bowing. 'You are very good.' He turned to Vanessa and said smoothly, 'I am desolated that I cannot go with you myself but there are pressing matters demanding my attention. I desire you will spend tomorrow night at the Court and then return to Lilian. I need hardly say that you will tell her nothing of all this?'

Vanessa smiled. 'No. We'd never hear the last of it.' She hesitated and then asked diffidently, 'And you? I shall . . . see you in London?'

His mouth grew rather grim. 'Perhaps. But you will not have time to miss me, I think. Doubtless Blanche will keep you fully occupied with her preparations.'

All the colour drained from Vanessa's face and she was suddenly very still. 'Preparations?'

He pushed the sword sharply into its sheath. 'Just so. The wedding takes place in ten days, does it not?' His tone was faintly abrasive and he forgot to drawl. Leaving her staring at him with wide, bewildered eyes, he cross to Charles and said simply, 'I owe you a great debt and it's one I doubt I can ever repay. No – let me finish. I have learned a good deal today – such as how you must have felt two years ago. On that occasion I believe I did not offer my apologies and, if it is not too late, I would wish to rectify that omission now. I most deeply regret the entire episode and hope you can come, in time, to forgive it. It is possible that I never quite understood. Now I do. That is all.'

There was a profound silence while Mr Maynard looked steadily into topaz eyes and saw an expression he had never thought to find. It was this which brought understanding and then a measure of respect. Charles' nature was not formed for the bearing of grudges and, smiling, he held out his hand. 'Gad, Francis – it's done and here's my hand on it.'

Slowly, almost hesitantly, his Grace put his own into it and their fingers gripped.

Just Revenge in a Manner Unforseen

Vanessa passed a sleepless night, pondering the inscrutable ways of her guardian. She had felt so sure he loved her – she *was* sure of it and yet he clearly expected her to go on with her marriage to Roderick Anstey. Nothing made any sense and it was with a drawn face and a heavy heart that she descended the stairs next morning.

In the parlour, Lyndhurst was already clad for his journey. He seemed eager to be off and Vanessa wondered bleakly if he would not have preferred to go without seeing her.

'You are leaving?' she asked lamely.

'As you see.' His tone was curt and his eyes frowned. 'I wish to reach London as early as possible.'

'Oh. You aren't riding?'

'No.' He found it an effort to reply. 'I shall take Wade's chaise and have hired another for you.'

'I see. And what of the horses, then?' She despised herself for finding no better way of keeping him with her, yet could not let him go. Desperately, she willed him to say something – anything; just a few words to tell her that he had not meant what he said.

'Charles will ride beside your carriage and lead Sultan.'

'Oh.' She looked down at her fingers. They could not keep still and restlessly twisted her handkerchief. His Grace watched her for a moment and then turned away to pick up his hat, silently damning the trivial miscalculations that had made him late. 'I . . . wish you wouldn't go,' she said. 'C-couldn't you travel to London with me?'

His mouth tightened. 'No. Charles will take care of you.'

'I know.' Her voice was husky. 'I know. But I want you.'

'That is . . . very proper. But you will accept my wishes and not argue. Is it not so?'

The lorn russet head drooped. 'Yes, sir.'

It was little more than a whisper and, flayed by it, he found it hard to maintain his light, even tone. 'It is well.' Crossing to her, he put his hands on her shoulders and dropped a swift kiss on her brow. 'It is best this way. Give Nicholas my love. Adieu, *mignonne*.' And he was gone.

He entered Lyndhurst House on Friday afternoon at a little before four and one glance at his expression was enough to warn Benson that he was holding his temper on a tight rein.

Having been relieved of his cloak, his Grace asked for burgundy, then disappeared into the library and, when Benson entered the room some five minutes later, he was seated in his usual chair, elbows resting on the arms, shading his eyes with his hands. Benson set the tray down and coughed discreetly. 'Shall I pour, your Grace?'

Rousing himself, Lyndhurst nodded curtly. Benson filled a glass and handed it to him. 'Will that be all, your Grace?'

'No – no. You may present my compliments to Madam Erskine and tell her to expect Mistress Vanessa at some time tomorrow. You will further inform her that she is to ensure my ward does not leave town again.'

'Yes, your Grace.'

'Instruct Alphonse that I shall require clothes for . . . a week's stay in the country and wish them placed in my chaise tomorrow morning. Strode will then take the chaise to the Three Crowns in Piccadilly where he will remain until I send for him. Lastly, I do not wish to see Madam Erskine . . . and, should anyone call, you have not seen me. That is all.'

He dined early and alone and then paid a visit to his sister whom he found putting the finishing touches to her toilet in preparation for an appearance at the Opera. In as few words as possible, he acquainted her with the facts of Vanessa's

211

abduction. Her ladyship listened with rapt attention and pronounced it exciting and romantic. His Grace did not share her raptures. Instead, he went on, in a tone devoid of expression, to explain that since he would not be remaining in town, he wished her to finalise all arrangements for the wedding. Blanche pouted a little at this and demanded to know if he would return in time to give the bride away. She did not see the little tremor which crossed his face but was surprised by the coldness with which he replied.

'You may presume it to be unlikely but I will advise you of my decision nearer the time.'

'Nearer the time?' she echoed crossly. 'Lud, Francis! The wedding's a week tomorrow. And who is to do it if you don't?'

'Ask Laurence – he has a fondness for Vanessa. I believe I should have asked Gideon, had he been in town – '

'But he is! They returned on Tuesday. It was such a surprise – '

His Grace stood up, suddenly alert. 'Where are they staying?'

'Half Moon Street – number sixteen, I think. Oh, Francis! You are not going already?'

'Why, yes.' He smiled mockingly. 'If I do not, you will miss the first interval and the opportunity to display your finery.'

He kissed her hand and then paused at the door, looking back. 'And Blanche . . . I wish my return to remain unknown for the present. You may tell Laurence but no one else.'

'But why?' She stared at him.

'I should have thought it obvious,' he sighed. 'I have no desire to visit Yorkshire and if Henley hears I am in town that is where he will doubtless go. As he did before.'

Blanche laughed. 'Of course! Oh, Francis, what will you do?'

He smiled, but with something in his face that made her shiver. 'That, my dear, I shall not tell you.'

Back in the library at Lyndhurst House, he seated himself at the escritoire and began to write steadily. Some ten minutes later he laid down his pen and read through what he had written. Then he folded the sheet, affixed a wafer and struck the handbell at his side. When Benson entered the room in response to this summons, his Grace handed him the letter.

'Have this delivered to Mr Vaughan at number sixteen, Half Moon Street. Tonight.'

On the following afternoon, the Duke left the house at about two o'clock and took a chair to Half Moon Street. He wore a coat of black brocade, extravagantly laced, and his satin vest was heavily embroidered with silver thread and diamond chips. Black lace foamed over his hands and his hair was confined by long silver ribbons. A smart tricorne was on his head and, from his shoulders, his silk-lined cloak fell in graceful folds.

He entered the drawing-room in his usual unhurried manner to find Gideon grinning at him from the hearth.

'Francis! My dear fellow!' He hastened to grasp the Duke's hand. And then, gesturing to his formal attire, 'But what's all this? Fancy dress at this hour?'

'Yes. Like Croesus in full array, is it not?' came the placid reply. 'Simply that I shall not be returning home before this evening.' He draped his cloak over the back of a chair and laid his hat and cane beside it. 'I must beg your pardon for thus incommoding your drawing-room but you see – I am not here.'

Gideon raised a startled brow and laughed. 'Really?'

A fleeting smile lit the Duke's eyes. 'I will explain later – but I must first offer my felicitations. I think there is no need to ask if the wedded state suits you?'

'None! I was never happier. And it's all due to Vanessa and Nick – which reminds me . . . where *is* Vanessa? We called in St James Square on Wednesday and Madam said a great deal but told us nothing.'

'How very like her,' sighed the Duke. 'I will endeavour to explain but it is a long story so perhaps we had best be seated.'

With a start, Mr Vaughan recollected his duties as a host and, waving Lyndhurst to a chair, poured two glasses of wine. His Grace frowned into the ruby-coloured liquid and said slowly, 'I think I must start by taking you back to the last time we met. We spent the evening at the Cocoa-Tree . . . you recall it?'

'Perfectly. It was the day before you went away.'

'Just so. I went, in fact, to Cornwall. And that, I suppose, is where the story began.'

So the Duke recounted, in concise but detailed terms, the events of the past few weeks. It was not to be expected that Gideon could hear him out without exclamations or questions but at length he sat back in his chair in silent amazement.

'I can't credit it,' he said at last. 'Wade must be insane.'

'Not insane, my dear. Just magnificently ruthless. But it should not have happened – and *would* not if I had not left town when, as I alone knew, her engagement would place her in immediate danger.'

Gideon's eyes narrowed a little. 'Why *did* you go?'

'Because,' came the bitter reply, 'I could not stay. No – do not try to understand. It is not important. It was selfish and – worse – it was stupid. But you will be pleased to know I was punished most appositely.' He paused. 'I did not . . . enjoy . . . those hours of knowing her in the hands of a man somewhat like myself. I knew only too well what she was facing . . . and the relief of finding her safe freed me from a burden fast becoming intolerable. Perhaps it was that,' he finished reflectively, 'that caused me to offer Charles Maynard a belated apology. Yes – I thought it would amaze you. I believe that he felt much the same.'

'Yes, he must have done,' said Gideon, not without difficulty. 'But I am glad you did it.'

'Yes. An apt ending, was it not?' drawled Lyndhurst. 'Though not quite the end, of course. There still remains the trifling matter of Carlton Henley who, as you will remember, was so foolish as to put a bullet into Nicholas.'

Gideon looked searchingly at him. 'You intend to deal with him yourself?'

'Naturally. I hope to do so tonight.'

'Not a duel, then?'

'Certainly not. Even if he had the stomach for it, do you suppose I would foul my blade with such as he?'

Mr Vaughan could not repress a smile. 'What then?'

'All in good time, my dear. First, I think I must practise a little deception or we are not likely to find him.'

'What deception?' asked Gideon warily.

His Grace helped himself to snuff and snapped his box shut. 'An ambiguously phrased note might do it. Unsigned, of course, and purporting to come from Wade or some other accomplice of his.'

Gideon frowned. 'I don't like it.'

'I am not enamoured of it myself,' sighed Lyndhurst gently. 'It's a thought unsubtle for my taste – but what is one to do? At this moment Carlton lives in fear. He does not know that I will pursue him but he fears I may. So he hides and hopes to elude me . . . but I do not think he must. I really do not think he must.' The smooth voice grew hard.

'Then wait. He must come out some time.'

'True – and at any other time it would suit me better to keep him guessing. But I want the business finished and that means luring him out. Come, Gideon . . . *exitus acta probat*, you know. And he deserves much worse than I shall do to him.'

Gideon thought a while and then gave in with a shrug. 'Very well. Where do we bring him?'

Rising, his Grace smiled and strolled to the desk. 'To Whites. Tonight at nine.' He indicated the writing materials. 'May I?'

It was a little after nine when Carlton entered the club and, beneath the rouge, his face was deathly pale. Up the stairs he went on legs which seemed likely to buckle under him and at the door of the large salon he paused, his eyes searching for a certain sinister black figure. It was not there. Sighing a little, Carlton walked through to the smaller card-room and found it empty save for old Lord Hardwick. Deaf and in his dotage, my lord was engaged in building a card house.

Carlton made his way to one of the alcoved tables and sat down in the shadows, repeatedly consulting his chronometer and wondering how soon he might leave. So it was that Lyndhurst and Mr Vaughan were with him almost before he

215

knew it and, starting violently, Carlton cowered back in his chair, clawing at the arms.

His Grace bowed with an insolent flourish. 'Why, Lord Henley,' he drawled. 'This is indeed a pleasure.' He sat down on the other side of the table. 'No – do not get up. I should be sorry to be deprived of your company so soon.'

'W-what are you g-going to do?' stammered Carlton.

'Why nothing in the least violent. Does that surprise you? It should.' Calton shivered. 'Not,' Lyndhurst went on, 'that I am not sorely tempted . . . but I have what is best described as a respect for my sword. It is therefore fortunate that you did not kill my brother – for, if you had, I am very much afraid that I should have had to . . . violate . . . my finer feelings.'

Green with fright, Carlton tried again to get up. 'Then y-you won't m-mind if I leave – '

'Sit down! I will tell you when you may leave and it is not yet. You have crossed my path once too often and I intend that you shall learn not to do so again. You will doubtless recognise that it is in my power to have you arrested for abduction and attempted murder?' Carlton twitched and gibbered unintelligibly. 'Quite. Then you will be relieved to learn that I offer you an alternative.'

'W-what? His teeth were chattering so that he could hardly speak.

His Grace leaned back in his chair. 'You will play with me exactly six rubbers of piquet . . . for stakes of my choosing.'

'And w-what if I r-refuse?'

'Then you will stand your trial,' promised Lyndhurst gently. 'My terms are generous – more so than you deserve. What is it to be? Piquet . . . or prison?'

Hatred vied with the fear in Carlton's eyes. 'P-piquet, damn you,' he said through clenched teeth. 'And m-may you rot in hell!'

His Grace did not reply. Turning to Mr Vaughan he said, 'Will you be so good as to order cards, Gideon – and claret.'

Although his glance never wavered from Carlton's face, the Duke did not speak again until Gideon returned and all was made ready. Then he said, 'I understand you are something of a gamester – and so am I. Therefore, I propose five guineas a point and five hundred on each rubber in addition.'

Caught in the act of sipping the wine, Gideon choked for this was more than deep play. It was little short of insanity. Carlton knew it too but he had no choice except to agree and the order of his mind was such that he could not help thinking that, with a little luck, he might arise from the table very much richer. He nodded and watched his Grace push the cards towards him.

'Cut.'

Carlton did so and drew the queen of diamonds. Lyndhurst reached across and exhibited the ace of spades. 'My deal, I think,' he said. And smiled.

It had begun. His Grace dealt *en deux et trois*, placing the talon between them and, with a shaking hand, Carlton picked up his cards. He held no diamonds or knaves. Biting his lip, he selected five cards, laid them down and drew five more to find himself the possessor of only one new card of any value – the ace of diamonds.

Calmly, his Grace laid down three and took the remaining cards from the stock. Then he waited for his opponent to declare.

'Point of five,' quavered Carlton.

'Not good.'

'Tierce major.'

'Not good.'

Carlton cleared his throat. 'Trio of aces,' he said desperately.

'Not good,' came the cool reply.

'Then nothing!' he snapped, throwing down the ace of hearts.

His Grace declared his hand and marked down the points. 'Point of seven, *septiéme, quatorze* of knaves. Repique.'

Gideon looked on with interest. Carlton was nervous and fidgety, the Duke suavely controlled. Gideon knew from experience that Carlton would need more than good cards for Lyndhurst was an exceptionally fine player possessed of an uncanny knack of accurately estimating his opponent's hand.

At the end of the first rubber, Carlton was already in debt to the tune of some sixteen hundred guineas. At the end of the second he was again the loser but by a smaller margin, having robbed his Grace of a pique. In the third, however, the cards he held were disastrous and when it was over he found himself quite severely rubiconed.

His hands were sweating so that the cards stuck to his fingers. Absently, he picked up his glass and drained it, his mind fixed on the silent, black-clad figure opposite. His nerves were screaming so he could hardly concentrate on his play and his neckcloth felt like an iron band. He tugged sharply at it, having for once no thought for his appearance.

Clumsily, he cut the pack and watched Lyndhurst win the deal again. Over by the door, Merton and Wickham were casting dice and he felt a ridiculous fascination for their proceedings. He wondered what the time was but dared not pull out his chronometer to look. Midnight at least, he thought; but time had no real meaning and might as well have stood still.

Miraculously it seemed, the fourth rubber brought him good cards. In the third hand he felt assured of obtaining repique and thought his luck had turned. Lyndhurst robbed him of it by declaring Carte Blanche. Yet again he went down; on that rubber and then on the next. His losses must be colossal – he dared not think how much. His Grace decided to enlighten him.

'You owe me something in the region of six thousand guineas,' he announced dispassionately. 'Do you wish to check my figures?' Carlton did not. He stared back, mouth agape. 'Very well,' continued the Duke. 'We have one more rubber still to play and I have a proposition to put to you.'

Merton and Wickham had crossed the room and were chatting easily with Mr Vaughan. Carlton heard them laughing. He giggled and saw Sir Gareth glance curiously at him.

'A proposition, is it?' And then, with a daring born of the claret bottle, said loudly, 'Well I'll wager it ain't like the one you made Hetty Wentworth, is it?'

Lyndhurst's hand clenched and Carlton exulted at having roused him. It was a brief joy, however, for the hand relaxed swiftly and his Grace was smiling again.

'Unless I am mistaken, you are indebted to your so-charming mama for that piece of information?' he queried gently.

Carlton shot him a glance malignant with loathing. 'I doubt there's anyone who don't know it. And that includes your bitch of a doxy.'

The topaz eyes blazed suddenly but the Duke's voice became disquietingly mellow. 'How very busy you have both been about my affairs, to be sure. It is difficult to know how best to repay you.'

The air seemed to hold something intensely dangerous and Merton, Wickham and Mr Vaughan fell abruptly silent, watching.

'The last rubber, then,' drawled Lyndhurst, 'and we will not play for points. If you win . . . I will cancel one half of your present debt. If you lose, I shall take all you have lost so far and . . . your house in Grosvenor Square.'

'Damn you! No – I won't!' Carlton leapt to his feet.

His Grace smiled. 'You have no choice, I think.'

Carlton subsided, a spot of brilliant colour burning in either cheek. The house was his mother's most valued possession and he realised that Lyndhurst knew it too and had proposed the stake quite deliberately. Now he saw where it had led him, he bitterly regretted that last foolish jibe but it was too late.

Reluctantly, he cut the pack and again lost the deal; yet strangely, as they played each hand, he found that somehow he was keeping pace with his opponent and, by the end of the fifth hand, was even a few points ahead. He began to breathe more freely. One more game to decide – and all he need do was hold on to that slender lead. Quickly, he dealt the cards, picked up his own and examined them. His heart sank with a sickening thud.

His Grace laid down three and drew three more. Then he waited. Frightened now, Carlton threw down five in the hope of averting the catastrophe that loomed over him. And, with maddening deliberation, his Grace declared his hand.

'Point of six.'

'Good.' Carlton's tongue cleaved to the roof of his mouth.

'*Sixième.*'

'Good.'

219

'*Quatorze* of aces.'

This time Carlton could not manage a reply. He felt as though he were in the grip of a seizure. His Grace smiled and, putting down his hand, finished his declaration.

'Also *quatorze* of kings. Repique. All the cards . . . capot. Unless you wish to play them out?'

He heard Gideon gasp disbelievingly. Carlton still made no reply but sat, apparently frozen in his chair. His Grace leaned back, smiling. Lazily, he consulted the score-sheet at his elbow. 'Six thousand, two hundred and forty guineas, then,' he said coldly. 'And . . . the house your mother values so highly.'

Suddenly something seemed to snap in Carlton's brain. With a choking cry, he leapt up and backed away, eyes fixed on Lyndhurst. 'You devil!' he cried, one hand at his pocket. 'You'll never have it – never!' He pulled out that tiny, gold-mounted pistol and levelled it.

His Grace did not stir and an odd expression flickered in his eyes.

'Devil!' shouted Carlton again. 'Go to hell where you belong!' He fired, but even as he did so Gideon threw himself forward, jerking down Carlton's hand; and the bullet, instead of passing through the Duke's head, caught his right arm.

Topaz eyes registering faint astonishment, Lyndhurst automatically gripped the wounded arm with his left hand. Within seconds, blood was seeping between his fingers but he paid it no further heed. He merely raised an ironic brow and gazed at Carlton, now standing still and lifeless between Gideon and Wickham.

'I think you have played your last game, my friend,' he remarked drily. '"*Ring down the curtain. The farce is over.*"' And, leaning back in his chair, he laughed softly.

Of Principles, Persuasions and Plots

His Grace of Lyndhurst was drunk. Not soddenly or incapably drunk, it was true, but more so than his butler had ever seen him and Benson felt faintly aggrieved for it not only spoiled a hitherto unblemished record but threatened to pose a tricky problem.

It was not that Benson did not understand for no one could fail to remark the change in Mistress Vanessa. Her spirits quite gone, she had become reluctant to set foot outside the house and, when she did go out, her return was always accompanied by the same question. It did not take a genius to draw the inevitable conclusion – astonishing though it was. And now, here was his Grace, staying away till the night before the wedding and then making a determined attempt to lose himself in brandy.

At that moment the bell gave a great peal and Benson guessed that his forebodings were about to be realised. He opened the door and Vanessa walked wearily inside. Her face was strained and she looked up at him as though she were almost afraid to ask.

'His Grace . . . ?'

Benson bowed. 'Yes, madam. About three hours ago.'

'Thank God!' Her voice quavered and she leaned heavily against the door. Then, composing herself, she said, 'The library?'

Benson's heart sank. 'Yes, madam. But his Grace . . . does not wish to be disturbed.'

'He said so?'

'Not exactly, madam. He is . . . a trifle indisposed.'

'He is ill? His arm – ?'

'Oh no, madam – nothing of that nature. Just not himself.'

Vanessa regarded him narrowly and then everything fell into place as she remembered the countless occasions when she had made similar excuses herself. 'I see. Is his Grace *very* drunk?' she asked calmly.

Benson's careful impassivity slipped a little. 'Miss Vanessa!'

'Oh, come now – it's pointless to stand on ceremony.'

Benson bowed, his face a picture of martyred resignation. 'I doubt he is very inebriated as yet but he has been drinking brandy this last hour and will not dine,' he said primly. Vanessa nodded and turned towards the library. 'Miss Vanessa – you can't!' Years of professionalism gave way to urgency.

'His Grace knows very well that drunkenness holds no surprises for me – in fact, it's likely that I'm more experienced in dealing with it than you are yourself. And drunk or sober, I *must* speak to him tonight!' And, turning on her heel, she walked quickly away to the library. For a second she paused, fingers on the handles, then, drawing a deep breath, she slipped quietly inside.

The room was lit only by the rosy glow of the fire and one branch of candles and the Duke sat in a large wing-chair a little way from the hearth. A half-empty decanter stood on the floor beside him and a glass was loosely cradled in one thin, white hand. His other arm was in a sling and he sat motionless, gazing into the flames.

Vanessa also stood still, watching him. Then, softly, she moved towards him on silent feet. Not till she stepped into the light of the fire did Lyndhurst become aware of her and then, turning, he sat up and his eyes blazed into hers. For an instant the frozen waste inside Vanessa was warmed and then heavy lids veiled the tawny depths and, rising, he made a deep, if slightly unsteady, bow.

'My charming ward!' he purred, with a certain bitter sneer that she had never before heard. 'What a delightful surprise. To what do I owe it, I wonder?'

Her heart sank but she smiled and said as lightly as she was able, 'I wished to see how you were. Gideon said you had been shot – and then you went off without a word. I was . . . worried. We all were.'

'But how kind of you!'

She looked searchingly into his face, unsure how to deal with him in this mood and then sat down, hoping it would pass. 'Won't you tell me about it?'

'There is nothing to tell. Gideon was there – I make no doubt he described the incident in detail.'

'Yes.' Vanessa looked down at her hands, still scalded by the memory of sitting beside Lady Alicia and hearing, not just of the shooting but also of the elaborate precautions he had taken to avoid seeing her. She swallowed and said, 'Then may I at least ask how your arm is? Or is that also a presumption on my part?'

He shrugged and leaned back in his chair. 'I shall live.'

'And Nick?'

'He will recover,' was the curt reply. 'If that is all you wished to say, I suggest you leave me. I am busy.'

'With what?' asked Vanessa, suddenly acidulous. 'Brandy? And, since tomorrow I shall be gone for good, may I not talk to you tonight?'

'My habits are not your concern. And I think we have nothing to say to each other.' His tone held both warning and dismissal.

'Then you are mistaken. Or have you forgotten that I am supposed to wed Roderick Anstey tomorrow?'

'Ah yes, of course.' He smiled, but not pleasantly. 'You will forgive me if I do not grace the ceremony with my presence – but Gideon will doubtless deputise for me.' He raised his glass mockingly. 'You will make a beautiful bride, my dear, and should set off the Anstey diamonds to perfection. I wish you every joy . . . and hope that Anstey's lovemaking is less dull than his conversation.'

'*Don't!*' Vanessa flinched and turned aside. 'I know you don't mean it – but I can't stand it.' She did not see the tremor which passed over his face, nor his start towards her, swiftly checked.

223

Rising, he walked away a little and, with his back towards her, said quietly, 'No. It was rather crude, was it not? You will be glad to leave my guardianship, I think.'

She looked across at him. 'No. Or only if . . . if the circumstances were different. If, for example, I left it not to marry Mr Anstey but to . . .' She stopped as he turned, frowning, to face her.

'These are mere bridal nerves, child. You will soon forget them, I promise you.'

'No,' said Vanessa again. Rising, she took a step towards him. 'I'm not a child. I know what I feel and what I am saying. And if you will have me, I would rather stay with you; as your ward if you wish . . . or anything else.'

Lyndhurst listened to the low provocative voice and glanced fleetingly into the tragic, downcast face. The firelight cast shades of dancing coral on her cream gown and tinged her hair with flame. He knew what she was offering him and her humility both hurt and shamed him. His hand clenched fiercely on his snuff-box and he said harshly, 'You do not have the remotest idea of the realities of what you suggest. There is perhaps a certain glamour attatched to me – or you are confusing gratitude with – '

'*No!*' The cry was wrenched from her. 'You can't be so blind!'

'Far from it, Vanessa. In a month, perhaps less, you will be thanking God for a lucky escape.'

'How can you know?' came the frustrated cry. 'Or is it yourself that you are trying to convince?'

'At the moment,' he hurled back in furious desperation, 'I am merely wondering if this sudden and rather ludicrous attempt to prostitute yourself is not your artless way of becoming a duchess!'

There was a catastrophic silence in which his words seemed to hang on the air. Frozen into immobility, he stared at her, seeing the blind shock in her eyes, luminous with unshed tears. '*Mignonne* . . . I am sorry,' he said hoarsely. She said nothing but gazed unblinkingly back at him. Flayed by her silence and his own weakening resolve, he took an involuntary step towards her.

'Forgive me. That was inexcusable. Sweetheart – don't cry. I am any kind of bastard you care to name – but please don't cry,' he exhorted unsteadily as the tears washed over her cheeks.

Vanessa did not move, nor did her glance waver from his face. 'I love you,' she said huskily, 'and I believe that you love me.'

Again his fingers gripped the snuff-box until the soft gold yielded to the pressure and was crushed. 'But perhaps your judgement is not completely to be relied upon,' he suggested at last.

She raised her hands and brushed the tears aside. 'It is. But if you tell me I'm wrong, then I will believe you.'

It was a long time before he spoke and then the hard mouth curled in something that was not quite a smile.

'Unfortunately . . . I cannot.' He paused. 'But it makes no difference, you see. For the simple fact is that I will not drag you down into my gutter.'

'Ah.' She nodded slowly, a wise little smile touching her lips. 'So that's it. I thought so. You'll crucify us both for a principle.'

He took a long, controlling breath. 'It's not the case.'

'No?' She looked down at her hands and concentrated on keeping her voice steady. 'You think I'm just infatuated – but you're wrong. You are my life.'

Again stillness and silence. Then he turned sharply away saying flatly, 'You don't know me. Neither do you realise that I've successfully made my name fit for decent people to spit on. Perhaps it's time I told you how.'

'Then tell me.'

He seemed to sigh and, bending his head, embarked in measured tones on the sordid tale of his past. Of the years of extravagant and licentious living; of seduction and of fleecing the foolish by his expertise at cards; of selfishness, verbal malice and unparalleled egotism. And finally, when it was done, he looked into drenched grey eyes and said harshly, 'Well? Now do you understand?'

With an effort, she swallowed and said, 'I've always understood – but I don't care!'

'Perhaps not. But I must.'

225

'*Why?* It doesn't matter. Nothing matters except that we belong together.'

Lyndhurst poured another brandy and drained the glass with a deft movement of his wrist. 'No.'

'You are selfish,' she said deliberately, out of her hurt. 'You may choose to sacrifice yourself, I suppose. You have no right to sacrifice *me*.'

It caught him on the raw and he snapped the glass down with a force which cracked it. 'Christ! Didn't you hear what I said?'

'Perfectly. But it's all in the past and it has no relevance to me – to us. Can't you forget it?' Then, her anger evaporating, she moved towards him, hands outstretched. 'Don't deny us both. Please.'

He did not look at her and his profile was stern. 'It is impossible, child. You will forget me because you must and – and Roderick Anstey will be good to you.'

Despair froze Vanessa to the marrow. 'You want me to marry him despite everything?'

'Haven't I just said so?'

Her head drooped in defeat. It was over. Incapable of thought, she said numbly, 'Very well. If – if that's what you want.'

He smiled crookedly. 'It's for the best, believe me. It seems I've already hurt you more than enough . . . and I don't wish to add disappointment to it.'

She did not reply but the russet head was shaking almost imperceptibly. Then she crossed to his side and sank down to kiss his hand. 'Goodbye,' she whispered. And then ran blindly to the door, leaving him staring intently down at his fingers on to which something brightly sparkling had fallen.

Shutting the doors behind her with a snap, she lifted her skirts in both hands and ran across the hall. Distraught, she did not see Gideon until he caught her shoulders.

'My dear! What is it?'

She raised tear-drenched eyes and clutched at his coat. 'Gideon . . . I don't know what to do!'

226

He gathered her cold hands into one of his and, slipping an arm round her shoulders, led her into the drawing-room. Closing the door, he drew her to a sofa and sat beside her. 'Now. Tell me.'

It was some minutes before she could manage this but eventually her sobs lessened and she resolutely blew her nose. 'I'm sorry. I'm being very stupid.'

Gideon shook his head and said grimly, 'I take it that Francis is home?'

She nodded and her hands moved restlessly in her lap. 'I told him I love him.'

'I see. And how did he take it?'

'He – he says I'll forget and – and that it's impossible because his name is f-fit to spit on,' she said bitterly. 'As if I cared for that! I'd be proud simply to be his mistress.'

'I trust you didn't tell him that?' asked Gideon, startled.

'I did – but he wouldn't listen. And there's no need for you to look like that. He loves me. I know he does.'

Gideon surveyed her thought. Then he said, 'All right. What do you want me to do?'

She stared at him for a long time before she answered and when she did, her voice was sharp-edged. 'What I should have done instead of tamely promising to marry Roderick. Attack.'

'*What?*'

Her smile went woefully awry. 'It's a hard thing to ask, I know – and I should have done it myself. I believe I came close . . . and he is near the brink. All you need do is push a little.' Gideon tried to visualise the possibility of manoeuvring Lyndhurst past his own defences and failed.

'Are you sure it's what you want?' he asked weakly.

She rose and walked away, her skirts rustling restlessly; then she stopped and, turning, laid her fingertips deliberately on a small table and looked austerly into his eyes.

'What else is there? I could try to seduce him but I don't know how. And, anyway, it's his reason I have to overcome. If I forced the issue by an appeal to his senses he'd feel guilty afterwards. The alternative is to lose him – and I don't think I can stand it. Will you try?'

There was only one answer to be made and, suppressing his doubts, Gideon bowed and made it.

In the library, his Grace of Lyndhurst and the sinister figure known to the world as Lucifer had dwindled away, leaving only the husk that was Francis Courtenay; a man who had tried to drown things best forgotten in brandy – and, who, having failed, swore long and fluently whilst pouring yet another glass.

Gideon entered in time to see him toss it off in one swallow. 'I doubt you will find that a help,' he said quietly. And listened while both he and his words were consigned to a place of great heat. Calmly, he sat down. 'I daresay. But, unless I'm mistaken, you are there before me.'

His Grace gave a grating laugh. 'You might say so.'

'Do you love her?' Gideon asked, watching him closely. Francis seemed not to be listening but then, with rare simplicity, he said, 'She is my life. I want nothing but her.'

Gideon drew a long breath. 'And Lydia Gwynne?'

'Nothing. A smokescreen to fool the credulous.'

'How long have you – cared?'

Francis smiled wryly. 'Who knows? I cannot recall a time when I did not. But how much I knew not till Anstey asked for her hand and then – '

'Yes?'

He shrugged with would-be carelessness. 'Oh, then I suddenly saw the bleakness of a future without her.'

Gideon was satisfied. 'She loves you, you know.'

'Damn you, of course I know! Do you think it makes it easier?'

'It should. I don't see your problem.'

'No? I had expected you to be the first to recognise it,' said his Grace, heavily sarcastic. 'You surely do not consider me a fit mate for her?'

'Odd as it may seem, I do.'

'Really? Two months ago you were aghast at the idea.'

'I was wrong.'

The admission was so placidly made that Francis abandoned his blighting tone. '"*Love bade me welcome; yet my soul drew back, guilty of dust and sin*",' he quoted. 'Delightfully appropriate, don't you think? And accurate enough to release me from the tedious necessity of elaborating the point.'

It was then that Mr Vaughan shocked himself by saying, 'Vanessa doesn't agree. She says she would be proud to be your mistress.'

'Does she?' The hard mouth twisted in bitter amusement. 'Then let us hope she does not say so to Anstey. Perhaps it was selfish of me to encourage her candour.'

'No,' replied Gideon, decisively. 'You just accepted her as she is. I doubt Anstey can do as much for she will offend his notions of propriety. Or do you want to see her moulded into conformity?'

His Grace frowned. 'The question will not arise. He loves her.'

'Have you seen him recently? He hasn't the look of a man betrothed to the girl he loves. Not that it matters since what Vanessa obviously wants is you – complete with faults and understanding.'

Francis turned away. 'Let it alone.'

'She needs you,' continued Gideon relentlessly, 'and Anstey can never take – ' And there he stopped as the Duke wheeled abruptly to face him and he saw what lay beneath the rigid control. With an effort, he forced himself to go on. 'She knows what you are and doesn't care. Turn aside from it if you will but you can't change it. Or is this thing you feel no more genuine than that which you felt for Judith Maynard and a dozen others?'

'Stop!' The Duke's voice cracked and, fighting for control, he continued more evenly, 'I accept that you mean well . . . but you don't know what you're meddling with.'

'Don't I? You encouraged her to love you – and now she's trapped. You've done well. In fact, you're so damned clever at providing us all with a taste of hell, you'd be hard-pressed to allow us a dull afternoon!'

And there he stopped as, bereft of every characteristic, practised grace, Francis Courtenay dropped into a chair, shading his eyes with a hand that was not at all steady. He did

229

not speak and Gideon suddenly knew that it was because he could not.

Discovering an unfamiliar constriction in his own throat, he strode across the room, poured two large brandies and handed one to his Grace. 'I beg your pardon. I'd no right to say that.'

Lyndhurst took the glass but made no move to drink. He stared at the amber-coloured liquid through half-closed eyes and, at length, he said, 'Gideon. I forfeited my chance to marry any innocent girl a long time ago – and you know it as well as I. The only thing you can justly accuse me of is not staying away.'

'Why didn't you?'

'Because I wanted to see her and hadn't the strength to deny myself. Pathetic, isn't it?'

'No. Vulnerability is new to you . . . but don't confuse it with weakness.'

His Grace achieved a sardonic bow. 'My mistake.'

'Yes. And it's not the only one. If you love her enough to give her up, then you love her enough to marry her.'

Francis gave no sign of having heard him. 'I should be grateful if you will . . . take my place at the ceremony tomorrow,' he said with careful detachment. 'I don't believe I can do it.'

Gideon sighed in exasperation. 'No. I don't suppose you can.' He paused, searching fruitlessly for words. 'For God's sake, man – marry her and forget your damned reputation! Since you met her it's been a thing of the past and it's certainly not worth ruining your life for.'

Francis said nothing but sat gazing into the fire, his expression enigmatic as ever. And, realising that he could do nothing more, Gideon dropped a hand on one black-clad shoulder and left.

Deep in thought, he retraced his steps to Arlington Street where he and Elizabeth had dined with Lady Alicia. The two ladies were anxiously awaiting his return and my lady scarcely allowed the door to close behind him before bursting into speech. 'Ha! He's back then? You've spoken with him? What had he to say for himself?'

Gideon smiled briefly at his wife and sank down beside her, saying slowly, 'I think, my lady, that you owe me fifty guineas.'

'She's to wed Anstey?' asked her ladyship sharply.

He nodded, his brow creasing in a frown. 'Yes. It won't do any good, but I will tell you what occurred.'

They heard him out in silence. Unable to bring himself to expose his merciless assault or its painful results, his account was skeletal and yet managed to convey the rawness of the encounter. When he had done, no one spoke for a full minute.

Then Lady Alicia brushed an impatient hand across her eyes. 'Drat the boy!' she said, in a voice that sounded suddenly very old. 'If he lets her go, he is a fool and I never thought him that!'

'Nor I,' admitted Gideon.

Her eyes brightened again and she nodded slowly. 'It's not finished yet. There is still time.'

He gestured hopelessly. 'The wedding is at two o'clock. I don't see what we can hope to accomplish before then.'

'He may change his mind,' suggested Elizabeth.

'It's possible,' agreed my lady. She paused and glanced shrewdly at her guests. 'Or there is one small thing we could try. It's a long shot and it won't serve on its own but it might tip the scales. And if there's another way, *I* can't think what it is.'

Jassy Makes her Contribution

Jassy yawned and passed a hand across her eyes. All her persuasions having failed to induce Vanessa to go to bed, she had elected to sit with her through the long hours of the night and had watched a tiny flicker of hope fade and die as time passed and the first fingers of dawn lit the sky. At a few minutes after seven the front door slammed shut and Jassy saw a strange quiver pass over Vanessa's still face. Silently, the maid slipped from the room and ran down to exchange hurried words with sleepy Thomas in the hall; then, with lagging step, she returned to the bedchamber and stood behind her mistress, watching her in the mirror.

'He's gone,' said Vanessa, in a queer hollow voice.

'Yes, Miss.' Vanessa's control cracked abruptly and, folding her arms across her waist, she leaned forward as if in pain. Jassy put her arms about the tense body and cradled it against her, murmuring futile words of comfort. 'There, there, Miss. Have a good cry and you'll feel better.' But Vanessa's hurt was too deep for tears and, churning with nerves and exhaustion she said baldly, 'I'm going to be sick.'

Later, when it was over, she sat still, weakened and shaking until her will reasserted itself and, opening a drawer, she pulled out writing materials and set them before her.

'Go and have your breakfast, Jassy. I need to be alone for a while.'

Reluctantly, Jassy went, leaving Vanessa gazing unseeingly into the mirror and gripping the pen in stiff fingers.

It was just after eight when Jassy returned bearing a tray of coffee to find Vanessa staring at the sealed letter while tears slid, unchecked down her cheeks. Swiftly, Jassy took charge. She removed the letter from her mistress's unresisting grasp and put a cup of coffee in its place. 'Drink that,' she said forcefully.

Obediently, Vanessa drank and when the cup was empty, Jassy replaced it on the tray and began brushing Vanessa's hair. After a while, Vanessa said, 'I wish that I could give him something to remember me by. He's given me so much . . . it doesn't seem right, somehow.'

'I doubt his Grace'll need any souvenir to remind him,' Jassy observed grimly.

'No . . . no, perhaps not. But even so . . . I should have liked to . . .' replied Vanessa vaguely. 'But how? If I had something to sell . . . but even the emeralds are not mine yet.' She frowned fretfully.

Carefully, Jassy brushed out the long gleaming tresses in which she often thought she had more pride than their owner. 'You could pledge the pearls and redeem 'em later.'

Vanessa shook her head irritably. 'No. If I give him something I must pay for it with something which is truly my own.' Her fingers twisted a lock of hair which had fallen over her shoulder. Then, gasping, she stood up. 'Get my cloak – and your own. We're going out.'

'Out?' echoed Jassy, stunned. 'Whatever for?'

'I'll explain on the way. Oh – do hurry!'

Relieved by such signs of normality, Jassy pulled a mantle from the closet and fled to collect her own. 'Where are we going?' she asked, as they set foot in the square.

'I'm not perfectly sure,' replied Vanessa, 'but I expect you'll know. Only don't try to dissuade me, for my mind is quite made up.'

The hall clock was striking eleven when they returned to the house. Vanessa held her cloak closely around her and, upon ascertaining that his Grace had not yet come back, she went

233

swiftly up to her room followed by a strangely silent and grim-faced Jassy.

Once inside, Vanessa went straight to her dressing-table and, gently drawing from her reticule a small, silver-wrapped parcel, set it down beside the letter. And, clearing her throat, Jassy said, 'Was it worth it?'

'Of course,' came the faintly surprised reply.

Looking up, Vanessa met Jassy's gaze in the mirror and only then did she raise her hands and put back her hood. Gone were the long, brilliant ringlets. Instead, her hair reached only the base of her neck where it seemed to cluster in forlorn curls. Vanessa touched it with curious but unrepentant fingers.

'It feels very odd – but I think I shall like it once I have grown accustomed. And it's certainly unusual. Maitre Jacques will be here soon – so let's hope Lady Blanche doesn't arrive first.'

Jassy resolutely held her tongue but promised herself the luxury of speaking her mind to the Duke when he finally deigned to return. She seethed with impotent fury and called down a silent plague on all men.

The diminutive hairdresser was lengthy in his abuse of Vanessa's perfidy but, by the time Blanche appeared, he had wrought a near-miracle and Vanessa's hair clustered in thick, seemingly artless curls. So well did it become her that her ladyship said a good deal less than might have been expected and, frothy as ever, set to work to dress Vanessa for her wedding.

'Benson tells me that Francis is back in town,' she said gaily. 'I can't wait to see him – it's all so exciting! Is his arm healed? And poor Nicky – how is he?'

'They are both well, I think.'

'It's so romantic,' sighed her ladyship. 'Indeed, I once thought that you might become my sister. Francis seemed so fond of you.'

Vanessa stiffened. 'I am his ward.'

Blanche glanced sharply at her but replied with unusual placidity, 'Yes, of course. That must have been it.'

By the time Elizabeth Vaughan arrived, Vanessa was ready.

Her deliberately simple gown of supple white satin was cut low across the shoulders and seemed almost severe in its unfashionable lack of trimming and laces. On her hair was a circlet of seed-pearls and his Grace's necklet lay around the base of her throat. The effect was breathtaking.

Blanche was effusive in her praise but Elizabeth, wise enough to see that Vanessa cared not how she looked, took the opportunity to ask Jassy if she had seen the Duke that day. Jassy shook her head. 'He went out about seven, ma'am, and he hasn't been back since. Mr Benson says as Mr Vaughan's called three times.'

'Elizabeth,' said Blanche, 'doesn't she look ravishing?' Elizabeth smiled and rustled over to where Vanessa stood. 'Indeed, yes. Quite charming.'

For an instant Vanessa clung feverishly to her hand, then she drew away and moved to the table where her bouquet lay. Absently, she picked it up and in doing so her eye fell upon the letter and silver package. Shivering a little, she turned to Jassy and said, evenly, 'Will you see that his Grace is given these on his return?'

'Don't you worry about it, Miss Vanessa,' replied Jassy, purposefully. 'I'll attend to it myself.'

'It's time we went down,' said Elizabeth gently. 'The carriage will soon be at the door.'

'Already?' Behind the white satin, Vanessa's insides contracted with cramp-pains.

'But yes,' Blanche assured her. 'Let us hope Francis is ready.' There was a sudden tense silence. Blanche looked at the three withdrawn faces. 'Well? Why do you stare so?'

It was Elizabeth who stepped into the breach. 'His Grace is not in the house, my lady, and he does not intend to be present at the ceremony. Gideon is to give Vanessa away.'

'Gideon?' echoed Blanche incredulously. 'But Francis is back now. Why can't he do it himself?'

No one replied but Vanessa's grip tightened on her posy until the delicate stalks were crushed.

'Oh, it's all of a piece!' exclaimed my lady crossly. 'I could scream with vexation!'

Vanessa walked swiftly to the door. 'I'm going down,' she said suffocatingly.

In the hall, Mr Vaughan paced back and forth in palpable agitation. He ceased abruptly as he saw the ladies and Elizabeth caught his eye and raised an enquiring brow. Almost imperceptibly, he shook his head.

Benson bowed before Lady Blanche. 'Your carriage is at the door, my lady.'

'Very well.' She nodded perfunctorily and turned to Vanessa. 'Elizabeth and I must leave now so mind you do not crush your gown in the carriage and – ' Quite suddenly she caught the girl in a quick embrace. 'And don't look so tragic. He isn't worth it.'

Elizabeth also kissed the pale, still bride and smiled anxiously at her husband before following her ladyship out of the house. The door closed behind them and Vanessa was left gazing wordlessly at Mr Vaughan.

'I've failed you,' he said starkly. 'I am sorry.'

She made a small dismissive gesture. 'What happened?'

'I did as you asked. It... wasn't difficult,' he replied frowning. 'I spoke to him in a way I didn't know myself capable of; stripped him of every facade, every barrier...'

Vanessa was very still, her eyes dark and drowning. 'Go on.'

He turned away a little. 'I couldn't do it. Perhaps I realised it wasn't my right to play God – I don't know; only that every man is owed some shred of privacy and the dignity of cloaking his hurt with silence if he chooses. What I attempted could only be done in love. Friendship wasn't enough.'

Slowly, he looked round at Vanessa. Her fingers were clamped hard over her mouth and tears slid weakly from under her closed lids. Swiftly he crossed to her side and put his arm about her shoulders. 'I shouldn't have told you.'

For a second she leaned against him and then, gathering the remnants of her self-control, disengaged herself. 'No. You were right. Don't worry about me – I shall do very well. But he... I think he will need you very much. You'll look after him?'

He nodded. 'As far as he makes it possible.'

Benson appeared smoothly at his elbow. 'The carriage, sir.'

Vanessa's eyes dilated. 'So soon?' Then, turning to the butler, she made an effort to speak normally. 'So this is goodbye, Benson – and thank you.' She held out her hand.

Taking it, Benson lost some of his impassivity. 'We shall miss you, Miss Vanessa.'

'And I you.' She laid her hand on Gideon's arm and together they descended the steps and entered the coach. It was ten minutes before two.

As soon as they had gone, Jassy slipped quietly across the hall and sat in a chair beside the door. In her hand was the letter and the silver-wrapped parcel. Not quite ten minutes later the door opened again and the Duke strode in. He was clad in riding dress and had abandoned his sling. His face wore a heavy frown and the marks of extreme exhaustion – all of which bespoke a black mood barely held in check. Many might have quailed at the thought of accosting him just then but Jassy was not of their number. Rising, she followed him to the library.

'Your Grace!' He swore and wheeled to face her. 'Miss Vanessa asked me to see that you had these,' she said crisply, holding the items out to him.

Slowly, almost reluctantly, he took them and, turning away from her, broke the seal and spread out the sheet. It said very little.

Dear Love,

I think you will not mind if I adress you so this once for I write to say goodbye. Also, I wish to thank you one last time for the happiness I have known with you. The companionship and laughter we have shared are very precious to me and I shall never forget them.

God keep you,
Vanessa.

His fingers tightened on the paper, crushing it.

'Oh, sweetheart!' he whispered, with infinite longing.

Jassy remained unmoved. 'Will your Grace not open the package?'

His head jerked round. 'You may go – you have served your turn.'

237

'Oh no!' said Jassy grimly. 'I've hardly begun – but I want you to see what she has left you first.'

The heavy lids were suddenly raised and his eyes seemed to pierce her, then he shrugged indifferently and removed the tissue from the small parcel. It revealed a silver snuff-box, heartshaped and bearing on the lid an exquisite, enamelled Aphrodite whose coppery tresses rippled to her knees.

'Open it,' said Jassy inexorably.

He did so and found inside one soft, russet curl. The breath left him and a nerve throbbed in his jaw. Gently, he touched the hair and watched it coil about his finger like a living thing.

Jassy glanced at the clock and said rapidly, 'And now I've something to say. What Mistress Vanessa sees in you I couldn't begin to guess – but she's breaking her heart for you and I think you know it. That box you're holding; she don't want you to know, but maybe it'll do you good to hear it. She wanted you to have something to remember her by – ' The Duke made an abrupt gesture with one hand but did not speak. 'Aye,' continued Jassy with dour satisfaction. 'God knows you'll find it hard to forget her, won't you? But, she wanted to give you something and she had no money. So this morning she visited the wig-maker and sold him her hair. Her beautiful hair – the only thing she said was truly hers. And, bless her stupid heart, she said it was worth it.'

Wincing, Francis looked from her to the box he held and, in a voice which cracked, said, 'You think I do not love her, but you are wrong. I am not . . . she deserves something better.'

'Well there, at least, we are agreed,' retorted Jassy acidly. 'Any man who'd sacrifice the girl he loves to his damned new-born principles ain't worth a candle. Best wrap your honour warm, sir, else it catch cold and die.'

He stared at her, a strange expression in his eyes. 'Is that what I am doing – sacrificing her?'

'God save us – yes! You're letting her pay for your filthy past while you escape, as always!'

He flushed suddenly. 'No. Not this time.'

'Well I hope not,' came the hard-hearted reply, 'but it takes more than fine words to convince *me*. All you're achieving is to add her to your list of victims. Maybe if you'd seen her sitting up all night like something on a tomb, you might believe me. And all that rubbish about not being good enough – why, it's like a line from a bad play!'

A change came over Lyndhurst's face. Vivid images flew through his mind; Vanessa in the same torment he suffered himself; Vanessa married to a man who, though enimently worthy, would never laugh with her, and a future filled with damnable meetings and unending pretence. The ashes that were all that remained of his past suddenly dispersed and with them his hagioscopic viewpoint of the last weeks. Clear-sighted at last, his eyes flew to the clock as it chimed the quarter.

'Oh God,' he said queerly. 'Oh God. I've left it too late.'

Weak with relief, Jassy said quickly, 'Not if you go now. They are celebrating mass before the wedding.'

In two strides he was before her, gripping her shoulders fiercely, topaz eyes blazing into hers. 'Mass! You are sure?'

She nodded, laughing shakily. 'Quite sure, your Grace.'

He released her. 'Then I may do it yet.' Unexpectedly, he raised her work-roughened hand and kissed it. 'I thank you.'

Equally unexpectedly, Jassy felt a pricking beneath her eyelids; but, before her gaze became too blurred to see, she watched him stride purposefully from the room. His elegant languor was gone and was replaced instead by a crisp youthfulness which made her wonder, irrelevantly she thought, if any of them had ever truly known him.

To the Devil his Due

The Mass was over and the marriage service about to begin. Vanessa and Roderick stood, side by side, at the altar-rail with Gideon and his Elizabeth a pace behind. And gathered, rank upon rank, the flower of English nobility decorated the Church like so many candied fruits in a dish.

Gloomily irritable, Lady Alicia's hands fidgeted nervously with her prayer-book. During the mass she had found the opportunity to question Gideon on the progress of her scheme and had been much disappointed in his reply. 'I've got the thing in my pocket,' he had whispered tersely, 'but Francis is out riding and he may as well have dropped off the face of the earth.'

They stood for a hymn. My lady's foot tapped impatiently to a rhythm of her own and she wondered whether they would put off the ceremony if she pretended to have a seizure.

The hymn came to an end, the congregation sat and the Reverend Bishop of Westminster began the service. 'Dearly beloved, we are gathered here in the sight of God . . .'

At the foot of the nave, Gideon glanced anxiously at Vanessa. She was so still she did not even seem to breathe and her cheekbones were thrown into stark prominence by the hollows beneath. Anstey, he noticed, looked little better and was plainly labouring under some mental strain of his own. Gideon debated the wisdom of devising some 'just cause or impediment' for use when the time came.

' . . . and therefore is not by any to be enterprised nor taken in hand, unadvisedly, lightly or wantonly . . .'

The swirling mists in Vanessa's brain seemed to clear and quite suddenly she knew that she could not do this thing – that it was wrong, absurd, offensive – and wondered that she had not seen it before. Bad enough in the beginning that, in love with one man, she had been prepared to marry another; but now that she knew her love returned – that all that stood in their way was an intangible barrier of ethics – it had more than a faint flavour of the ridiculous.

'Thirdly, it was ordained for the mutual society, help and comfort that one ought to have of the other . . .'

Reality struck her forcibly at last and she tried to speak but the words stuck in her tinder-dry throat.

Then, some way behind, she caught the sound of a crisp footfall and a rippling stir in the congregation. Her heart gave a great thud and, sweeping round, she gazed down the aisle. Midway between the chancel and the great tower, stood his Grace of Lyndhurst, his dark, magnetic presence dominating the scene and causing the good Bishop to falter and stop.

The silence was absolute. Vanessa's head spun dizzily and, seeing her sway, Gideon started towards her – but she needed no help. With a swift, apologetic glance at Mr Anstey who responded with a smile so broad it was almost a grin, she began to descend the steps.

Reaching the aisle, she gathered her skirts in both hands and fled towards the Duke, light as a bird, only the soft tapping of her slippers and the swish of her satins breaking the unnatural stillness. Some half-dozen steps away she hesitated, poised as if asking a question. Their eyes met and his smile was her answer. He opened wide his arms and, as Vanessa closed the space between them, his mouth found hers.

Their audience began to recover from its hushed amazement and a rustle of whispers grew slowly into a buzz of shocked chatter. But for possibly the only time in his life, Francis Courtenay was oblivious to the sensation he was causing. Holding Vanessa crushed in his arms, his mouth against her hair, he murmured inarticulate endearments in half a dozen languages. Vanessa's heart was too full to speak. She smiled shyly at him, touching his cheek with unsteady fingers.

He looked deep into her eyes. 'It . . . is what you want, sweetheart?'

She laughed shakily. 'I think you need not ask!'

His embrace tightened and, lingeringly, he kissed her again before looking around with his peculiar, glinting smile. 'Then I think we should leave,' he drawled, 'for we appear to be causing something of a furore.' Effortlessly, he lifted her into his arms and began to carry her up the aisle.

'No! Your arm – ' she began, concerned but laughing.

'Damn my arm,' he retorted succinctly. 'Think of my reputation.'

Lady Alicia waved frantically at Gideon who hurried to her side.

'Quick! Follow 'em and give Francis the papers. And Gideon – ' He halted again and looked back at her. 'You owe me fifty guineas,' she grinned.

Mr Vaughan laughed. 'I do – and gladly!'

Once out of the church, he saw that, inside the carriage, Vanessa and the Duke were extremely and pleasantly occupied. Strode made no move to drive off, his Grace having apparently neglected to give him any instructions. Gideon smiled in unholy amusement and walked to the box.

'Take them to All Saints in Chelsea and when you get there, be sure to give his Grace this.' He put a slim white packet in Strode's hand.

'Yes, sir.' The man touched his hat and set his horses in motion.

Neither occupant of the carriage noticed that they were moving, so lost were they in each other. Held close within Francis' arm, her cheek pressed against his velvet-clad shoulder, Vanessa entertained a thought.

'Are we eloping?'

'Not quite,' he replied in something approaching his normal tone. 'I am abducting you. Do you mind?'

'No. I like it. But did you *have* to leave it so very late?'

242

'It seems I did . . . but I meant well, you know. And that is more than I ever did before.' His fingers sought her shortened curls. 'But, my heart . . . I am not worth such a sacrifice.'

'You've been talking to Jassy,' said Vanessa resignedly. 'She sees me as an Early Christian Martyr – and if you are going to do the same, we shall quarrel. I'm ordinary and selfish and I need you. And if you were not who you are I probably wouldn't love you as desperately as I do. So don't talk to me of worthiness – it has no meaning.'

'You . . . are sure?'

'Quite sure.'

He seemed to sigh and took her hand in his. 'Then I give you my word that you will never have cause to regret it,' he said simply, raising her fingers to his lips.

'I know.' She smiled and then said, 'Now perhaps Roderick will marry Sophy.'

'Sophy?' enquired his Grace, at a loss.

She nodded. 'Sophy Brandon. Roderick only proposed to me when he believed all at an end between them.'

'He never loved you?'

'No. Never.'

'Good God!' said Francis feelingly as he realised how nearly they had all courted disaster. 'I had no idea.'

'Well, you see,' she admitted with slightly heightened colour, 'I didn't *want* you to know. I accepted him because I . . . because I thought you were in love with Lydia Gwynne.'

The topaz eyes exhibited astonishment, quickly followed by amusement. His shoulders began to shake. 'Oh, *mignonne, mignonne*,' he said, hugging her close, 'the one possibility I never envisaged! I must have been more convincing than I knew.'

Vanessa sat up very straight. 'You pretended?'

'Alas, I did,' he confessed, still laughing.

'Why?'

'To divert attention from the fact that I had, quite unethically, fallen hopelessly in love with my ward.'

She blushed but said with mock severity, 'You are shameless! Upon my word, I don't know what you deserve.'

His mouth curled in that rare, attractive smile. 'Don't you?' And he drew her into an embrace which brooked no refusal.

Just then the carriage came to a stop and they looked out of the window in surprise. Turning back to Francis, Vanessa burst into helpless laughter at the discovery that they neither knew nor cared where they were. Having descended from the box, Strode opened the door and stared at them perplexedly.

'Where are we?' asked Vanessa unsteadily.

'I really have no idea,' drawled the Duke. He turned to his driver. 'Perhaps you can enlighten us, Strode?'

'All Saints Church in Chelsea, your Grace. Mr Vaughan said to bring you here and to give you this.' He held out the packet.

The black brows rose. 'Did he so? Very well, Strode. You may close the door again – for the moment.'

Francis surveyed the envelope through his glass. 'Now what, I wonder, is this?'

'Open it and see,' advised Vanessa eagerly.

He eyed her quizzically. 'Thus the female mind. So impatient!' But he broke the seal and drew out a large folded document and a gilt-edged card. This latter he held out and they read it together.

To the Duke of Lyndhurst and his future Duchess.

Lady Alicia Marchant and the Honourable Gideon and Elizabeth Vaughan beg to extend their warmest felicitations on the occasion of your approaching nuptials and hope that the enclosed document will be of some small assistance.

On the back was a small and less grandiloquent note.

It may be of some interest to you, Francis, to know that my Lady's felicitations are particularly warm owing to the trivial sum of fifty guineas which your marriage removes from my purse to hers.

Gideon.

'I really must remember to tell Gideon,' said Lyndhurst pensively, 'that, in my experience, it is never wise to bet against a woman on matters of the heart.'

'And your experience is sufficiently wide, is it not?'

He met her teasing glance with a look that sent fire licking through her veins and said, 'Not quite. But I hope to rectify that.' And, smiling at her confusion, covered his own by flicking open the document and scanning it. Then, throwing back his head, he gave a crow of uninhibited laughter and held it out to her.

'A special licence, sweetheart, for the marriage of Francis Eugene Courtenay and Vanessa Anne Tremaine. How very like Gideon. Less a bride-gift than a reminder that I must safeguard your reputation!'

'Do you think,' asked Vanessa brightly, 'that I still have one? I rather thought that I must be quite ruined.'

'Oh beyond all question,' he agreed, the laughter dying on his lips. And, growing rather pale, 'I fear it must be marriage, my heart. If you feel yourself abe to take me.'

Oddly breathless, she gazed back at him. 'Is it *really* what you want?'

His smile answered her. But he said, 'I love you. Do you think I could settle for anything less? Beside which . . . how else can I hope to improve my standing with Bates?'

Her brows rose. 'Indeed, your Grace? Well, in *that* case, I suppose I can't refuse.'

But Francis had looked into her eyes and was not deceived. 'How kind of you!'

The breath caught in her throat as she met his look. 'Ah, no . . . no. The truth is that I can't live without you,' she whispered, raising her face to his.

When he released her, she managed a teasing smile. 'And shall you be a gentle husband, sir?'

The light eyes grew suddenly dark. 'I may not always be gentle . . . but I swear that I shall love you till I die.'

They gazed, each at the other, in silent avowal and then he threw open the door.

> *"Come live with me and be my love*
> *And we will all the pleasures prove . . ."*

They left the carriage behind them and, hand in hand, entered the church.